Praise for *Undressed*

"Readers will enjoy Cook's latest lively Regency-era romance featuring a feisty, intelligent heroine."—*Booklist*

"Even with its lighthearted plotline, there is a depth of emotion and passion in Cook's tale that's sure to pull on your heartstrings and place her next to Julia Quinn and Stephanie Laurens on your shelf."—*Romantic Times*

"Passionate and stunning . . . Kristina Cook has stripped the romance novel down to its glorious bare essentials. She has combined a superb story, authentic characters, and profound passion to create a novel perfect in its vulnerability. *Undressed* exposes Kristina Cook for what she is—an original storyteller with a talent that needs no dressing up!" —*Romance Junkies*

"Always count on Kristina Cook to deliver intriguing tales filled with interesting characters and vivid settings. She continues to captivate and charm her readers with her Ashton/Rosemoor series and *Undressed* is just as entertaining as the first two books."—SingleTitles.com

Praise for *Unveiled*

"Happily, the promise so evident in Cook's debut, *Unlaced*, is fulfilled . . . mesmerizing as once again Cook provides thoroughly enjoyable entertainment."—*Booklist*

"*Unveiled* is touching and tender, with just enough pathos-tinged humor to win our hearts."—*Romantic Times*

"A totally charming tale . . . sexy and delectable . . ."—Historical Romance Writers / Romance Designs

Praise for *Unlaced*

"Sexy and entertaining."—*Booklist*

"I was totally charmed . . . This reviewer gives *Unlaced* my highest recommendation."—The Road to Romance

"The breath of fresh air that I have been waiting for!"—RoundtableReviews.com

Also by Kristina Cook

UNDRESSED

UNVEILED

UNLACED

Published by Zebra Books

To Love a Scoundrel

Kristina Cook

ZEBRA BOOKS
Kensington Publishing Corp.
www.kensingtonbooks.com

ZEBRA BOOKS are published by

Kensington Publishing Corp.
850 Third Avenue
New York, NY 10022

All Kensington titles, imprints, and distributed lines are avail-
able at special quantity discounts for bulk purchases for sales
promotion, premiums, fund-raising, educational, or institu-
tional use.

Special book excerpts or customized printings can also be created to fit specific needs. For details, write or phone the office
of the Kensington Special Sales Manager: Attn. Special Sales
Department. Kensington Publishing Corp., 850 Third Avenue,
New York, NY 10022. Phone: 1-800-221-2647.

Zebra and the Z logo Reg. U.S. Pat. & TM Off.

ISBN-13: 978-0-8217-7981-1
ISBN:10: 0-8217-7981-8

First Printing: June 2007
10 9 8 7 6 5 4 3

Printed in the United States of America

Prologue

Oxfordshire, 1793

"May his soul, and the souls of all the departed, through the mercy of God, rest in peace. *Amen.*"

Frederick squeezed his eyes shut, somehow hoping it would block out the sound of clods of earth thumping against the casket. His sister Maria reached for his hand and held it in hers while she sobbed quietly beside him.

Valiantly, Frederick blinked back his own tears. He would not cry. He was almost ten now; nearly a man. A man didn't cry, no matter how badly the unshed tears burned behind his eyelids. Shuffling his feet uncomfortably, he opened his eyes and peered down the line of weeping girls—his sisters, all five of them, and all of them bigger and older than he was. His eldest sister, Katherine, stood beside his father who was ramrod straight, staring dead ahead at the gaping hole in the earth.

And then bedlam broke loose. Next thing Frederick knew, his father was on his knees, reaching toward the shiny mahogany box, wailing like nothing Frederick had ever heard. Instantly his sisters gathered like soldiers, plucking at their father's sleeves while they sobbed, pleading with him to get up. Aunt Esther flew into action, motioning for the girls to retreat while she spoke forcefully to her brother in a commanding tone Frederick had never before heard her use.

"He was my son, Esther," his father blubbered, and Frederick recoiled in horror. His father, crying? No, it could not be. "He's all I had of worth in this world since Fiona was taken."

"Hush now, you foolish man. We're all of us hurting. We all loved Charles, each and every one of us. But you've still a son—an heir—and five lovely girls, besides."

Frederick took two steps backward, his boots sinking into the muddy ground as his father spun around, no doubt searching for him amongst the mourners.

When his father's gaze landed on Frederick's trembling form, one long finger lifted to point toward him accusingly. "You think that one's worth a farthing to me? He killed her—he killed my Fiona. All these years, and I can't stand to look at him. And now with Charles gone . . ." He broke off, shaking his head wildly. "No. No, damn it. Get him out of my sight!"

Frederick's bowels began to roil, and for a horrible moment he feared he might soil himself, right there in front of everyone. His sisters flocked around him, forming a protective circle as he vomited all over himself instead. Tears of shame immediately welled in his eyes as Maria wiped his mouth with her handkerchief, but he did not let them fall.

"Do not listen to him, Freddie," Maria whispered. "Go on, back to the carriage."

But he couldn't move, couldn't force his feet to follow his mind's command. Instead, he took a deep, steadying breath, but it did nothing to soothe him. A strange, metallic scent hung heavily in the air—the scent of death, of loss.

Aunt Esther's voice, laced with disgust, carried on the cold, biting wind. "Get ahold of yourself, brother. It is not the boy's fault. Dear God, the poor child has never known his mother and now he's lost his brother, too. You've no right to blame him."

"Fiona wouldn't rest easy till she bore me a second son," his father keened. "A 'spare,' she said. Five girls after Charles, and each and every time I said 'no more.' Charles was the perfect son in every way; I had no need of another. I told the midwife—" His voice tore on a sob. "I told her to save my wife, not the babe. To do whatever it would take to spare her life. But look," he said, spittle flying from his mouth. "There he stands now, with the audacity to look just like her—to remind me daily of my loss. Take him to Ireland, to Fiona's family. I want no more of him." His father broke down then, sobbing on the ground at Aunt Esther's feet. She looked on helplessly but a moment before signaling the footmen to retrieve him and carry him to the waiting carriage.

At once it all made sense to Frederick—everything became crystal clear. His father's cool detachment, his complete and utter disinterest in his youngest child. His refusal to look him in the eye, to look at him in any way. The man hated his own son. Hated *him*.

He tugged his hand from Maria's grasp and turned and fled then, running as fast and as far as his legs would carry him. Through the woods beside the churchyard he flew, branches whipping his face and plucking at his clothing. A hot, sticky trickle of blood traced a path down one cheek, but he dared not stop to wipe it away. All at once the heavy, gray sky opened up, rain pelting him and stinging his face, washing away the blood as he ran toward nothing but away from everything.

At last he could run no more. His trembling legs buckled beneath him and he sank to the muddy ground beside the road, his clothes wet and torn, his lungs burning painfully from the exertion.

A bubble of despair swelled in his chest, tightened his windpipe, and a horrified Frederick realized he was crying—deep, gulping sobs full of anguish. For a quarter hour the tears flowed unchecked down his cheeks, his body curled tightly into a ball, till the tears dried up and he could cry no more. At last spent, he picked himself up off the ground, brushed off his ruined clothes, and walked home—knowing in his heart that his life would never again be the same.

The carefree days of boyhood were forever lost to him. He was the heir apparent now, the future Baron Worthington. And yet, in his father's eyes, worthless.

Chapter 1

Essex, 1806

"Marry him? Dear Lord, Papa, no. You cannot mean this." Lady Eleanor Ashton shook her head, her stomach clenched into an uncomfortable knot. For a moment, she feared she might begin to retch.

"Of course I mean it, Eleanor dearest." Her father rose from behind his massive mahogany desk, leaning against the blotter with his palms. "It's all settled between myself and Lord Worthington. You're to be married by Christmastide. Young Frederick has already agreed. Come now, daughter, I thought you would be pleased."

"Pleased?" Eleanor's voice rose a pitch as she clutched her skirts in angry fists. "Why ever would I be pleased? He's . . . he's the worst sort of rake, Papa, a . . . a rogue," she stuttered, the heat rising in her cheeks. "Not at all the type I said I would consider."

"Is that so? Well, your mother tells me all the unattached young ladies are swooning over him. She expected you would be delighted that he's accepted you."

Whatever was he talking about? No well-bred young

ladies swooned over Frederick Stoneham; how could they? He had not ventured out into polite society, not once in the six months he'd been in Town. Indeed, Eleanor had spent the entire Season in London, and had not had even a glimpse of him. Nor had anyone of her acquaintance.

There had been rumors, of course. The *ton* had been rife with gossip and innuendo, with eagerly whispered tales of his misbehaviors, his many conquests and exploits. To say that the young ladies of the *ton* were swooning over him was, at best, a gross exaggeration. Indeed, it was patently untrue. Her mother must have been mistaken, confusing him with someone else. Unless . . .

Her thoughts shifted guiltily to her diary, and her palms dampened at once as her gaze darted to the doorway, toward her mother's favorite sitting room just down the corridor. Was it possible that Mama had somehow found the slim volume Eleanor kept safely concealed beneath her feather mattress? Had her mother read the silly, childish scribblings? *Dear God, no*. It would be far too mortifying to bear.

"But I'm *not* delighted, Papa," she said, finding her voice at last. "Not in the least. He cares nothing for me nor for anyone, save himself. I cannot fathom why he would accept such an arrangement as he is not the type of man to accept his father's wishes and do his duty."

"It would seem that you are mistaken, as Lord Worthington claims to have his full agreement on the matter. Come, now, Eleanor. Do not fret so. Haven't you always said you've no wish to marry for love? You haven't changed your mind on that count now, have you, daughter?"

"No, of course not." One hand rose to her temple,

massaging the hollow beside her brow. If only her papa knew the irony of the situation.

"Then I don't understand your hesitation. It's an excellent match, a fine one, indeed. Lord Worthington's estate in Oxfordshire is large and lucrative, as are his holdings here in Essex. I've no doubt that marriage will settle young Frederick and, besides, you'll be made a baroness one day."

A baroness? No, it didn't signify. She could *not* be betrothed to Frederick Stoneham. It was far too cruel a twist of fate.

And why ever would Frederick agree to the betrothal? He was far too young to settle down and marry, and Eleanor knew just what he thought of her—she'd been cringing over the memory of his cruel words for more than four years now. "A horse of a girl," he'd called her, and that had been the *most* complimentary thing he'd said.

Oh, she'd known all along that her infatuation was hopeless, ill-considered at best. Never in a million years would she have confessed her shameful secret to anyone, not even her brother. Henry would have thought her out of her right mind. She was a smart girl, a sensible girl. Practical and pragmatic. She wasn't prone to flights of fancy or silly romantic notions. She'd readily agreed that her father should choose her husband, but she'd never imagined he'd choose so poorly.

No, she'd imagined a match with a studious, upstanding nobleman, a scholar, perhaps, like Papa—an heir to an earldom at the very least. Not some reckless youth whose rakish exploits were near legendary. A mere mister, with only a barony in his future! Whatever was her father thinking?

She closed her eyes, sighing deeply. Frederick's devilishly handsome visage swam into focus in her mind's eye—deep brown eyes the color of drinking chocolate; sensual, full lips curved into a wicked grin; sun-bronzed skin that might fool one into believing he led a healthful, sporting life rather than one consumed with debauchery. With a shake of her head, she opened her eyes, banishing the images.

Despite every rational thought to the contrary, she'd wanted Frederick Stoneham to want her—wanted it so desperately she'd thought she might go mad with longing. But she hadn't meant like this—not for no other reason save her dowry, and what other reason could there be? Her stomach lurched as she rose from her seat on trembling legs. "You must excuse me, Papa," she called out, fleeing blindly from the room through a veil of tears.

"I'll tell Lord Worthington you've agreed, then," her father called out after her. "Tomorrow, before I leave for Kent."

Tell him whatever you wish, she thought, hurrying up the wide marble stairs to the sanctuary of her bedchamber. *I'll never agree to this. Never. Not while I've breath left in my body.*

"Married? How positively dreadful, Frederick." Molly tossed her long blond curls over one deliciously curved shoulder, her bow of a mouth drawn into a pout. "Why would you want to do such a thing? Don't I please you well enough?" She trailed one manicured nail down his bare torso as she gazed up at him, her round eyes shining.

He reached down to cup her bottom, drawing her closer. Her skin was warm and soft, and she smelled invitingly of rose petals. "Aye, you please me immensely, love. Perhaps I should show you just how much." He dipped his head toward her neck, his tongue skimming across her leaping pulse.

She pushed him away. "Then why must you marry? Why now? You're far too young to take a wife. It's . . . it's positively *unnatural*."

Frederick sighed. "She has a huge portion behind her, and I could use the blunt. To buy trinkets for you, among other things. Besides, think how much more time I'll have to spend with you once I'm free from the marriage-minded mamas."

"Hah! As if any respectable mama would consider *you*. And, besides, have you forgotten that you'll be expected to spend time with your wife?" Molly asked petulantly. "Time that could be spent with me, instead?"

"Not overmuch, I assure you, love. This is simply a duty, a marriage of convenience to a perfectly respectable, wholly unattractive woman. She cares nothing for me nor expects much, I vow."

She tucked a lock of hair behind one ear with a huff. "Don't be so sure of that, Frederick. You said the same of that tart in Shropshire."

Her tone struck a chord of annoyance with him, his mood souring at once. He owed Molly nothing. Lovely though she was, she was a drain on his finances and a hindrance to his pursuit of pleasures where pleasures could be had. And they could be had quite easily, he'd realized.

That 'tart' in Shropshire had given him exceptional pleasure for more than a fortnight. An experienced widow nearly twice his age, she had surely taught him a thing or two, and he'd been loathe to end the association and return to London and Molly's bed. But, truly, one kept mistress at a time seemed sufficient, especially now that he planned to take a wife.

An unremarkable wife at that, he thought with a

grunt of displeasure, recalling the lady in question's form and features. She'd been no more than sixteen the last time he'd laid eyes on her—uncommonly tall with a long face and round, skittish eyes. A Long Meg, not the slightest bit delicate or graced with feminine charm.

Still, he'd liked her well enough, as he remembered. She'd been a hoyden then, outspoken, not yet formed into the gentle lady she would likely become. Indeed, he'd first stumbled upon her romping with a pair of hounds in the meadow near her home, dashing this way and that, tugging on the end of a stick while one of the enormous hounds tugged back. The sight had amused him; it seemed something a wild Irish lass might do, not the high-born daughter of an English lord.

As he'd become better acquainted with young Lady Eleanor Ashton, he'd learned that such behavior was nothing out of the ordinary for her. He'd lifted her up into his saddle once and raced across a gently rolling field, while Eleanor laughed gaily, her shouts of "faster!" carried on the warm, summer breeze. Now that he thought about it, he had enjoyed her company very much.

Still, he was a man who enjoyed beautiful women, and she had been so unremarkable in appearance that he could not even recall the color of her eyes.

He'd find out soon enough, he supposed, as he was traveling to Essex on the morrow to complete the marriage agreement with her father, Lord Mandeville. He only hoped their business would be concluded efficiently and expeditiously, for he had no intention of remaining in his father's company any longer than necessary. He had no reason to tarry in Essex and subject himself to his father's displeasure for more than a day or two at most. God help him.

"I should go," he muttered, rising from the bed

and stalking to the chair where his breeches lay in a rumpled heap.

"Don't be cross with me," Molly snapped, sitting upright in a huff. "You can't very well expect me to delight in your betrothal. Really, Frederick. Must you go?" She leaned forward, her delectable breasts pushed forward invitingly. "I don't think I've had quite enough of you yet."

With a scowl, he stepped into his breeches. "I'm afraid it will have to do for now. Surely you'll survive a sennight without me. I have no doubt you'll find someone else to warm your bed in my absence."

"Is that what you think of me, Frederick? That I entertain other men, here in the home that's paid for with your coin?"

He shrugged as he reached for his shirt. Hell, it didn't matter to him if she did. With a start, he realized that he had no feelings whatsoever for the woman, save an appreciation for her carnal talents.

Which, he had to admit, were considerable. No, perhaps he wasn't quite ready to cut her loose—not just yet.

Reaching for his coat, he fished in the pocket and retrieved the ruby and diamond bracelet he'd purchased only that morning in Bond Street while he'd been out choosing a betrothal ring for his intended. In haste, he'd taken the bracelet and a matching ruby and diamond ring without much consideration. The ring remained tucked safely away in his traveling case, but he'd shoved the bracelet into his pocket before heading off to the townhouse he shared with Molly on Jermyn Street— indeed paid for by his own coin.

With a flick of the wrist, he tossed the bracelet to the bed. "Here, let this bauble smooth your ruffled feathers."

Just as he expected, Molly squealed in delight. She dangled the bracelet between her forefinger and thumb, the waning sunlight reflecting off the jewels, casting flame-colored prisms of light across the smooth, white walls.

"Oooh, Frederick! It's simply exquisite." Her eyes danced with greedy pleasure as she slipped it over her wrist. "Come now," she purred, patting the bed beside her. "Must you really go so soon?"

"I'm afraid I must." His father did not expect him for a fortnight, but it wouldn't do at all for him to arrive as expected. No, timely comings and goings were far too respectable for Frederick.

Besides, it would vex his father greatly to have his only living son and heir arrive quite unexpectedly, and Frederick took perverse pride in vexing the man. And why not? The Baron Worthington was universally displeased by his son regardless of what Frederick did or did not do. Therefore, he might as well put a bit of effort into earning his censure. He hastily pulled on his boots, then turned to face Molly once more. "But don't fret. Soon enough I'll be back in Town and in your bed."

The sooner the better, he thought, making an exaggerated bow to the lady before striding purposefully toward the door.

"*Au revoir, mon amour*," Molly called out after him, as if she were a French courtesan instead of the Whitechapel-doxy-turned-stage-actress that she was.

More than he deserved, really.

Chapter 2

Eleanor sighed as she clipped a brilliant red aster and laid it gently in the basket she carried on her arm. A sparrow dipped beside her ear and she looked up, watching the bird's flittering path through the branches that fanned gently in the breeze. Tipping her face up to the sun, she smiled, allowing the golden rays to heat her skin.

It was pleasantly warm for early September, with only the smallest trace of autumn chill in the air. She inhaled deeply, filling her lungs with air redolent with the sweet scents of the garden around her. No sounds save the buzz of insects, the chirruping of birds, and the occasional bleating of sheep in the distance spoiled the fine afternoon.

And yet Eleanor was restless. Dissatisfied. Why did her life have to change so? She'd been happy enough with the sometimes dull routine of her days—too happy, in fact, to have taken a husband before now. Two Seasons had passed rather uneventfully, and yet she hadn't seen fit to accept any of the offers of marriage she'd received. Not that there had been all that many offers, but still . . .

She shook her head. Just what had she been waiting

for? She hadn't sought love—that much was certain. Or at least she hadn't thought she'd sought love. It seemed to her that, more often than not, love was a one-sided affair, leaving one party unaffected and the other pining away miserably for an affection that would never be requited. Her own parents were a perfect example, and theirs was not what Eleanor would term an agreeable marriage.

Instead it seemed perfectly reasonable to allow her father to choose her husband, now that two Seasons had passed unsuccessfully—at least her mother had termed them 'unsuccessful.' Eleanor had found them perfectly pleasant and diverting, even without an acceptable proposal.

However had her father managed to choose the one man who would put his daughter in danger of suffering the same fate he did? Eleanor tried to deny any knowledge of her mother's infidelities whenever her brother was vulgar enough to bring them up, but she knew. And she knew how her father suffered for it.

There must have been a dozen eligible bachelors he could have chosen from, gentlemen who might have accepted her. Men who fit the carefully detailed description she'd given him of her ideal husband. Why had fate seen fit to play such a cruel trick on her?

The distant sound of hooves drew her attention toward the road. Perhaps she'd call on Selina today—it was nearly an hour's walk to Marbleton, but some exercise would do her good.

She clipped another fragrant bloom and added it to her basket. Yes, she would go to Marbleton, but perhaps she'd take the carriage, instead. It seemed a silly indulgence as she generally enjoyed the walk, but her anxiety mounted most uncomfortably by the hour.

Frederick was expected in less than a fortnight and

Eleanor was going mad with nervous anticipation. Selina's soothing presence and sisterly advice might help settle her nerves and lend her the confidence needed to defy her father's wishes.

Were she to flatly refuse to marry Frederick, she supposed her father would not force her to do so against her will. No doubt his intentions had been well-meaning. Mama had told him that Frederick Stoneham was the most elusive and secretly desired bachelor for miles about, and Papa had no doubt delighted in securing such an eagerly sought match for his only daughter. *Foolish, foolish man*.

But were she to confess the truth to him—tell him exactly why she could not marry Frederick—then he would surely understand and extricate her from the agreement. Of course, to confess that she harbored such silly, romantic notions about a man who hadn't given her a second thought would be humiliating at best.

Yet the alternative—marrying Frederick—was simply out of the question. Her only hope was that the past few years had robbed him of his near-legendary good looks, leaving him fat, prematurely balding, and wholly unappealing. Entirely unlikely, of course, but if it were so, then perhaps she would be immune to his charms.

For there was no denying that it was only his appearance that attracted her so, that stirred her blood beyond reason. Nothing more. There was certainly nothing of merit to his character—nothing whatsoever to recommend him. Which, of course, made it all the more puzzling that her parents should think this a suitable match.

She resolved to speak with her papa immediately upon his return from Kent. When he'd first given her the news, she'd been far too stunned to put forth an effective argument. She must do so at once, before Frederick arrived.

Grasping the stem of a flowering chrysanthemum,

she savagely ripped off its blossom and tossed it into her basket with a scowl.

"Might I ask what that flower did to deserve such cruel mistreatment?" a decidedly male voice called out, surprising her so completely that she dropped the basket to the gravel path at her feet.

"Oooh, sir, you frightened me half out of my wits," Eleanor cried, bending down to retrieve the basket.

"Pray forgive me for startling you," the deep voice said silkily beside her ear, the hint of an Irish brogue vaguely evident. Their hands met on the basket's handle and, at last, Eleanor's gaze rose to meet the stranger's.

No! Eleanor snatched her hand back, rising to her feet with a small gasp. No, it couldn't be. He was not expected for a fortnight—Lord Worthington had said so quite plainly only two days past. Yet, inexplicably, there he stood—an older version of the boy who'd haunted her dreams. And, dear Lord, looking more darkly and devilishly handsome than she'd remembered.

Grinning at her discomfiture, Frederick Stoneham bent into an exaggerated bow. "Allow me to introduce myself. I'm—"

"I know who you are," Eleanor snapped.

One black brow arched in surprise. "Is that so? Well, then, I see my reputation precedes me. In that case, might you direct me to Lord Mandeville? We've some business to discuss."

Eleanor swallowed hard before replying. "I'm afraid Lord Mandeville is not at home. He has removed to Kent, and isn't expected back for a sennight. Good day, Mister Stoneham." More than anything, Eleanor wished to quit his company as expeditiously as possible.

"Ah, but you have me at a disadvantage, one which I cannot abide. Would it be too much to ask for your name?"

"My name?" Eleanor asked, her voice faltering. Did

he not remember her? Her fingers rose involuntarily to her lips, her cheeks burning with remembered shame and humiliation.

"Aye, I was under the impression that Lord Mandeville has but one daughter, and you are clearly not that lady." His eyes narrowed slightly as his gaze slid up her body, pausing briefly at her décolletage, then rising to her face. "Though there is a familial resemblance. A cousin, perhaps?"

Eleanor shivered slightly, uncomfortable under the weight of his impenetrable stare. His eyes, a darker brown than she'd remembered, unnerved her. Must he look at her so directly? She shifted her gaze lower, to his full lips, to his chiseled jaw in desperate want of a shave.

His unruly hair reached his shoulders—terribly broad shoulders—in soft black waves. He looked positively . . . *uncivilized*. She found herself taking two steps back, wanting to increase the distance between them. Looking around wildly, she realized she hadn't even a proper chaperone about. Wherever had Mama gone off to?

And then the full weight of his insult descended upon her consciousness. She was clearly *not* that lady? He'd stolen a forbidden kiss when she'd been naught but a girl—a kiss that, try as she might, Eleanor hadn't been able to banish from her thoughts, even after all these years. And now he did not even recognize her? Had she changed so much since then? Or was she just so very forgettable?

A heated flush climbed her neck as she straightened her spine and tilted her chin up to meet his gaze. "I am Lady Eleanor Ashton," she said, her voice as haughty and cool as possible. "And I'll ask that you remove yourself from my presence at once."

Frederick was sure his mouth hung open like a

blithering fool's, yet he could not help but gape. No, this could not be her—Lady Eleanor, his intended. The Lady Eleanor he remembered was tall, ungainly, unexceptional at best. But this woman . . . *No*. He shook his head. Was his memory so very faulty? For this woman was the essence of feminine grace, the epitome of classic beauty. Drape her in folds of white and she'd be a goddess. Or a mere mortal Helen of Troy.

She *was* tall; that much hadn't changed. Frederick was a solid six feet in height, and yet the top of her head reached his shoulder. But ungainly? No. Her slender neck was long and proud as a swan's, her limbs perfectly proportioned. If the generous swell of creamy bosom that rose from her bodice's neckline was any indication, he was certain that beneath the folds of her gown lay a deliciously curved figure, exactly as he preferred. The body of a courtesan—not the willowy frame exalted by the *beau monde*.

Still, she was every inch the lady. Her carriage exuded grace and noblesse, even as she glared openly at him with eyes the color of indigo ink. Round and thickly lashed, he'd never before seen eyes quite the same hue. Only a fool would have forgotten them.

Her skin was likely too tanned to be considered fashionable, yet it lent her an air of healthy vigor and vitality. Her face was a perfect oval, not in the least bit long, as he'd so uncharitably remembered it. Her mouth was wide, her lips sensually full and rosy, even while curved into a frown. And her hair . . . her hair was as black and glossy as a raven's wing.

Bloody hell, she was nothing as he remembered. *Nothing.* It sent his mind reeling in confusion even as his thoughts rambled on in silent appreciation. With a concentrated effort, he at last recovered his composure and mercifully found his voice. "You cannot be Lady

Eleanor Ashton," he said, realizing how foolish the words sounded even as he said them.

"Perhaps, then, you should find my papa in Kent and give him the news. He'll surely be surprised, won't he? After all these years, thinking I was indeed his daughter." She shook her head as she knelt and reached for her basket. Setting it into the crook of her arm, she rose to face him once more.

Silently, he studied her face again, seeking something recognizable in her countenance—for her disposition had surely changed. "You must forgive me, but you are not at all as I remembered. Not the girl I knew." Sweet. Compliant. So easy to coax into a kiss in order to win a wager.

"Don't presume to know me, Frederick Stoneham," she snapped. "It's been four years since we last met. I was naught but a girl then."

Fours years—had it really been so long? Time enough for a girl to grow into a woman. "Might I be so bold as to ask your age?"

"I am twenty," she answered coldly. "And what is your age?"

Impertinent woman. Still, he answered her. "Three and twenty."

"You see, then, far too young to marry. Are you just out of university?"

He nodded. "Two years."

"What? No Grand Tour? No sowing your oats? Why ever would you wish to marry now? It's not sensible, a gentleman your age agreeing to take a wife." Her brow knitted with a frown. "Naturally, I use the term 'gentleman' quite loosely in this case."

"I'll brook no argument with that. I never claimed to be a gentleman."

"At least we agree on that point. I *do* wish you'd go."

Eleanor glanced over one shoulder, toward the house. "You weren't expected for a fortnight, and this is most irregular."

Her cheeks pinkened delightfully. God help him, but he'd made a mistake. A terrible mistake. He could not marry this woman, after all. She was, no doubt, a bloody paragon of genteel grace and breeding, and he was . . .

He allowed the thought to trail off, his stomach pitching uncomfortably in his gut. "I will take my leave," he bit out. "I'll speak to your father—"

"You needn't bother," she interrupted. "I won't have you, despite the agreement our fathers struck. It . . . it was rash and ill-advised, and I cannot possibly—"

"Allow me to set your mind at ease, Eleanor. I won't have *you*."

It was her turn to gape in surprise.

No, he couldn't marry her. She represented everything he wasn't; everything he couldn't have.

And how very charitable of her to rub it in, like salt in a wound. He'd be damned if he'd let her treat him like a bloody tinker. Perhaps someone needed to bring Lady Eleanor Ashton to heel—and perhaps he was just the man to do it.

"What the devil are *you* doing here?"

Frederick turned toward his father's flinty voice. "Ever the warm welcome, I see. As always, Father, a pleasure. I believe I was called here to attend to business. A betrothal contract, if my memory serves me."

"You weren't expected for a fortnight. Mandeville isn't even in residence at Covington Hall."

"Yes, I know. I've just come from Covington Hall where I had the opportunity to briefly reacquaint myself with my intended. I'm afraid that, when Mandeville returns, you will have to tell him that I wish to beg off. I've had a change of heart, you might say."

An angry flush climbed up his father's neck. "You *will* marry her. I'll not renege on a deal made in good faith with a man like Mandeville just to suit your capricious nature. You're damn lucky he agreed to the match in the first place."

Frederick strode to the sideboard in the room's corner and reached for an opaque blue glass bottle. Removing the stopper, he poured a generous amount of his father's finest brandy into a tumbler, then drained the contents in one long draught.

His father's eyes narrowed, studying Frederick closely as he set the empty tumbler on the sideboard. "Haven't I enough troubles as it is without you coming here—quite before you were expected, I might add—and trying to destroy what's been accomplished on your behalf? After what's happened to Maria—"

"Maria?" Frederick's stomach did an uncomfortable flip-flop.

"Surely you recall your sister Maria? I realize that devoting oneself to a life of debauchery might cloud one's memory, but still—"

"What the hell has happened to Maria?" Frederick snapped, his patience worn thin.

"That vile husband of hers has left her, that's what. Taken off with his mistress to God knows where, leaving her all alone, with child, and without a farthing. She arrived here not a sennight ago, in a sorry state, indeed. And now you burst in, declaring that you won't honor your betrothal agreement. Tell me, is Lady Eleanor not coarse enough, not vulgar enough to suit your tastes?"

His father's insult barely registered. Eckford had left

Maria? The bastard. The blood roared in Frederick's ears, a near-deafening din. "I'll kill him!"

"Eckford? You'll have to find him first, though there are rumors he's hiding out near Plymouth."

"Oh, I'll find the bloody bastard, and when I do I'll put a bullet through his head." Frederick's hands closed into fists by his sides. "Where is Maria?"

"Upstairs. Well-sedated, I'm told."

With a nod, Frederick turned and strode off toward the door.

"Where the devil do you think you are going?" his father called out after him. "Come back here, I'm not yet through with you."

Ignoring the command, Frederick continued on toward the sweeping staircase. "I'm going upstairs to see my sister, that's where."

"Not till you tell me what imbecilic reasons you have for rejecting Lady Eleanor Ashton. If you've seen her, then surely you cannot claim to find fault with her. You should be grateful to Mandeville for even considering your suit, much less agreeing to it."

He paused and turned toward his father. "I'm in no mood right now to feel anything but concern for my sister's welfare. Now if you'll excuse me."

"Perhaps if you'd been in Mayfair these past six months, amongst the quality rather than holing yourself up with your whore on Duke Street—"

"Actually, she resides in Jermyn Street," he corrected. "Close enough to Duke. Somewhat shabby, I suppose—"

"Drinking, gambling, challenged to more than one duel, I'm told," his father continued, ticking off his sins on his fingers. "And off piddling away your time in Ireland before that."

"Aye, but I had pressing business in Ireland."

"You had no pressing business in Ireland." His

father's scowl deepened. "Four years at Cambridge, and still you speak like one of *them*."

"One of them? I have nae idea what ye mean," he said with a shrug, forcing the thickest brogue imaginable into every syllable.

His father rose to the bait. "You know exactly what I mean. I expected they would raise you like a gentleman, not like some filthy little heathen who cannot even speak the King's English in a civilized fashion."

"Strangely enough, I find the familiarity of your criticisms somewhat comforting. You *do* realize, don't you, that my mother—your wife—was one of those 'filthy little heathens'?"

His father approached him menacingly, his eyes narrowed and one finger pointed at Frederick's chest. "How dare you say such things about your mother!" he sputtered, his face a mottled red. "You, of all people."

Frederick folded his arms across his chest. "Actually, those were your words, not mine."

Ignoring his reply, his father continued on in a strangled voice. "Fiona was an angel here on earth, and if it weren't for you—" His words broke off as one fist rose to cover his mouth. At once the color drained from his face, leaving him pale, ashen.

"Pray continue," Frederick drawled, waving one hand in the air for emphasis. "If it weren't for me, she'd still be alive. That *was* what you meant to say, was it not?" Despite his flippant tone, Frederick's throat constricted, making him feel suddenly as if he were suffocating.

"Indeed not," his father managed at last, the color returning to his sagging cheeks. "I only meant that . . . well—"

"Don't insult me, Father. I know exactly what you meant. Now if you'll excuse me, I'll take my filthy half-Irish self off and see to Maria."

Frederick excused himself with a bow, delighting in the displeasure so evident in his father's cold, hard features. There was nothing he liked so well as having the last word, particularly where his father was concerned.

He would see that Maria was well-recovered, and then he would find her bloody bastard of a husband and take care of him, once and for all. Only then could he return to London in peace—to the shabby, cramped accommodations he shared with his mistress. Where he belonged.

Far away from his father, and even farther away from Lady Eleanor Ashton, bloody paragon that she was.

Chapter 3

"Blasted arrogant man," Eleanor muttered, raising her skirts as she stepped carefully over a fallen branch in her path. She had decided to go to Marbleton on foot after all, hoping the exertion would help tamp down her wildly overwrought emotions.

It hadn't, of course. She'd traversed a full mile, and still she stomped along the dusty road, seething at the injustice of it all.

All these years he'd haunted her dreams against her will—and he'd forgotten her. Entirely. There he'd stood, not three feet away, and he hadn't even recognized her. A familial resemblance? *Hah.*

As if that weren't enough, he'd had the nerve to scrutinize her from head to toe and then declare that *he* wouldn't have *her*. Why in heaven's name had he ever agreed to the match in the first place? So that he could have the pleasure of rejecting her yet again? Was he so cruel, so heartless as his reputation suggested, that he would tease her with an offer which he fully intended to break off?

Pity he couldn't have waited to break it off in

public where he could have had the full enjoyment of her humiliation.

With a sigh of frustration, she ducked under the fence's wooden rail, at last entering Marbleton's neatly manicured park. Eleanor stopped to admire the scenery, forcing away her dour thoughts. *Forget him,* she chided herself. Do not let him ruin this fine day.

As her eyes took in the green, gently rolling landscape before her, her furrowed brow began to smooth, her frown to disappear. She had far too many fond memories of Marbleton and its inhabitants—past and present—to allow thoughts of Frederick Stoneham to ruin her appreciation.

Many years ago, Marbleton had belonged to Sir Gregory Bradstreet, a baronet of limited means but the kindest of hearts. His wife, Lady Bradstreet, was equally kind and generous, and the Bradstreets had four children, the youngest being the same age as Eleanor and her twin.

Eleanor had spent many a fine summer day right here in this park, running and skipping with the Bradstreet children, served lemonade and sandwiches there on the lawn with Henry beside her smiling happily—something he did rarely at home.

No, at home he cowered beneath their mother's criticism, forced to while away his days indoors for fear that he might overtax himself. But here at Marbleton, Henry blossomed under the gentle nurturing of Lady Bradstreet, fully accepted and genuinely liked by her children despite his weaknesses.

But then, just before her and Henry's tenth birthday, Sir Gregory had fallen upon hard times. He'd been forced to sell Marbleton, and the Bradstreets had packed up their belongings and left, never again to return to the district. Eleanor had cried for days, not for her own loss of playmates, but for Henry's loss—acceptance, encouragement, nurture. Things he did not receive at home save her own childish attempts.

Eleanor closed her eyes and inhaled deeply, summoning the memory of the happy sounds of children scampering about these very same grounds. In her mind's eye, she could see Henry sitting there on the lawn, his deep blue eyes dancing with delight, free from the sadness that usually darkened them.

Oh, Henry. Dear, beloved Henry. If only her brother were here with her now, instead of off at university. How cruel that their difference in gender forced a separation at a time like this, a time when she was most in need of her brother's companionship. She'd missed him terribly when he'd gone off to Eton, but at least then he'd returned home for holiday breaks. Now that he was at Oxford, he never came to Covington Hall.

He was, of course, a faithful correspondent. Not a week went by without a letter, detailing his studies, his art, his life. Still, it wasn't the same—would never be the same. With whom but Henry could she share her hopes and dreams, even her silly poems, without fear of being laughed at? Certainly not her mama, and not even Selina, her dearest friend.

No, no one knew her as her brother did, and it was unlikely that anyone ever would. Eleanor sighed, watching as three fat geese waddled by, honking loudly in unison.

Her thoughts now fully returned to the present, Eleanor pushed aside the childhood memories and continued on toward the main house where Selina and her husband, Lord Henley, now resided.

Yet her feet slowed not a dozen yards away when she reached the tall honeysuckle hedge beside the old, towering oak—this had been their favorite spot for dining *al fresco.* The ground beneath the oak was soft and shady, the air filled with the sweet scent of honeysuckle. They would kick off their shoes and roll hoops or dance about the springy lawn, their stomachs full and their hearts light. More than anything, Eleanor yearned for those carefree days. If only she could taste such freedom again, such lighthearted playfulness.

Did she dare? No, it was foolish. And yet . . . the day was so lovely, the lawn so inviting. Surely there was no harm in it. Looking around furtively, she reached down and unlaced her half boots, smiling in anticipation as she did so.

Seconds later she stood in her stocking feet, the tall blades of grass tickling her ankles. She untied her bonnet and tossed it to the ground beside the oak's massive trunk, onto the old, gnarled roots that protruded from the earth, covered with spongy green moss.

Hurrying to the hedge, she plucked a single honeysuckle blossom and tucked it behind her ear. She inhaled its scent, gaining courage from the familiar fragrance.

And then she began to dance. Not the carefully modulated, reserved steps of a country dance, but the relaxed, inventive movements of a child. She hummed a lively tune as she twirled and flitted beneath the oak's drooping branches, her heart beating a happy rhythm. The gentle breeze caressed her cheek as the birds chirruped in harmony, and for the moment Eleanor was free—free from worries, from marriage contracts, from her parents' discontent and her brother's melancholy.

A hint of gray in the otherwise verdant surroundings caught her eye, and Eleanor spun toward it, her breath hitching in her chest.

"Oh!" she cried out, one hand rising to cover her mouth. Mortification coursed through her, making her cheeks burn and her breath come fast. She was far too horrified to do anything but gape at him, her eyes blinking rapidly as she attempted to regain her equilibrium.

Wearing a long, gray overcoat and leaning indolently against the tree's trunk, Frederick stood there watching her with an amused gleam in his eye. "Do not stop on my account, Lady Eleanor. I was quite enjoying the performance. Though I do apologize for startling you twice in one day."

At last she found her voice, however tremulous. "I believed myself to be alone, Mister Stoneham. You might have made your presence known."

"And deprived myself of such a delightful sight as this? No, never."

"A gentleman would have done so."

"And yet I've already conceded that I am no gentleman."

"There is certainly no doubt of that. What are you doing here in Lord Henley's park? Besides skulking about like a panther, spying on those unaware."

"As much as I hate to dispel your illusions, I'm afraid the truth is far more pedestrian than that. I have an appointment with Lord Henley, and, as the day seemed fine, I chose to walk. A panther? Hmmm, I rather like that image."

"I did not mean it as a compliment."

"No, of course you would not. Still, I'll take it as one. But you"—his dark eyes skimmed over her figure—"look like a pagan priestess, performing some sort of ancient rites. Though I hoped in such a circumstance one might remove more than just one's boots and bonnet."

Frederick watched as the color in Eleanor's cheeks deepened to crimson. He longed to gather her trembling body in his arms and kiss her, just for sport—but she did not follow the same set of rules as the women with whom he normally associated. No, she would never allow such an impropriety as a meaningless kiss. It was too bad, really, as she *was* quite lovely.

Then again, she had allowed his kiss before—almost eagerly, if he remembered correctly. He studied her face, still unable to believe this was the same girl. A woman now, and not one with whom he should trifle. "Perhaps you should retrieve your things and allow me to escort you to Lord Henley's house. I suppose that is your destination?"

"Indeed it is." She reached for her boots and leaned against the trunk of the tree while she pulled them on. His eyes were involuntarily drawn to the curve of her ankle as she laced the boots, her long, elegant fingers efficiently accomplishing the task. "I came to pay a call on Lady Henley," she said, smoothing down her skirts.

"Lady Henley?" Dear God, he hadn't even realized that Henley had taken a wife.

"Did you not realize that my friend Selina Snowden is now the Viscountess Henley?"

Selina? The little blond slip of a girl who always trailed about in Eleanor's shadow? "No, I did not realize that was so."

"Yes, they only just wed in the spring. Anyway," she said with a shake of the head, "I can find my way without your escort. Pray, go on ahead." She tilted her head toward the house, the sun-weathered beige stones looming just beyond the treetops.

"After you," he retorted with the sweep of one hand.

Her eyes met his briefly, her gaze steady and sure, before she nodded. "Very well. Good day, Mister Stoneham."

With the bearing of a queen, she swept off, trailing the sweet scent of honeysuckle and lemon verbena behind. Her bonnet, a wide straw contraption trimmed in a pale green silk that matched her frock, lay forgotten on the grass beside him.

Smiling broadly, he bent down to retrieve it. Her clean scent wafted from the straw, sending his pulse into a full gallop. Deuce it, what was the woman doing to him? He'd never before been attracted to someone like her— a lady by all accounts, and an innocent at that. Yet here he stood, grinning like a schoolboy as he watched her retreating form.

A challenge, perhaps? Indeed, nothing more.

"Lady Eleanor," he called out after her. "Haven't you forgotten something?"

She froze, her shoulders rising and falling with two deep breaths before she turned to face him. He could sense her wariness, her distrust, charging the air around her. *Smart girl*.

He held the bonnet aloft, dangling it from its wide, silk ribbons. *The forbidden apple*. Would she take it?

She said nothing in reply, not moving an inch in his direction. Was she so desirous of removing herself from his company that she was actually considering abandoning her bonnet and continuing on without it? Leaving him standing there holding it, like a fool?

Not bloody likely. In several long strides, he closed the distance between them. "Here," he said gruffly, "I can't very well allow you to compromise your complexion simply to spite me." He plucked the honeysuckle from behind her ear, tucking it into his lapel instead.

She stood as still as a statue, as if she were carved from marble, watching him, transfixed. One ebony lock had escaped her hair arrangement and fallen across her flushed cheek, and he reached down and pushed it back from her face, tucking it behind her ear.

There was something hypnotic about the way she silently stared at him—looking right at him, yet somehow past him. With precise movements, he planted the bonnet firmly on her head. Not yet willing to end the physical contact, he trailed one fingertip down her neck, eliciting a shiver in response.

"Do not touch me, sir," she said at last, her voice a near whisper.

"No? Perhaps I should kiss you, then. To refresh my memory. It's been so very long, hasn't it?"

"Don't you dare!" she cried, her eyes widening with alarm.

"Don't fret, love. I can accomplish it without touching you, if that's what you desire. Here, my hands shall remain firmly by my sides the entire time." He leaned in toward her, her rapid breaths warming his cheek as his mouth slanted over hers.

For no other reason save to torment himself, he allowed his lips to brush against her firm, unwilling ones—coaxing them into softening, into opening for him. He heard her whimper, the quietest of sounds yet still discernible over the din of his pounding heart.

He kissed her gently, tenderly, his hands balled into fists by his sides with an enormous effort of restraint. The kiss was near-chaste and yet flames of desire coursed through his blood, urging him to crush her to him, to possess her with his mouth. Instead, he commanded himself to retreat. He took a step back and watched curiously as her eyelids fluttered open, her eyes seemingly unfocused and dazed.

And then her hand flew out and struck him firmly across one cheek. "How dare you kiss me so without my permission?" She glared at him, her entire body quivering.

Frederick smirked as he rubbed his smarting cheek. "Soon, my lady, you'll be begging me to kiss you like that."

"Not as long as I live." She shook her head so hard that he feared her bonnet would become disengaged.

"Shall we strike a wager on it? One hundred pounds that you beg for my kiss before the year is out. Are you game?"

"Oooh," she cried, stomping one foot with a huff. "You *are* a rogue. I didn't want to believe it, but everything they say about you is true, isn't it?"

"I haven't any idea. Perhaps you should tell me just what it is they say about me, and I'll answer each charge. Might as well get it all out in the open. 'Air my dirty laundry,' as they say."

"Very well." She folded her arms across her breasts, meeting his gaze with her own. "They say that you are a defiler of innocents."

"Innocents? Do they really say that? You may rest easy, as that that one is indeed false. I do not trifle with innocents. *Ever*. What else?"

"That you keep a half-dozen mistresses."

"The current count is a mere one, unless you count a recent though regrettably brief interlude with a widow in Shropshire. Do you honestly think I should pay to keep half the *demimonde* in style? I've not that much blunt. No, I think one kept mistress is sufficient, even for a man with my, er, appetites. Have you anything else?"

Her eyes narrowed perceptibly as her color rose once more. "That you've fought two duels of honor these past six months alone, called out by angry husbands for dallying with their wives."

"Ah, that one is true. Partially. I have fought two duels and—"

"And wounded an innocent man who sought only to avenge his wife's honor after you coldly and calculatedly seduced her," she interrupted, her blue eyes blazing.

"In the hand. I shot the fool in the hand, only to keep him from killing me without just cause."

"So you deny seducing two married women?"

He nodded. "I seduced only one married woman, and I hadn't any idea she was married at the time. In fact, she told me quite plainly that she was not. Is that all?"

"Isn't it enough? You're lucky you haven't gotten yourself killed."

"I must say, your concern for my reputation is touching. But why should you care if I do get myself killed?"

"In case you have forgotten, our fathers have signed a betrothal agreement on our behalf. They expect us to wed by Christmastide."

"Ah, yes. That. And yet you told me just this morning that you would not have me, and I was in full agreement. So, you see, you needn't worry."

"No, a man like yourself could not bear to associate with a woman like me, could you?"

Had she any idea how close to the truth this statement was? No, he could not bear it—to taint her so. He might not be a gentleman, but he did possess *some* scruples.

"Good day, Mister Stoneham," she said, interrupting his thoughts. With a tip of her head in his direction, she turned and walked away from him, leaving him there alone beside the honeysuckle hedge, thinking that perhaps the world would be a better place if he hadn't shot the dueling pistol from that fool's hand.

Chapter 4

"Dearest Eleanor, it cannot be true." Selina set down her teacup so abruptly that it clattered against the saucer, sloshing the caramel-colored liquid onto the fabric that covered the table. Her blue eyes were full of concern, her mouth drawn into a frown. "Why ever would your papa do such a dreadful thing to you?"

Eleanor traced the blue design on the fabric with one finger, unable to meet her friend's sympathetic gaze. "I can barely credit it, but I think he believes he is doing me a favor."

"A favor?" Selina's voice rose shrilly. "Marriage to Frederick Stoneham a favor?"

"Apparently Mama told him that all the young ladies are swooning over him. I suppose my father thought him . . . desirable." Eleanor almost choked on the word. Dear lord, he'd kissed her. Was he now having a chuckle about it out in the stables with Lord Henley? Saying how easy it was to bend her to his will?

Selina shook her head. "No one of our acquaintance has swooned over him since we were girls. Why, I haven't so much as laid eyes on him in years. Why ever would your mother suggest such a thing?"

"I've no idea, Selina. It's driving me mad, wondering if somehow she *knows*."

"How could she know? Have you told anyone—Henry, perhaps?"

Eleanor shook her head. "Of course not, and even if I had, Henry would never speak of such things to our mother."

"True." Selina nibbled on her bottom lip, looking as if she might cry. "Oh, Eleanor, I so wanted you to find happiness in the married state, as I have with Henley. This . . . this will never do."

"I plan to tell Papa that I will not honor the agreement. It's just as well; Frederick says he won't have me, after all."

Selina inhaled sharply. "How dare *he* refuse *you*? He's not fit to wipe your boots."

"I don't understand why he ever agreed to the betrothal in the first place." Eleanor shrugged, her attention drawn to the sound of voices in the front hall—male voices. Moving closer.

She leaned forward in her seat. "Why ever is he here?" she whispered.

Selina's eyes narrowed. "Imagine my surprise at learning that Henley considers Mister Stoneham a friend. A *friend*, Eleanor—can you believe it?"

"I cannot," Eleanor answered. "Henley is nearly ten years his senior. How have they come to know one another?"

"It would appear that Henley was well-acquainted with Mister Stoneham's elder brother, Charles. Poor Henley was hunting with Charles Stoneham the day the man was killed, and I'm afraid Henley feels somewhat responsible, though it was an accident, of course," she added hastily. "Henley says that, with Charles's dying breath, he begged him to watch over Frederick, and so

Henley has endeavored to do so. It hasn't been easy, of course, not with Frederick's character as it is."

"Surely not," Eleanor murmured, fiddling with the hem of her sleeve.

The men's voices continued past the closed door of Selina's sitting room, toward the viscount's study. Eleanor met her friend's questioning gaze but a moment before averting her own to the marble-topped mantel crowded with decorative cherubs of all shapes and sizes.

Selina's eyes narrowed a fraction. "There's something you're not telling me, Eleanor. I can sense it."

Her friend knew her far too well. Almost as well as Henry did. Of course, Selina was privy to the one secret that Eleanor dared not share with her brother, close as they were. Heaven forbid that Henry know what had happened between Eleanor and Frederick so many years ago—he'd likely call the man out and get himself shot in the process. No, he must never know.

"Eleanor?" Selina asked, interrupting her thoughts. "You're woolgathering. You must tell me what it is you're keeping from me. I cannot bear not to know."

Eleanor sighed, dropping her hands to her lap. Very well, she might as well confess it all. Selina would eventually root it out of her, anyway. "Just now, out in the park. Frederick, he . . . he kissed me."

"Kissed you? Surely you jest."

"I'm afraid I'm entirely serious. I've no idea why, considering he finds me as attractive as a horse, but he did. A small kiss, nearly chaste, but a kiss nonetheless."

"Please tell me you did not allow it."

"Of course not! Once I regained my wits, that is."

Selina bit her lower lip, looking toward the door. Returning her gaze to Eleanor, her curiosity was unmistakable. "You must tell me, what of his looks?" she said, her voice barely above a whisper. "Have they diminished at all? Is he still as terribly handsome as before?"

"Selina!" Eleanor cried, feigning shock. "Weren't you just chastising me for kissing him?"

"Oh, Eleanor, I will be the first to admit that Frederick Stoneham is precisely the kind of man one can't help but daydream about. But he's certainly not the sort of man a gently bred lady like yourself marries. Still, you must describe his appearance. I'll see for myself soon enough, but I'd best be prepared."

Eleanor sighed heavily. "If you must know, his looks have only improved with age. He's far too handsome for his own good, and well aware of it, I'll wager."

"His hair? Still as black as midnight?" Selina laid a hand on Eleanor's wrist.

"Yes, and far too long to be fashionable, though he no longer wears it in a queue. His skin is tanned, his shoulders broad, and he has a wild, near-dangerous look about him now." Eleanor nodded to herself. "More so than before, though I wouldn't have believed it possible."

"No. Oh, no, Eleanor, this is far worse than I'd imagined." Selina rose and hurried to her side, clasping Eleanor's trembling hands in her own. "Even now, after all this time, after everything wicked you've heard of him . . . you still fancy him, don't you?"

"Of course I do not fancy him. Don't be silly. Why, I have not spared the man a single thought in all these years," she said, amazed that the lie slipped so easily off her tongue.

"But . . . but you kissed him," Selina pressed.

"Not on purpose, I vow."

"You cannot say it was an accident, Eleanor. Am I to believe that you inadvertently fell upon his lips, then?"

Eleanor sighed in exasperation. She should never have told her about the kiss. However would she explain it? "Nothing as foolish as that. Truly, I cannot explain it except to say that he somehow caught me unaware. Almost as if he'd . . . he'd . . ." Eleanor cast her gaze wildly about the room, searching for the right word to describe the indescribable. "He'd transfixed me, somehow. Hypnotized me, like a viper does its prey. I'd taken off my bonnet and boots, you see, and—"

"Taken off your boots?" Selina interrupted, releasing Eleanor's hands. "Whatever for?"

Eleanor raised her gaze heavenward. "It's far too embarrassing to discuss."

Selina clasped her hands to her breast, her eyes shining with gathering tears. "We must find you someone right away. A suitable man. Someone honorable and kind, someone to divert your thoughts from Frederick Stoneham as quickly as possible."

Eleanor nodded her agreement. "But who? I've already had two Seasons, you know."

"Yes, and perhaps you should not have been so choosy," Selina scolded. "After all, nearly any gentleman is better than Frederick Stoneham."

Eleanor could not argue that point.

"I cannot sit idly by and watch your poor, fragile heart get trampled on once more by that scoundrel." Selina patted her on the shoulder. "Do not fret, Eleanor. I *will* think of something."

Eleanor only hoped she'd be quick about it.

"Devonshire? What would he be doing in Devonshire?" Henley poured a generous amount of brandy into an intricately cut glass and handed it to Frederick.

"My fear is that he plans to set sail from Plymouth. Of course, it's entirely possible that he's not in Devonshire at all. Maria's in no shape to determine just what information is credible right now." Frederick took a long draught of the brandy, savoring the full, smoky flavor as it burned a path to his stomach. "I've no idea where she obtained her information, though she claims a reliable source."

Henley nodded sharply. "Still, the lead is worth pursuing. My youngest brother George resides in Devonshire. He has a lovely estate south of Plymouth, on the coast. He'll have no objection to aiding us."

"Us?"

"Of course. I'll travel there with you."

"I cannot ask that of you, Henley, with you so newly wed. And to lovely little Selina Snowden—however did you manage it, a cowhanded old chap like yourself?"

Henley raised one dark brow. "You're acquainted with my wife?"

"Since long before she put her hair up. Gloriously fair hair, if I remember correctly." Frederick attempted a lascivious smile.

"It is, indeed." Henley eyed him coolly, clearly taking Frederick's bait.

There was no need to involve Henley in such unpleasant business. He would take care of Eckford himself. "I must say, I'm eager to reacquaint myself with your wife," he said with a leer. "Is she home at present?"

Henley's scowl gave way to a wry grin. "I say, you had me going for a moment there, Stoneham. Indeed, you shall reacquaint yourself with my viscountess, and we shall all travel—together—to Devonshire. I will hear no more objections."

Frederick shook his head. "Despite any promises you might have made my brother before his untimely demise, you owe me nothing." Henley was a good man, a man of worth. Frederick knew he did not deserve such a champion.

"Charles was a very good friend, indeed, but he's been gone more than a decade now. You've been my friend in his stead, all these years."

"Not so good a friend as to get invited to your wedding, I see," Frederick grumbled.

Henley had the good grace to look uneasy. "I'm sorry about that, Stoneham, old boy. But with all the talk surrounding you these past months, I decided it best—"

"Do not worry yourself over it, Henley. I shall do my best to overcome the slight," he quipped.

"Yes, well. Ahem. Anyway, Charles did ask that I watch over your welfare in his absence, and it has been an honor and privilege to do so, though God knows I've failed you more than once. I *will* aid you in this."

Frederick shifted his weight uncomfortably, wishing he could dissuade the man, yet grateful for his tenacity at the same time.

"Now," Henley said, clapping him on the back. "Shall we go and find my wife?"

"I'd like nothing better. I hope you don't think me ungrateful, Henley. I do appreciate your support. I only wish I could spare your involvement in such an unpleasant situation as this."

"Nonsense, old boy. Come now, let's adjourn to the sitting room. I'm willing to bet Selina is wearing the carpet thin, awaiting to receive you."

Frederick wasn't sure the woman would be quite so pleased to see him. Still, he nodded and followed Henley down the narrow corridor, vaguely wondering if Lady Eleanor remained in the woman's company. If so, his reception would no doubt be icy indeed.

Henley paused beside an arched oak door. "Here we are," he said, reaching for the brass handle and pushing open the door. "My dearest, my business is concluded with our guest here and—oh, good day, Lady

Eleanor. What a pleasant surprise." He bowed toward the room's far corner.

Frederick stepped across the threshold and saw Eleanor there, standing before a plum-colored damask chair, glaring at him.

"Henley, dear, you near enough frightened us to death," Selina chirped, hurrying to her husband's side.

"You remember Frederick Stoneham, do you not? The Baron Worthington's son?"

Selina raised her cornflower blue eyes to his face, her eyes widening perceptibly. "Oh, dear! Goodness, it *is* true."

Frederick quirked a brow, then executed an exaggerated bow. "Lady Henley. How good to see you after so many years. I didn't believe it possible, but you have grown even more lovely than I remembered."

A giggle escaped her lips, and Frederick smiled inwardly. It would seem that she, at least, hadn't changed all that much.

"You flatter me, Mister Stoneham. And where have you been all these years? We've missed you in this district."

"In Ireland, madam. At my father's estate in Connemara, though I've spent these past six months in Town." He couldn't keep his gaze from straying to the corner where Eleanor still stood, mute. Ah, but he'd affronted her maidenly sensibilities with his kiss. How very charming.

"Lady Eleanor," he added with a bow in her direction.

"Mister Stoneham," she bit out in reply.

"You two are acquainted, then?" Henley asked.

"We are indeed," Frederick said.

"Good, very good. I say, Stoneham, you must concur that the two loveliest and most charming ladies in all of Essex stand right here before us, do they not?" Henley smiled jovially as he rocked back on his heels, his hands thrust into his pockets.

"That cannot be argued otherwise," Frederick agreed with a nod. "How very fortunate for us both. Why, only this very afternoon, out in your park—"

"Only six months in Town, you say, and already your reputation is near-legendary," Eleanor interrupted. The air around her was charged with tension, her eyes flashing dangerously. "However did you manage it in so short a time?"

"A natural talent for scandal, I suppose."

Eleanor smiled archly. "And how proud you must be of such an accomplishment."

"Aye. Amazing what one can do, when one focuses his efforts."

She took two steps toward him, and he noticed that her cheeks had flushed deliciously. With anger, no doubt. "I was surprised to learn you were so well acquainted with Lord Henley," she said.

"Oh, I do occasionally venture out in respectable company. Keeps the tabbies guessing. I wouldn't want to become too predictable."

"No, I suppose you wouldn't. That explains, then, why you would so rashly agree to an arrangement that you never intended to honor."

"Actually, I had every intention of honoring it until just this morning."

"What the deuce are you two talking about?" Henley's gaze swung from Frederick to Eleanor and back again. Beside him, Lady Henley's eyes were wide as saucers.

Frederick reached down to straighten his waistcoat. "Nothing of consequence. Perhaps it's best to let the subject be, if you'll pardon me, Henley."

Henley cleared his throat, looking flummoxed. "Yes, well. Ahem."

An uncomfortable silence ensued. Eleanor retreated toward the sofa, her temper evidently subsided.

"Well, Stoneham, shall we give my wife the news?" Henley asked at last. Frederick said nothing in reply. "Selina, dear, you must arrange to have your trunks packed at once. We shall travel with Mister Stoneham to George's estate in Devonshire in two days' time."

"To Devonshire? Whatever for, Henley? We've only just returned from Town, and I'd hoped—"

"I've some business to attend there with Stoneham. We shall stay no more than a month, I vow. I say, I've an idea." Henley thoughtfully stroked his whiskers. "Perhaps Lady Eleanor might join us on our journey. Otherwise, you shall have no female companions there, and Lady Eleanor's company will no doubt enliven the party— George can be so very dull. Say you'll come, or my wife will surely perish from boredom whilst Stoneham and I are away, attending to our business."

Eleanor's gaze snapped up and she shook her head, horrified by the suggestion. Travel to Devonshire with the devil himself? *Never.* "I thank you for the kind offer, Lord Henley, but I simply cannot."

"You must reconsider," Lord Henley interjected. "I cannot bear to leave my wife behind, yet I do not wish to drag her there and leave her with no one save George to entertain her."

Selina reached for Henley's sleeve. "Really, dear, George is not so bad."

Henley's brows drew together. "Isn't he?"

"No, not at all." She turned toward Eleanor, reaching for her hands. "I vow, George Whitby is an amiable and sensible man. A fine sportsman, and quite handsome, too. I think you'll enjoy his company. Perhaps you *should* join us."

Eleanor shook her head. Had Selina lost her wits? Did she realize what she was suggesting?

Just then, Selina looked furtively over her shoulder at

Frederick, who was standing by the bookcase and idly examining a brass kaleidoscope that sat on one of the shelves. Returning her attention to Eleanor, Selina leaned toward her. "This might be the perfect solution to your predicament, Eleanor," she whispered. "Oh, why did I never before think of it? We could be sisters," she added breathlessly.

Sisters? Whatever did she mean? Eleanor allowed the thought to trail off before realization dawned on her. *Of course.* It would not be the advantageous match she had hoped for, not to a viscount's younger brother, but if this George Whitby was as amiable and handsome as Selina suggested, then it would be a far cry better than marrying Frederick Stoneham. And what could be more pleasing than gaining Selina as a sister-in-law?

Yes, perhaps it might work—if only Mister Whitby might come to admire her. Feeling trapped, she resolved at once to accept Henley's invitation. Her mother would gladly give her permission for Eleanor to travel with the Henleys to Devonshire, though her father would be cross at her for leaving Mama alone. Still, desperate means required desperate measures.

If Mister Whitby was everything Selina said he was, she would put forth her best effort to secure the man's affections as expeditiously as possible. If she managed to succeed, she could return triumphantly to Essex and beg her father's approval of the match. If he refused his consent . . . well, there was always Gretna Green.

"Yes, then," she said with a nod. "Thank you, Lord Henley. I will be delighted to join you."

She only hoped the decision would not prove disastrous.

Chapter 5

"I can't believe I allowed you to talk me into this. I must have been mad to ever have agreed to it," Eleanor huffed, settling herself into the traveling coach beside Selina. "Pure and utter madness," she added under her breath, watching as the less elaborate coach carrying their luggage and an assortment of personal servants clattered off.

"Come now, Eleanor. It's not as bad as all that. Truly, we shall have a fine time." Selina fiddled with the closure on her plum-colored satin spencer, looking somehow hopeful and apprehensive at the same time. "I do believe you shall like George, and I have no doubt that he shall like you very much."

Eleanor smoothed down her bottle-green skirts with visibly trembling hands. "Which is precisely why this is madness. It seems so cold, so calculating."

"Why should you think so? As I said, Mister Whitby is a sensible man; that's precisely why Henley finds him so dull. He's not at all prone to flights of fancy or romantic notions. It's not in his character, you see. He'll appraise your wifely potential based upon practical matters—your dowry, accomplishments, family connections. Is that any less cold or calculating than your reasons for wishing to meet him?"

"I suppose not," Eleanor murmured, hoping that her friend was correct. Still, the words did nothing to assuage the prick of guilt that niggled her mind.

"Here now, if it will make you feel better, I'll tell him straightaway why I wanted you two to become acquainted. I'll say quite candidly that you were hoping to avoid an unacceptable match arranged by your father, and that I thought the two of you might suit instead."

"No, that might make him uneasy, as if he's been put on the spot." How desperate it sounded, when Selina explained it so. Oh, what a horrid position to find oneself in, as if she were naught but a piece of horseflesh, offered up on the block in order to avoid slaughter.

If only she could turn back time—accept the suit that had been offered by Lord Eldridge last Season. She'd had no real reason to refuse him—nothing besides a nagging suspicion that they would not find happiness together. In retrospect, what did it matter that he was near enough bald, with beady eyes and sweaty palms? With a sigh of defeat, Eleanor shook her head.

No, it would never do to be quite so forthcoming about her situation with Mister Whitby. It would make becoming acquainted far too forced, too full of expectations. "Perhaps we should let events take their natural course," she murmured, "and see what develops in due time."

Selina tilted her head to one side, appearing to weigh Eleanor's words. "Very well," she said at last, "but only if you'll promise not to fret so."

Eleanor reached over to pat Selina's gloved hand. "Agreed, then. You must forgive me. This is just all so terribly irregular, so unsettling. If only Henry were here to advise me."

Selina shook her head. "Do you not think that matters of the heart are best left to females?"

"I suppose they are," Eleanor agreed. In truth, she and her brother had rarely discussed the notion of romantic love—at least, not without scorn. They'd both seen how their father had suffered for it, and neither held the emotion in high regard. If only her own heart hadn't betrayed her and led her astray so many years ago, when she'd first come to know Frederick Stoneham.

Selina turned toward the window, and Eleanor followed her gaze. Henley stood in the drive with his steward, Frederick a few paces behind wearing a long, black traveling cloak and a tall beaver hat. *And looking quite dashing, of course.* Eleanor groaned inwardly, dreading the long journey to Devonshire. It had rained heavily during the night, and the roads would be slow.

Eleanor wondered briefly what she'd done to deserve such ill fortune. Once they arrived at Mister Whitby's estate, she expected Frederick would be occupied with whatever business brought him there, but until then she'd have to endure long hours in the coach with him, in far closer company than she desired.

Just what business *did* Frederick have in Devonshire, anyway, and how did it involve Henley? No one had ever said as much, and Eleanor briefly wondered if Selina knew the answer. Had she even questioned her husband on the matter? She closed her eyes and inhaled sharply, suddenly wishing she was back home at Covington Hall, strolling through the garden or curled up on her favorite window seat with a book of poetry.

"Here they come now," Selina said, and Eleanor started in surprise as the coach door swung open, the scent of wet earth rushing inside and mixing with the smell of the coach's leather interior.

Moments later, Henley stepped inside and took a seat

on the bench opposite Selina. Eleanor's breath hitched in her chest as Frederick's form appeared in the doorway, the air before him rippling with his very presence. With a nod in her direction, he shouldered his way inside and took the unoccupied seat on the bench directly opposite her.

Eleanor kept her gaze trained on the place where his biscuit-colored breeches met the tops of his knee boots, silently cursing the heat that flooded her cheeks, undoubtedly staining them red.

"Well, then, our party is all assembled. Shall we set off?" Henley asked conversationally. When no one dissented, he rapped the roof of the coach with his walking stick. "Drive on."

At his words, the coach lurched forward, slowly gaining speed. Eleanor trained her gaze on the window, watching as the gently rolling countryside became nothing more than a soggy blur. Nearly a quarter hour passed in blessed silence.

No longer able to bear the weight of Frederick's stare upon her, Eleanor looked his way, her gaze colliding with his. For several seconds, they regarded one another in silence. He was, no doubt, likening her appearance to a horse again.

"You look lovely today, Lady Eleanor," he said at last.

"Neigh," Eleanor replied, feeling churlish.

Selina suppressed a giggle with one hand.

"Pardon me?" Frederick asked, his brows drawn.

Did he consider it his duty as a rake to pay ladies compliments he did not mean? She allowed herself to be fooled into believing his pretty words once; never again would she be so careless.

"Dreadful weather for traveling," Eleanor offered, ignoring his compliment altogether.

"Isn't it, Lady Eleanor?" Henley said, nodding his

agreement. "Positively frightful. I fear the roads shall be difficult today. Ah, well, at least I'm in agreeable company," he added with a wink in Selina's direction. "I shall endure."

Eleanor smiled weakly. "As shall we all, though not as cheerfully as you, I should say."

"I do apologize for putting such a blight on your mood, Lady Eleanor," Frederick said with a wry smile. "Perhaps you'll find Mister Whitby's company more endurable than mine upon our arrival in Devon."

"*If* we ever arrive," she muttered under her breath as the carriage hit a rut in the muddy road and lurched to the left.

"Ah, yes. George." Henley stroked his whiskers. "I hope he has planned some sort of amusement for you ladies while Stoneham and I attend to our business in Plymouth."

At Henley's words, Frederick's gaze darkened perceptibly, shifting toward the window, his hands suddenly fisted in his lap.

Eleanor's curiosity was piqued further. "Might I be so bold as to inquire about the nature of your business there, Lord Henley?" she asked, unable to curb the words. "I do hope it's nothing too unpleasant."

"Oh, I shall take great pleasure in killing the bastard when I find him," Frederick growled. The simmering rage that he had tried to suppress for days threatened to bubble up, out of his tightly guarded control. Henley shot him a warning glance across the width of the coach, but he did not heed it.

"We're going in search of my bloody lout of a brother-in-law," he added, "who was last seen in Plymouth, by some accounts. And when I find him—"

"Yes, well, we've already established that," Henley interrupted. "Perhaps the man can be reasoned with, instead."

Frederick's chest tightened uncomfortably. "Not after what he's done to my sister."

Eleanor sat forward in her seat, the dark arch of her brow startling against her fair skin. "Just what *has* he done to your sister?"

"Come now, Stoneham. This is not fit for ladies' ears, is it?"

"He's left her destitute, that's what." Frederick ignored Henley's protests. "Abandoned her, carrying his child, to run off with his mistress. He's taken everything of value, including her jewels, and left her saddled with enormous debts and no way to satisfy them."

"How dreadful!" Selina cried. "Oh, the poor thing."

"You must forgive my prying, Mister Stoneham," Elea-nor said, her voice soft. "I had no idea—"

"No, it's best that you know." He collapsed back against the squabs, hoping to relieve the tight bunching of muscles at the base of his neck. "If you hear anything about him while in Devonshire, you should let me know at once. His name is Eckford, Mister Robert Eckford. Though it's likely he's traveling under an assumed name, with his mistress posing as his wife."

A shadow flickered across Eleanor's features. "I believe I have met this Mister Eckford. Your sister Maria is his wife?"

"Yes," he bit out. "What do you know of him?"

"Only that we met once, at a house party in Kent. I found him . . . most unpleasant. Though Missus Eckford seemed lovely. I was surprised to observe that she seemed . . . well . . ." she trailed off, shaking her head.

"Pray, go on. I would appreciate your candor on this subject."

Indecision flicked across her features, but only for a moment. "Well, it was only that she seemed so smitten with her husband, oblivious to the fact that he appeared to seek the . . . er, attentions of other women in the party. Quite openly, too."

"Yes, it would seem Maria had no trouble turning a blind eye to Eckford's faults, though I've no idea what he did to earn such devotion from her."

"Have they children?" Selina asked. "Beyond the one she carries now?"

"Indeed. Two young daughters, now being cared for by my eldest sister and her husband. Maria hasn't the means to support them, nor is she in any state to do so. She can barely see to her own needs at the present. She's back under my father's protection, for what that's worth." Very little, as far as he was concerned.

Their father was, after all, the man who allowed Maria to marry Eckford in the first place. Had Frederick been in his father's place, he would never have allowed it. Hell, if he'd been a few years older at the time, he would have made damn sure that the marriage had not proceeded as planned. As happenstance would have it, he'd only been a boy, unable to do anything but form an immediate and intense dislike of his sister's husband. He hadn't trusted him. And he'd been right not to. *By God, Eckford will pay.*

"I do hope you are able to locate him," Eleanor said quietly. "He should make proper restitution. No woman should suffer so. But surely you do not plan to murder the man?"

"Give me one good reason why I should not," Frederick countered.

"Well, for one thing, it's against the laws of England to do so," Eleanor offered.

"It's not as if I plan to shoot him on sight, Lady Eleanor. Have no fear; I shall throw down my glove in the proper fashion."

"A duel?" Selina asked, her voice rising shrilly. "You plan to challenge him to a duel?"

"Now, now, Selina darling," Henley said, laying a hand on his wife's slender wrist. "I say, Stoneham, enough of this talk. You've gone and upset the ladies, and I simply won't allow it to continue. Perhaps we should discuss something more appropriate. Hmmm, let's see . . . well, then." He nodded to himself. "How is your brother faring at Oxford, Lady Eleanor?"

Eleanor hesitated before responding, her gaze meeting Frederick's. He sensed something there in her eyes, an understanding of sorts. Something indescribable yet comforting nonetheless. A familiarity flickered in the depths of her deep blue eyes, and the recognition startled him.

Yet the flicker disappeared as quickly as it had emerged, and she returned her attention to Henley.

"He's having a marvelous time at Oxford, Lord Henley, and I could not be more pleased for him. If only I didn't miss his company so dreadfully."

Frederick was glad for the change of topic. He no longer wanted to think about Eckford—it only made his blood boil. The past few days had been tortuously exhausting, in no way resembling the brief jaunt to Essex he'd expected when he'd departed London not a sennight ago. In fact, he'd expected to be on his way back to Town by now—back to Molly's warm bed and soft body, her uninhibited sensuality and keen desire to please.

He shifted in the seat, feeling cramped. The conversation continued on around him, nothing but a hum now as he allowed himself to study the two ladies sitting across from him. What a study in contrasts they were, with Selina so tiny and bland, and Eleanor so tall and vivid.

Both were impeccably attired in voluminous traveling

costumes that concealed nearly every inch of their flesh, their hair intricately arranged, without a single lock out of place. So refined, so restrained. Likely repressed, as well, he added a bit uncharitably.

He did not belong in their company, and it was foolish of Henley to insist the ladies accompany them to Devonshire. At best they would be an annoyance; at worst, a distraction. He only hoped he would be able to locate Eckford easily and expeditiously so that he could be on his way back to London before the month was out.

Frederick shifted again, moving closer to the side of the coach so that he could stretch his legs a bit without inconveniencing Eleanor. He rubbed one aching temple, then wearily closed his eyes and allowed the coach's rhythmic movements to lure him into a deep, dreamless sleep.

The coach lurched violently, and Frederick sat up with a start. How long had he been sleeping?

With one more jolt, the coach came to an abrupt halt, tilted to the left at an improbable angle. Vaguely aware of the gasps of the other passengers, Frederick pressed his palms to the seat, steadying himself. "What the deuce?"

Carefully leaning forward, he peered out the window. They appeared to be in a rut on the side of the road.

"Is anyone harmed?" Henley asked, turning toward his companions. "It would seem we've lost a wheel."

"Oh dear, I think I've injured my neck," Selina said weakly.

The next few minutes passed in a frenzied blur. Both Henley and Lady Eleanor saw to Selina's injury while Frederick stumbled out to speak with the stunned driver. They had indeed lost a wheel—stuck in the thick mud not twelve paces away from where the coach had come to rest. It would have to be replaced before they could proceed.

"Blimey, milord," the driver said, shaking his head. "I done what I could but there were no avoidin' it."

"Have you any idea how far we are from the nearest village?" Frederick asked, craning his neck to see beyond the trees lining the road behind them.

"Not so very far, thank the Maker. We shouldn't be more'n three miles from the coaching inn at Dalton. Planned to stop there to change the horses."

"Very well. Here—" Frederick dug inside his pockets, retrieving a coin purse. He pulled out several heavy coins and handed them to the driver. "Take this. And take one of the footmen with you—that one, over there." Frederick pointed toward a tall, liveried youth who stood at the foot of the coach, watching them. "See if you can hire a cart to return with the necessary parts for repair, and ask about for a physician to accompany you. It would appear that Lady Henley has sustained an injury."

"Bloody 'ell, it ain't so very bad, is it?"

"I don't believe it's all that serious. Still, she should be examined."

"Aye." The driver nodded, then reached into the band of his dusty breeches for his pistol. "Take this. I don't want no ruffians touching the horses, and that footman there don't look so good hisself." He tilted his head toward the second footman, who sat on the grassy slope leading up from the road, rubbing his head and looking stunned.

"No need." Frederick shook his head, refusing the gun the driver held out to him. Pulling back his coat, Frederick revealed his own weapon, tucked safely into his braces. "You may rest assured that no one will touch the horses."

The driver eyed him sharply. "I suppose ye know how

to use it, too. A man don't carry 'round a weapon that fine jest for show."

Indeed. The custom-made, ivory-handled pistol had cost him dearly. It was a fine piece of workmanship and, more importantly, it could hit its mark with astonishing accuracy.

"I'll jest be off, then," the driver said, stuffing his own gun back into his waistband. "I 'spect we won't be back fer hours."

Frederick watched as the man grunted instructions to the youth who would accompany him. A moment later, the two trudged off down the road.

"Stoneham!" Henley called from the open door of the coach, now hanging crookedly from one hinge. "Has the coachman gone for help?"

"Indeed he has." Frederick heaved a sigh as he made his way back to the disabled conveyance. It was going to be a long morning, no doubt.

Chapter 6

Carefully lifting her skirts above her ankles, Eleanor picked her way through the mud, up the embankment at the side of the road, and into the grassy field beyond. Her limbs had grown cramped from sitting inside the disabled coach for nearly an hour. She needed to walk, to stretch her limbs and breathe the fresh air.

Besides, as soon as the coachman had departed in search of help, Frederick had stalked off, leaving her alone with Selina and Lord Henley. Eleanor was beginning to feel as if she were trespassing on their privacy as Henley whispered soft, soothing words in his wife's ear and gently massaged her aching neck.

Her own neck was beginning to ache, if truth be told. Eleanor tilted her head from side to side, testing it, and winced as a pain shot down her shoulder and across her back. Sighing deeply, she continued on toward a shady copse of trees in the distance, hoping the exercise would alleviate the discomfort.

Tugging at the neckline of her gown, she glanced up at the sky, pleased to see a hint of blue. At last the bright sun emerged from behind the clouds, warming her skin and drying the moist air that rippled about her as she made her way across the high grass. Now that the weather had cleared, her traveling gown seemed far too heavy, too constricting. Of course, she'd imagined herself tucked safely into the carriage throughout the day, not traipsing about the countryside on foot. Ah, well. At least she was no longer forced to sit there, directly across from—

Frederick. There he sat, on the folds of his cloak beneath a tree—in his shirtsleeves, no less. His back rested against the massive trunk, his scarred boots crossed at the ankles, and his head bent over the leatherbound book he held in one hand. Beside him lay his coat and tall beaver hat, his discarded gloves looking as if they'd been tossed carelessly aside.

Eleanor stopped dead in her tracks, afraid to even breathe lest he hear her approach. Was he actually reading? The notorious Frederick Stoneham, reading a book? Indeed, it appeared he was, as unimaginable as it seemed.

She took two steps backward, wishing to get away before she was discovered.

Crack. Her heart skipped a beat as she stepped on a twig, her half boot breaking it in two.

Frederick's head snapped up and he twisted his torso around to face her, dropping the book as he did so and reaching one hand inside his waistcoat. Spotting her standing there, his mouth curved into a grin. His warm chocolate eyes, sparkling mischievously, met hers. "So, you came looking for me, did you? I'm flattered." Scrabbling to his feet, he mock-bowed to her, one hand across his heart.

Eleanor's lips twitched with the hint of a smile. "Of course I didn't come looking for you, you arrogant beast." Try as she might to curtail it, her smile widened. She couldn't help it. Standing there beneath the trees' drooping branches, stripped of gentlemanly trappings, he looked more like a mischievous boy than a man of three and twenty—like the boy who had stolen her heart. And then trampled it beneath his boot, she reminded herself, forcing the smile from her lips.

"I had no idea where you had gone off to. I only wished to stretch my legs and perhaps ease the pain in my neck."

"I thought you unharmed," Frederick said, his brows drawn. "Is it not so?"

"I . . I'm not entirely certain. Perhaps it's just a stiffness."

"A stiffness? Ahh, I know just how uncomfortable that can be. Most painful." His smile was nothing short of lascivious.

"In my neck," Eleanor bit out, inwardly cursing the heat that flooded her cheeks.

"Of course. To where else would I be referring? Here, let me see." In a split second, he was beside her, his fingers tracing the column of her neck.

Eleanor attempted to sidestep him, her breath hitching in her chest. "Please unhand me, sir."

He dropped his hand and eyed her sharply. "You, my dear, are decidedly no fun."

"I never claimed to be fun." Her gaze moved to the book he'd dropped, lying at his feet. "What were you reading?"

He hastily bent down and retrieved it. "Nothing of any import."

"Might you share the title?" Eleanor pressed curiously. "I must say, you looked entirely engrossed."

It was her turn to enjoy his discomfort.

"It's just a book of . . . ahem . . . poetry."

"Poetry? Is that so? What poet? I'm a great lover of poetry myself."

"Oh, er . . . two Irish poets, actually. Brian Merriman and Oliver Goldsmith."

"Goldsmith? You enjoy pastorals, then?"

"I suppose I do. You know Goldsmith?"

Eleanor nodded, and then began to quote from memory.

Sweet Auburne! loveliest village of the plain,
Where health and plenty cheered the laboring
   swain,
Where smiling spring its earliest visit paid,
And parting summer's lingering blooms delayed.

She sighed in appreciation, then added, "I'm quite fond of Irish poets myself. May I see it?" She held out her hand for the volume he clutched by his side.

He hesitated, eyeing her warily as he shifted his weight from one foot to the other. He rubbed his chin and then nodded, placing the book in her outstretched palm.

Eleanor opened the heavy cover, her eyes widening in surprise as she flipped through the pages. "It's entirely in Gaelic," she said, looking up to meet his gaze.

After a pause, he nodded.

"You read Gaelic?"

"Yes. My mother was Irish, you know."

"Yes, I suppose I did know that. Would you"— Eleanor swallowed hard—"I mean, that is, might you read me a line or two?"

When he said nothing in reply, Eleanor added, "It would give me great pleasure."

"If you insist," he muttered, flipping through the pages with a scowl. At last he nodded to himself, cleared his throat, and began.

Ba thaitneamhach leabhair an crobhaire mná í,
Bhí seasamh is com is cabhail is cnámha aici,

Casadh ina cúl go búclach trilseach,
Lasadh ina gnúis go lonrach soilseach,
Cuma na hóige uirthi is só ina gáire, is cuireadh
ina Cló chun póige is fáilte!
Ach chreathas le fonn gan chonn gan chairde
Ó bhaithis go bonn go tabhartha i ngrá dhi.
Is dearbh gan dabht ar domhan gur díoltas
Danartha donn dom thabhairt ar m'aimhleas
D'fhearthainn go trom ar bhonn mo ghníomhartha
Ó Fhlaitheas le fonn do lom do líon mé.

"That's lovely," Eleanor said breathlessly. "Such a beautiful language." The unfamiliar words had slipped off his tongue so effortlessly, so artfully. "But what does it mean?"

He quirked a brow, then began to recite in English.

She was a pleasant and graceful strip of a lass
Her posture and presence betokened class
The toss of her head showed off ringlets and curls
And the sheen on her cheeks fairly glowed like
*   pearls,*
She had the vitality of youth and a smile of bliss
And all her demeanor invited a kiss.
I shook with desire, my mind did reel
I fell besottedly in love, head over heel.
It's certain, no doubt, it was retribution
For all my bad actions, my dissolution
Which fell with a vengeance for my transgression
From heaven above with cruel repression.

For a brief moment, Eleanor was rendered entirely speechless. "Surely it doesn't say that," she finally managed to say.

"Oh, I assure you it does. Precisely that."

"Hmmm, well. Imagine that." She supposed she should be thankful that the passage hadn't been even bawdier than it was.

Frederick snapped shut the book, glancing over his shoulder toward the carriage. "It's taking the coachman an interminable time to return. Perhaps I should have gone with him."

"Well, why didn't you?"

"Henley is so busy clucking over his wife that I thought it best I stay to offer protection. The roads can be dangerous, you know."

"And what good are you over here? Someone could make off with the horses without you even knowing it."

"Not likely. You'd be surprised how accurate one can shoot from this distance."

"Shoot? Whatever do you . . ." Her voice trailed off as she noticed the glint of steel peeking out from the hem of his waistcoat. Of course. He'd reached for it when she'd stepped on the twig and startled him. A pistol. Good God! "You don't really mean to shoot your brother-in-law when you find him, do you?"

"Of course I do, though I've dueling pistols for that. You spoke of your own brother with a great deal of fondness. Do you not suppose he would do the same, had a man mistreated you as vilely as Eckford has mistreated my sister?"

"Henry?" No, of course he wouldn't. Would he? "I've no idea, though I find it difficult to imagine him shooting a man in cold blood."

"No? Not even if the man had left you destitute? Robbed you of your jewels? Left you at the mercy of creditors, some more disreputable than others? Left bruises on your body, even while you carried his child?"

"Bruises?" Eleanor asked, horrified by the thought. "Did he really raise his hand to her?"

"According to Maria he did not, but I saw the bruises myself. She's protecting him, as she always has. Now tell me, what would your brother do in my place?"

"I . . . I cannot say." She shook her head. "But Henry is not a violent man—"

"As I am?"

"Well, you *have* fought duels. You admitted as much yourself."

"Yes, I suppose I did. In any case, yes, I do intend to shoot the bastard. Are you sure you're not injured?" he asked suddenly, leaning toward her with narrowed eyes.

Eleanor took a step back from his scrutiny. "Why do you ask?"

"You're holding your head at an odd angle, and you look as if you're in pain."

"I confess, it does hurt. It didn't at first, but now . . ." She trailed off, reaching up to rub the dull ache.

"Come, sit down." He reached for her hand and led her to the cloak spread out on the ground. "Let me see."

"No, I—ouch!" Eleanor winced as his fingers found the tender spot where her neck joined her shoulder. "Yes, right there. Is it swollen?"

"You've an enormous knot. Does this hurt?" He pressed his fingers into the spot, kneading ever so gently.

"A bit." The heat of his bare hands against her flesh made her heart race dangerously fast. Heavens, but she must summon the strength to make him stop. *Now.* "Really, you shouldn't touch me like this. Perhaps we should start back to the coach."

He peered over her shoulder, pressing himself against her back as he did so. "Why? Do you think I might try to take advantage of your injury and seduce you, right here? By the side of the road?"

She tried to force herself to move away from him, but found she couldn't. Instead, she licked her lips and said,

"Well, that *is* what you do, isn't it? Seduce women. You're quite accomplished at it, from what I hear."

He said nothing, but continued to massage her neck, his fingers surprisingly gentle and tender, easing out the pain as if he possessed some sort of magic. How many nights had she lain awake, dreaming of his touch? Of his strong hands on her bare skin . . .

"I must get up." She struggled to gain her feet, but he prevented it with his steely grip.

"Come now, I should just let you suffer? Stay. Tell the truth—my massaging it does make it feel a little better, doesn't it?"

"I suppose it does," she answered, her voice strangely tight. "Still, it's really not proper for us to be out here like this without a chaperone."

At last he moved away, rising to stand before her. "Good God, woman, are you really so priggish as that? In case you have not noticed, our carriage is shot to hell, you've got a knot the size of an egg on your neck, we're stranded here for God only knows how long, and you're worried about propriety?" He folded his arms across his broad chest and glared at her, his gaze sweeping down her form and back up again, the muscles in his jaw flexing perceptibly. "Do you know what you remind me of, Eleanor?"

Eleanor rose, feeling slightly dazed as she stood facing him. "I'm sure you're going to tell me. And please, quit calling me Eleanor as if we were intimates. You know it isn't proper, and you do it just to vex me."

"You remind me of a horse with too sharp a bit, too tight a bridle."

Ah, again with the horse comparison. "Is that so?" she bit out.

"Indeed. In fact, I've only seen you on one occasion

where you actually seemed free of the restraint—unbridled, so to speak."

"And when was that?" she asked, brushing a few stray blades of grass from her skirts.

"That day at Marbleton, when I found you dancing beneath the tree without boots or bonnet. It was truly an amazing sight, watching the transformation."

"I wish you wouldn't mention that . . . that . . . *indiscretion* on my part. It's quite embarrassing."

"I don't see why it should be," he said with a shrug. "There's no shame in doing something simply because you *want* to. Taking pleasure where it can be found. Doing what you please."

Eleanor began to pace, making a circuit beneath the trees. "That's what you do, isn't it? Whatever you please, regardless of the consequence, regardless of what people think or whom you might hurt."

"You're beautiful when you're angry, you know. Your cheeks turn crimson and your eyes roil like the sea in a storm."

She stopped her pacing a mere three feet from Frederick, who was now leaning indolently against a tree, one boot propped against the trunk.

"Is that so?" she snapped, her hands fisted by her sides. "Have you any more practiced lines to use, something more original, perhaps? I do believe I heard my eyes likened to the sea, oh, at least a half-dozen times over the course of the Season."

He shrugged. "It may not be original, but it is the truth. You're as lovely as any woman I've ever seen."

"Your pretty words have no power over me, Frederick Stoneham. It's a game you play, nothing more. Though I will say you're good—quite good," she added with a nod. "No wonder your conquests are plentiful."

He reached up to rub his cheek with his palm. "You doubt my sincerity?"

"I don't simply doubt it. I know your words are false, a means to an end."

"You're damn lucky I *don't* do whatever I please, regardless of the consequence. Otherwise, I'd show you just how sincere I am. Right here, by the road."

Eleanor considered his words, the innuendo finally sinking in. "Would you, now?" she asked, fully piqued.

"Indeed I would. Of course, then your brother would be forced to come after me with a pistol in *his* hand."

"I presume I'm supposed to be shocked by your scandalous talk? Is that your intent?"

"Aren't you? Shocked, I mean? After all, a lady of your circumstances—"

"Not in the least," Eleanor interrupted, deciding at once to put on a show of complete and total disaffectedness. "In fact, I find your predictability boring, to tell the truth."

The corners of his mouth curved into the barest hint of a smile. "I'm boring you, then?"

"No, I simply said your predictability was boring. In fact, in some ways I find you amusing."

"First I was boring, now I'm amusing? Well, I suppose I should be grateful for the improvement."

And now her trump card. "In fact, it's almost pitiable how one-dimensional you are. Have you nothing on your mind when you're with a woman besides how to get her on her back as expeditiously as possible?"

His faced blanched, and she knew her words had found their mark.

"You pity me?" he asked, his voice laced with incredulity.

She boldly met his gaze, folding her arms across her breasts. "You didn't answer my question."

"A lady shouldn't ask such a question. Perhaps I should report your impertinence to your father." He was smiling once more, but the smile was tight. Forced, perhaps.

"Oh, but you won't." Eleanor answered gaily, finally feeling as if she had the upper hand in the conversation.

"And why won't I?"

"Because you enjoy it. My impertinence. I can see it in your eyes."

His response startled her—he threw back his head and laughed, a deep, reverberating, purely male laugh. Finally, he returned his gaze to her, studying her face for what seemed like forever. "What game are you playing at, Eleanor Ashton? I'm beginning to think you a tease."

She shook her head. "I'm no tease. I'm simply stating facts, nothing more. I've no reason to be coy with you, of all people."

"And what does that mean, me of all people?"

"Just that it's not worth my while to trifle with you."

"No, I suppose it is not," Frederick said, carefully studying her. Not that he was such an expert on women, but she completely baffled him. One moment she was haughty and condescending, near-flirtatious the next. And now her hands were trembling, even as she tried to hide them in the folds of her skirts. Her cheeks were flushed and her eyes flashed, her chin tipped in the air contemptuously.

Damnation, but she was near to shaking with anger. What in God's name had he done to inspire such potent feelings of dislike? "We used to be friends, you and I," he said softly.

Eleanor bit her lower lip, then turned to look back toward the road. He could see the rapid rise and fall of her shoulders as she considered his words. At last she turned back to face him, her gaze fluttering up to meet his. "I suppose we were friends. But that was eons ago;

we were but children. We're adults now, and I do not think it wise that we . . . well, that we have overmuch to do with one another."

He took two steps toward her, wanting to reach for her hand, but deciding it was best if he didn't. "And what, exactly, have I done to sink so low in your estimation? After all, you informed me that you did not wish to marry me, and I agreed that it was not prudent for us to do so. Call me what you will, a rake or a rogue, but what difference does it make to you if I am the worst sort of libertine? I've done you no wrong, besides rejecting a match that you yourself rejected first."

"Why did you ever agree to it in the first place?" she asked, her voice wavering slightly, her bravado fading at last.

How could he explain it? How could he tell her that he'd remembered her as nothing more than a companionable yet utterly unexceptional woman? A woman he could tuck safely away in the countryside whilst he continued to enjoy himself in Town, his pockets made heavier by her dowry.

I can't, his mind countered. He couldn't say such hurtful things to her, no matter how snappish she was, no matter how much she deserved the comeuppance. He was tired of arguing with her, tired of the tension that crackled between them whenever they were in each other's company. Damnation, but he needed some peace in his life, some tranquility. The time spent in his father's company of late had drained him, leaving him feeling empty, barren.

Despising his own weakness, he realized that a part of him—a small part—had hoped that once, just once, he'd walk through his father's door and hear warm words of welcome instead of scorn and disdain. Disappointment. Rejection. Those things were his constant companions.

And then it dawned on him. *Rejection.* Eleanor felt he had rejected her. A woman's pride was fragile, and he'd hurt hers when he'd said he wouldn't marry her. He'd meant to hurt her pride, of course. Initially. A natural reaction to her snobbery, nothing more. But considering she'd been right to reject him, it suddenly seemed unjustified, even cruel. He resolved at once to make it right, to make her understand *why* he had rejected her.

"I cannot explain why I agreed to the match, Eleanor. But surely you don't think I decided to beg off because I found you lacking in any respect?"

Eleanor simply raised one delicately arched brow in response, and Frederick realized he'd been correct, that that was exactly what she had thought. Of course she would have. A wave of remorse washed over him, and he reached out to tuck an errant ebony lock behind her ear. "My God, entirely the opposite is true. I thought . . . I thought you realized that."

She shivered and stepped away from him. "I . . . I don't know what you mean."

"Simply that I'm not of your ilk, Eleanor Ashton. You deserve far better than me. As soon as I saw you, standing there in your garden, I knew you were far too good for the likes of me."

Her eyes widened a fraction, but she said nothing.

"Come now," he said jestingly. "Don't protest *too* heartily."

"I . . . Truly, I don't know what to say," she murmured, and he heaved a sigh of relief.

"That it's the truth, of course. You've accurately sketched my character, and I've no apologies for it. I enjoy women, take pleasure in my conquests. I drink too much, live too dangerously. My reputation is well-earned.

My father thought that perhaps my marrying would rein in my . . . excesses. I, of course, assumed that I would simply take a wife and continue to live my life as I wished to live it—doing whatever I please. I had no reason to object when my father suggested you as my prospective bride, and it's actually a compliment to you that, once I became reacquainted with you, I realized you did not deserve such a lot in life as that." Bloody hell, he'd never felt so emasculated, so damned vulnerable as he did at that moment, confessing the truth to her. Yet, the unshed tears that shone in her indigo eyes told him that he had been right to tell her.

"Anyway," he continued on, "a leopard cannot change its spots, and I've no desire to do so. You don't have to approve of the way I live my life, but I do wish we could call a truce. I've enough to worry myself right now with Maria and her predicament. Truthfully, I could use a friend, not another enemy. I've enough of those as it is."

"Very well," she said, her voice soft, full of caution. "A truce, then."

As soon as the words left her lips, his heart felt immeasurably lighter. No, he truly did not deserve her. She was a starburst of light—bright, passionate, full of life and spirit. If they were to marry, he would surely extinguish that light.

"Friends?" he asked, holding out a hand to her.

"Friends," she answered with a nod, offering her hand and allowing him to raise it to his lips.

He brushed a kiss across her knuckles and felt her shudder in response. Damn, but she really *was* lovely. It was too bad she was such an innocent, because he knew with a surprising certainty that he would enjoy her in his bed, warm and naked beneath him.

Bloody hell, enough with the gentlemanlike behavior. He could only be a kind, sensitive soul for so long.

Still clasping her hand, he met her gaze and grinned wickedly. "And as my friend, you'll surely forgive any attempts I make to get you . . . how did you so delicately phrase it? Ah, yes, *on your back*, that was it. You'll forgive any attempts I make to get you on your back before our journey is through, won't you?"

Her eyes began to flash, and she jerked her hand from his grasp. "You're incorrigible," she snapped. With that, she turned and stomped off through the grass, back toward the coach.

"As I said," he called out toward her retreating form, "a leopard cannot change its spots."

He heard her huff indignantly, and all he could do was smile.

Chapter 7

Eleanor reached for Lord Henley's hand and alighted from the coach with a weary smile. The journey to Devonshire had been long and arduous, and she'd never been so glad to reach a destination as she was at that very moment.

As she stepped down onto the gravel drive, she glanced up at George Whitby's home with appreciation. Whitby Hall, they called it. It was lovely, just as Selina had said it would be—a white-columned Greek revival structure surrounded by a lush, gently rolling park that stretched all the way to the sea. Eleanor inhaled the crisp scent of the sea as terns circled lazily overhead, calling to one another as they glided through the clear skies.

Returning her attention to Whitby's home, she watched as a line of servants assembled at the foot of the front stairs. She knew that the well-dressed gentleman standing two steps above the servants and adjusting his cravat must be Mister Whitby himself, and she studied him carefully as she waited for her remaining traveling companions to alight and the introductions to be made.

The man appeared broad of shoulder but not terribly

tall, with a trim waist and muscular legs. He wore no hat, and wavy hair the color of cinnamon shone in the waning sun, reaching just below his ears and complementing his neatly trimmed, wide whiskers. While his fawn breeches and bottle-green coat were not the height of fashion, they were well-cut and finely made, and he wore them with ease. Two hounds sat at his feet, one a mottled gray and the other solid black, both so large that their muzzles reached their master's waist, even while sitting.

"My dear Mister Whitby," Selina called out, joining Eleanor on the drive, and the man sprang to life at once, hurrying down to greet them with a broad smile.

"Ah, Lady Henley!" he said, reaching for Selina's hand and brushing a kiss across her knuckles. "How very grand to see you. I say, marriage suits you well. You look positively radiant."

"Enough flirting with my wife, Georgie," Henley said with a scowl. "Haven't you a word of greeting for your own brother?"

"Always a pleasure, Henley," Whitby said, and the two men embraced warmly.

"Indeed," Henley replied, smiling fondly at his brother. "And now you must meet my guests. May I present my wife's dearest friend, Lady Eleanor Ashton. Lady Eleanor, my brother, Mister George Whitby."

Eleanor executed a small curtsey, then allowed Mister Whitby to take her hand.

"Enchanted," Mister Whitby murmured, raising her hand to his lips. "It is a pleasure to welcome you to Whitby Hall."

Beside her, Frederick cleared his throat impatiently.

"And may I also present Mister Frederick Stoneham," Henley added, an amused note in his voice.

Mister Whitby released Eleanor's hand and reached

for Frederick's. "Any friend of Henley's is a friend of mine. Welcome, Mister Stoneham."

Frederick only grunted in reply as the man pumped his hand.

"Shall we?" Mister Whitby asked, moving aside and motioning toward the stairs. "Your servants arrived yesterday with your trunks, so your things are unpacked and awaiting you in your rooms. Come, meet my staff, and then you ladies can get settled in before dinner."

Minutes later, Eleanor was shown to her room, where her lady's maid had already laid out a fresh gown for dinner. It was an attractive room, the furnishings well-made if not a bit rusticated. It only lacked a woman's touch, she told herself. As the maid arranged for a bath to be drawn, Eleanor sat on the plump feather bed and exhaled slowly, suddenly wishing she could lie down and rest, if only for a moment.

Her eyelids felt heavy, and she allowed them to close, leaning back against the bed's fluffy pillows. At least her neck no longer felt sore. The physian summoned to the scene of the carriage accident had assured them that neither she nor Selina had suffered anything more serious than a mild strain. It would seem the man had been correct, as they'd both felt remarkably improved the following day, despite the discomfort of the jouncing coach and inferior accommodations. She hadn't slept well on the lumpy beds offered by the coaching inns they'd patronized along their route, and she was near enough exhausted.

Still, she was glad she had come. On first inspection, Mister Whitby seemed everything Selina had promised—handsome, well-mannered, charming. She couldn't for the life of her imagine why Henley thought him a bore, as he seemed quite lively. Perhaps he *would* prove to be the answer to her troubles, after all.

As Solange bustled back in, Eleanor sat up and rubbed her eyes, glancing over at the dress that the servant had laid across the chaise in the room's far corner. The gown's fabric was a flattering purple-puce gauze, but the cut was the prim, full-bodiced cut she generally preferred. She knew instantly that it wouldn't do, not if she hoped to capture Mister Whitby's attention in so short a time. She must showcase her assets, as her mama would say.

Rising from the bed, she strode across the room to the wardrobe, flinging open the doors and fingering the gowns that Solange had hung neatly inside. *No, not this one, nor this one, either.* She shook her head as she regarded several almost-identically cut gowns.

And then her gaze fell upon the peacock-colored sarcenet and velvet evening gown that her mother had insisted upon last month in Town. Eleanor had refused to wear it thus far, embarrassed by the shocking amount of décolletage it exposed—so much so that she had to have specially cut-down stays to wear beneath it.

Still, it was her best choice if she wanted to capture Mister Whitby's attention straightaway. Indeed, her mother would no doubt applaud the choice, which immediately made the rational side of her wary. Yet if she did not have a reasonable alternative to marrying Frederick before she returned to Essex—

"Solange, I think I'll wear this gown instead," she called out before she had time to change her mind. She held the brightly colored gown out to her maid, who plucked it from her fingers with a delighted smile.

"Indeed, mum, it'll look lovely on you. With the matching velvet band in your hair, perhaps, and York tan gloves?"

"Very well," Eleanor answered with a nod. "Haven't I some matching velvet slippers?"

Solange produced them from her trunks with a triumphant gleam in her eye. No doubt Selina's eyes would pop from her head when she saw her in this uncharacteristically revealing gown. Well, no matter, Eleanor thought dismissively. It only mattered what Mister Whitby thought.

And as to Frederick Stoneham . . . Blast it. It shouldn't matter one bit what he thought. But of course it did—oh, how it did.

I must fight this, she thought, her pulse quickening despite her resolve. *I must, and I will.* Her foolish heart depended upon it.

Frederick stood on Whitby's terrace, a snifter of brandy clutched in one hand as he watched Eleanor throw back her head and laugh, the moonlight illuminating the hollow at the base of her long, slender neck. The soft notes of her laughter floated on the sea-scented breeze, intoxicating him. Everything about the woman intoxicated him, if truth be told.

What particularly stymied him was the fact that she did not seem to have the same effect on George Whitby. Oh, the man seemed attentive enough on the surface; he said the right things, laughed at her witticisms, attempted to indulge her every whim. She'd had him in the palm of her hand throughout dinner, Whitby hanging onto her every utterance like a lapdog.

Yet, strangely enough, what Frederick did not sense was the man's lust—and what man in his right mind could help but lust over her in that blasted gown? Good God, outside the circles of the *demimonde*, he'd never seen a woman so blatantly and overtly sexually inviting as she was in that damnably indecent frock.

He'd nearly had to run back upstairs and relieve his

own needs the moment he'd seen her standing there at the top of the stairs, her dark hair piled high on her head and encircled in a band of velvet the same exotic blue-green shade as her gown. With her hair swept up, there was nothing to distract the eye from the astounding display of creamy, rounded breasts that peeked out from the oval-shaped cut-out that decorated her gown's bodice. How her undergarments didn't show was beyond him, and for a moment he wondered if perhaps she wasn't wearing any.

But intimate knowledge of the woman's form told him that such lush, full breasts could not possibly sit so high, so rounded, without support. It was a mystery, one that would distract him throughout the entire evening meal. Thankfully, his urgent erection had remained hidden beneath his napkin, and only intense mental concentration had forced it to subside before he'd been compelled to rise and join his companions there on the terrace for an after-dinner drink.

Even now, all he could think of as he watched her was removing that gown and discovering just what lay beneath. And while it certainly appeared that Whitby was enjoying Eleanor's company, his gaze never once lingered on her décolletage or traveled longingly up the column of her neck. No, the man appeared completely unaware of the fact that she was doing her damnedest to seduce him.

The realization that Eleanor was, indeed, attempting to seduce Whitby crashed down upon his consciousness. Of course. That was why she had come. He remembered Lady Henley going on about how handsome and amiable her brother-in-law was just before Eleanor had agreed to accompany them.

Frederick took a long draught of brandy, allowing the smoky liquid to slide slowly down his throat as he considered the situation. He studied her more closely, sitting upon a wide stone bench and gazing up at Whitby with approval, even as the man droned on about a fox hunt. Henley and Selina sat beside her, the party forming an image of genteel respectability.

And he was an outsider, an interloper. They'd all but forgotten his presence there, in the terrace's far corner, cloaked in shadows beneath the drooping branches of a willow. It was better this way. He could watch her from a safe distance, gauge Whitby's reaction to her practiced charm.

Suddenly Lady Henley rose, reaching for her husband's hand. "You must excuse me," she said, stifling a yawn with one gloved hand, "but I believe I shall retire now. I'm positively exhausted from our travels."

"Of course, my dear," Henley said, rising and tucking her hand into the crook of his elbow. "The day has been long, indeed."

Eleanor and Whitby followed suit, rising to stand before the French doors that led back inside.

"Shall I show you upstairs, as well, Lady Eleanor?" Whitby asked.

Eleanor shook her head. "No, I . . . I think I shall remain outside a bit longer, if you don't mind. I thought I might take a brief turn in the park before retiring." She looked up at Whitby hopefully, her cheeks flushed a delightful pink.

"What a fine idea," Whitby answered enthusiastically. "Unfortunately, I've some business to attend to with my steward, but perhaps Mister Stoneham would be so kind as to accompany you?"

Frederick raised a brow in surprise. Devil take it, what was wrong with the man? Was he blind? Or simply a fool?

Eleanor whirled around to face him, looking startled

to see him standing there. "I . . . well, perhaps I should retire after all," she floundered, watching the Henleys' retreating forms with a panicked look about her.

Before he could think the better of it, Frederick strode across the terrace and offered his arm. "Nonsense, Lady Eleanor," he heard himself say. "It's a lovely night, and you shall have your turn in the park. I don't bite," he added when she hesitated.

"I'm not so certain," she muttered under her breath, even as she took his arm. "Very well, then. Thank you, Mister Stoneham," she added, no doubt for Whitby's sake. "And good night, Mister Whitby. Thank you for a most pleasant evening."

"The pleasure was entirely mine," Whitby said with a bow.

There was nothing left to do but escort Eleanor down the wide, stone steps and through the fragrant garden below.

For several minutes they walked in silence, nothing but the distant crash of waves interfering with the hush that surrounded them. The full moon lit their path, illuminating the silvery lawn beneath their feet and casting an ethereal glow upon Eleanor's skin.

Frederick chanced a glance down at her, his gaze involuntarily drawn to the rise and fall of her breasts. If the fabric of her bodice were to move just an inch in either direction, the cut-out would expose a nipple, and he couldn't help but wonder if that nipple would be rosy, or dusky pink instead. Bloody hell, but he wanted to know.

He expelled his breath, forcing away the lustful thoughts as best he could. *Molly . . . Think of Molly instead,* his mind pressed. Her long, blond hair fanned out upon her shoulders, her eager mouth willing to please. Damnation, but it was no use.

A salty breeze rippled the branches above them as they passed through a grove of short, dense, fruit-laden crabapple trees, and Frederick felt Eleanor shiver beside him. He paused, turning to face her. "Are you cold?"

She nodded in reply. "A bit. I should have brought something warmer than my shawl," she said, releasing his arm and tucking the fringed shawl more tightly about her shoulders.

"Here," he said, unbuttoning his coat and shrugging out of it. "Take this."

"No, I cannot. Put it back on, someone might see—"

"Who? George Whitby?"

"Well, perhaps," she said, glancing back over one shoulder toward the house.

"And what if he did? Do you suppose he would prefer I let you catch a chill?"

"Perhaps not. Still—"

"Do you care so very much what the man thinks of you, Eleanor?"

"It's none of your concern," she said, then strode off toward the line of chestnut trees in the distance.

He caught up with her easily, falling into step beside her, his coat tossed over one shoulder. "It would seem that you care very much what he thinks of you, if that dress of yours is any indication."

"And just what does that mean?" she asked, hurrying her step.

"You know exactly what I mean. And you'd best slow down. If you exert yourself any further, your breasts are surely going to spill right out of that gown. And if they do, you cannot possibly hold me responsible for what I might do with them."

She turned on him then, her eyes flashing. "How dare you say such coarse, vulgar things to me!" The breeze stirred, and she shivered again, violently this time.

Again, he held out his coat to her. "Put the coat on, Eleanor. You're cold."

"No, thank you," she said, turning away from him.

He could see the gooseflesh on her arms, stubborn woman. "Damn it, Eleanor. Put the coat on."

She said nothing, but he saw her ball her hands into fists by her sides. Silently, he moved behind her, so close that his chest pressed against her back. When she did not protest, he gently laid the coat across her shoulders, and then stepped away from her before it was too late—before he did something he shouldn't, like gather her soft body in his arms and kiss her senseless. His breath coming ragged now with the effort of restraint, he watched as she pushed her arms through the sleeves without making a sound.

Eleanor inhaled the masculine scent of him, lingering in the folds of the coat, and her heart accelerated alarmingly. This was precisely why she had refused it—this, and the fact that he now stood beside her, his wild, dark hair blowing softly in the breeze, in nothing save his shirtsleeves and waistcoat. Looking dangerous—far too dangerous—with the hint of a beard darkening his chin and angular jaw. Why had Mister Whitby refused her and pawned her off on Frederick? Whitby's attentions had seemed so enthusiastic, so authentic, if only slightly detached. She had enjoyed his company well enough, and felt sure he had enjoyed hers equally so.

Yet, now Frederick stood here in the moonlight beside her, precisely the man she'd sought to avoid. Worse still, something about the way he was looking at her frightened her. No one had ever looked at her like Frederick was, and she didn't know what to make of it.

"For the record, Eleanor, I could refuse you nothing in that frock. If you asked me to jump off a cliff, I would do so, and willingly."

"I'm not certain if I should be flattered or offended by those sentiments," she said, endeavoring to slow her breathing.

"Flattered, no doubt. You see, you've found my weakness. Wear that gown, and you have me at your mercy. Your slave, so to speak."

"Interesting," she murmured, wanting to believe the veracity of his words but knowing she could not. "As always, Frederick, such pretty words. Tell me, do you ever encounter resistance? Any at all? Or do they all just simply fall at your feet?"

He threw back his head and laughed.

"What's so funny?" she asked, feeling foolish.

"You. Doubting my words. Haven't you noticed that I've barely been able to pry my eyes off you all evening?"

Of course she had noticed, and it had made her pulse leap and her palms dampen every time she had caught him looking her way. Was it truly desire she saw there, burning in the dark depths of his eyes? Or only wishful thinking on her part?

"Tell me about Ireland," she said, wishing to change the subject. "About your family's estate in Connemara."

For several seconds, he said nothing. When he finally spoke, his voice was soft, near reverent. "The Abbey is perhaps the most beautiful place on earth. It is nestled between a lake and a mountainside, terraced in old oak-woods and more often than not shrouded in mists. The house is slate-gray stone, rectangular and rambling, with exposed beam throughout. Behind it lies a walled garden, one side a flower garden and the other a kitchen garden. I spent many hours playing there as a boy—there, and rowing on the lake. My grandparents lived nearby, in a pink-washed house traced with vines, over-looking the grounds of the Abbey."

"It sounds lovely. Do you travel there often?"

"Not often enough, I'm afraid. It's isolated, and not an easy journey. I was sent there as a punishment, you know. As a boy."

"It doesn't sound such a punishment."

He shrugged. "I missed my sisters terribly. Maria, especially, and Katherine, the eldest. She was like a mother to me. But no, it wasn't such a punishment as my father thought it to be."

"You'd a brother, too, hadn't you? An older brother?"

"Indeed. Charles was my father's heir, his pride and joy. Killed quite tragically before I reached the age of ten. Is there anything else you wish to know?" he asked, his voice tight.

Eleanor shrugged, unable to meet his probing stare. "I only meant to be conversational."

He reached for her chin and tipped it up, forcing her gaze to meet his. For a moment she was spellbound, unable to think of anything save the sight of the moon, reflected in his eyes.

"Don't cast me as the tortured hero, Eleanor," he said at last, breaking the spell. "I'm nothing as romantic as that."

She turned her head, prying her chin from his grasp. "I've no idea what you mean."

"I'm glad to hear it." He eyed her sharply, his gaze traveling the length of her and back up again. He took a step in her direction, and she took an equal step away. "Are you always so anxious, so tightly strung as this?" he asked, noting her stiff posture.

"Is that how I seem to you?" she asked, wondering if she was really as transparent as that. "Anxious?"

"Indeed. It's like the air around you is charged with nervous energy. Even when we were younger, I felt it."

Eleanor swallowed, carefully measuring her words

before replying. "I suppose I am a bit anxious at times. I'm a . . . a worrier at heart."

"A worrier?"

"Well, just as you said that your sister Katherine was like a mother to you, I mothered my own brother in much the same way."

"Why? Your own mother is alive and well."

"Indeed, but my brother, well . . ." She trailed off, wondering briefly if she was revealing too much. Likely so. Still, she felt compelled to continue. "My brother suffered a weakness in the chest as a boy. He was much smaller and weaker than I was." How to phrase this delicately? "My mother, she was impatient with him, often unkind," she said, amazed that she was actually speaking these words aloud—words she often had a hard time admitting even to herself. "I do not blame her, of course. She was busy with her own interests, you see—"

"Yes, I've heard tales of Lady Mandeville's . . . er, interests."

Eleanor's cheeks burned with mortification. Was it really such common knowledge? Much as she tried to deny the ugly truth, she knew that her mother took many lovers—very *young* lovers—and did little to hide her conquests. Did everyone in all of Essex know about it, laugh about it, behind her back? Anger welled in her breast.

"My mother is not what one would call an affectionate woman," she said bitterly, "but she particularly withheld her attentions from Henry. I worried over him every single day; I still do, if truth be told. His health has been much improved since he went off to school, but I cannot help but worry." A painful lump formed in her throat. "I know that must sound silly, as he's a grown man now, off living his own life."

He reached for her hand, and Eleanor allowed him to

clasp it tightly within his warm one. "Not in the least. It only sounds as if you are a loving, devoted sister. He's lucky to have you."

"Thank you," Eleanor murmured, her voice thick with emotion. Why did his approval mean so much?

"Now let's get you back inside," he said softly, wrapping one arm about her shoulders and pulling her close. "It's late, and you're cold."

Eleanor nodded, allowing him to lead her back toward the garden. "I *am* cold, thanks to this ridiculous gown. I've no idea how I let Mama convince me to buy it."

"I've no idea, either, but I shall have to kiss Lady Mandeville in thanks next time I see her."

"Is it really as shocking as that?" Eleanor asked with an easy laugh, clutching his coat more tightly about her shoulders.

"Suffice it to say I shan't soon forget it. I'll no doubt ride off to Plymouth tomorrow, entirely weak with exhaustion for lying awake all night wondering just what you're wearing beneath it."

"I've almost a mind to tell you, it's so absurd." Her mouth curved into a smile as his gaze snapped up to meet hers questioningly. "But I won't," she added. "I'll let you suffer instead."

"Cruel woman."

"Nothing more than you deserve," she answered, realizing with a start that something had shifted in their relationship, something small but important nonetheless. The banter, the teasing . . . something about it reminded her of Henry, of the comfortable, easy relationship she shared with her twin. And if she were thinking of Frederick in brotherly terms, that could only mean one thing—that she was free at last from the infatuation that had held her heart prisoner for four long years.

"Will you promise to behave yourself, when I leave

you here tomorrow in the care of the honorable Mister Whitby? Honestly, you shouldn't rush the man's affections. No doubt he'll succumb to your charms in the end."

"Is that so?"

"Indeed. Only a fool would not."

"Well, there's hope, then. I suppose I shall have no choice but to behave. But only if you'll promise me you'll be careful, once you find him. Eckford, I mean. There must be another way, besides a duel."

"Will you shed a tear for me if I'm killed?" he asked, capturing her wrist and bringing her palm to his lips.

Despite his mocking tone, Eleanor felt her throat constrict uncomfortably. "Don't jest about something so serious, Frederick. It isn't at all funny."

"No? I apologize, then. I'm an excellent marksman, Eleanor. Have faith in that."

She pulled her hand from his grasp and swallowed hard, her gaze trained on her slippers. "I don't like it one bit, despite the horrible things that Mister Eckford has done."

"No, I don't suppose you would. Well, the least you can do is send me off with a kiss."

Eleanor inhaled sharply. "You cannot be serious."

"Aye, I'm entirely serious. Just a small kiss?"

Her heart began to pound—her theory was being tested. If her infatuation had died a quiet death, then what harm could come from a chaste, sisterly kiss?

"Like sending a lover off to war," he pressed, leaning in toward her, his breath warm on her neck.

"You're not going to war, and I'm not your lover," she countered, knowing full well that she would kiss him in the end. *A test,* she told herself. Nothing more.

"Ah, but my current *inamorata* is in London at present," he said, his hands encircling her waist, drawing her closer still. "And I'm here in Devonshire. What's a man to do?"

"Oh, very well." Taking a deep, fortifying breath, Eleanor raised herself on tiptoe and cautiously pressed her lips against his. She gasped when she heard his sharp intake of breath, just before he crushed her to him.

She knew precisely then—the moment his lips parted hers—that she'd failed the test. God help her, but she'd failed.

Chapter 8

Damnation, where had she learned to kiss like this? Frederick's mind reeled as he deepened the kiss, exploring Eleanor's soft, yielding mouth with his tongue. Her own tongue boldly met his, eager and inviting as she tangled her fingers in the hair at the nape of his neck. His breathing now ragged, he traced her bottom lip with his tongue, all but intoxicated by the feel of her in his arms, her breasts pressed against his chest, her heart pounding furiously in rhythm to his own.

He should have known she would be as tempting as Eve, once he broke through that tightly guarded restraint of hers. His lips trailed down her throat, lingering on the spot where her pulse thrummed against her skin. She tipped her head back, a soft moan escaping her lips. His mouth moved lower still, across her collarbone, to the base of her throat, and back up again to her trembling lips.

Taking her with him, he stumbled back a few paces and pressed her back against the solid trunk of an oak, his own feet planted wide. She did not resist as he parted her lips once more, his hips pressed against her belly, his erection throbbing against her.

Allowing his hands to freely roam her body, he brushed his palms across her breasts, nearly exposed now in her bodice's opening. Unable to resist, he slid one hand inside, across her smooth, silky skin to her hardened nipples. One flick of his fingers made the sensitive skin pebble tightly, and he felt a shudder run through her body.

Bloody hell, but he wanted her. Hard and fast, against the tree. He couldn't, of course. But damn, how he wanted to.

He had to stop this—now. *Now*, his mind screamed, his entire body afire as she squirmed against him, pressing urgently against his erection and driving him mad, even through the layers of fabric that separated them.

Groaning fiercely with the effort, he tore his mouth from hers. "Dear God, Eleanor," he said, his voice laced with unquenched desire. "Are you trying to kill me yourself?"

For a moment she said nothing, leaning against the tree for support, her legs visibly shaking. She looked dazed, slightly disoriented as she tugged the bodice of her gown back to its rightful place.

An innocent—he'd finally sunk so low that he'd trifled with an innocent. It took him a moment to find his voice.

"I apologize, Eleanor. It's that damned frock of yours."

Still she said nothing.

"Will you say something, love?" he prodded, reaching for her trembling hands. "Did I hurt you?"

"N . . . no," she stuttered, her eyes finally appearing to focus. "I'm not hurt. I'm only . . . Dear Lord, what did we just do?"

"We stopped; that's what matters. I did not compromise

you. And even if I had, we're still betrothed, technically speaking, are we not?"

"No. *No*," she repeated, her voice rising. "I hope to marry Mister Whitby."

"You barely know the man," Frederick countered.

"I know him well enough to know he would not do . . . what we just did . . . this."

She was probably right; the man seemed to be a bloody eunuch. "No, likely not," he conceded. "And that is what you want in a husband?"

She nodded. "Precisely so."

A burning anger rose in his breast, though he could not credit it. "Then that's what you'll have," he said curtly. "If you'll excuse me." He bowed sharply, dismissing her. Reaching up to straighten his cravat, he turned and strode toward the house without so much as a glance back in her direction.

Only when he stepped into his guest chamber and closed the door behind him did he realize that he'd forgotten his coat, no doubt still draped across Eleanor's shoulders. Bloody hell, but he was losing his mind.

Cinching the belt on her dressing gown, Eleanor sleepily padded across the room, drawn to the window as if spellbound. She pulled back the drapes and peered out the glass as the first light of dawn penetrated the murky shadows below. Lord Henley stood in the drive, holding the reins of a dappled gray horse. Beside him, a groom stood with an enormous bay. Eleanor held her breath as Frederick appeared, striding across the drive with his greatcoat billowing out behind him. The brim of his hat shielded his eyes from her view, but she could picture them, a warm chocolate brown and sparkling wickedly, in her mind's eye.

She pressed one palm against the glass, cool and smooth beneath her skin, as she watched him swing up onto the horse's back and take up the reins. For several minutes the two men appeared to converse atop their mounts. Finally, Frederick nodded, wheeling his horse's head toward the road. A shudder ran up her spine as he dug his heels into the animal's flanks and rode off in a cloud of dust.

Only when his form was reduced to a barely discernible speck in the distance did she allow her gaze to drop, her chin dipping down toward her breastbone as she let out the breath she hadn't realized she'd been holding.

It was good that he was leaving, she reminded herself. Definitely for the best. Now she could become better acquainted with Mister Whitby without the distraction Frederick created just with his presence alone. Turning from the window, she swiped the back of one hand across her forehead, allowing her gaze to travel across the room. She'd tossed and turned all night long, entirely unable to sleep, and now the bedcovers were a tangled jumble upon the bed.

She hurried over to the carved maple bed, thinking to straighten the linens a bit before Solange awakened and came in to ready her for the morning meal. With a tug, she pulled the bedcovers up, frowning at the lump that remained at the foot of the bed. *What on earth?* She flipped up the edge of the delicately embroidered counterpane and peered beneath it.

Frederick's coat! Her hand flew to her mouth, muffling the gasp that escaped her lips. She'd entirely forgotten she'd been wearing it until she'd entered her bedchamber last night and saw her disheveled reflection in the looking glass. Hearing Solange's footsteps approaching in the hallway, she'd hastily shrugged out of it and stuffed it beneath the bedclothes only seconds before the maid had entered to help her undress.

Warily, she dragged the coat out from under the counterpane, involuntarily bringing it up to her nose and inhaling the scent of him that lingered still in the soft folds of fabric. Memories of his kiss came flooding back, and she sank to the edge of bed with a groan of frustration. What a fool she'd been, thinking she could resist his kiss, that her girlish infatuation had been replaced by a more sisterly affection.

What a silly, stupid thing she had done, kissing him. If anything, it had only proven that her infatuation had grown stronger, more potent—more dangerous. Because now it was more than simply a senseless appeal, a mere physical attraction. Despite Frederick's rakish ways, she was beginning to actually *like* him. She could not fathom why—perhaps it was simply that he spoke so lovingly and protectively of his sisters.

Whatever the reason, she now found Frederick far more amiable than before. She'd best not confess as much to Selina, or her friend would surely insist she have her head examined. And perhaps she should. What sort of woman had she become, kissing one man while hoping to ensnare the affections of another? How could she so easily dismiss Frederick after allowing him such liberties?

On the other hand, Frederick surely had no qualms about sharing a passionate embrace with one woman, then moving on to another. In fact, he'd made a habit of precisely that. She'd only suffered a moment of weakness, nothing more, and it would never happen again. Never. A wave of remorse washed over her. Mister Whitby deserved better.

But what to do with Frederick's coat? How could she possibly explain its appearance in her bedchamber?

Even if Solange didn't discover it, a chambermaid surely would. Her mind cast about frantically for a solution, but none came immediately to mind. *Oh, fustian.* What was she to do? She brought it to her nose once more, inhaling deeply. For a moment she thought to put her arms through the sleeves, to wrap herself up in it and slip back into the soft, warm bed.

Reaching a hand to her mouth, she stifled a yawn. Perhaps she would lie back down for a spell. The sun had only just arisen, after all. She scooted back toward the headboard, still clutching Frederick's coat to her breast. Sliding her legs beneath the bedclothes, she reached around to plump the feather pillow behind her.

Crash! Eleanor started in surprise, staring down at the ceramic pitcher she'd inadvertently knocked from the bedside table. It had broken cleanly, cleaved into two brightly pattered pieces that lay there on the polished floorboards below. Her heart began to thump against her breastbone as she held her breath. Had anyone heard? She found her answer in the sound of footfalls, gaining in volume. Oh no, not Solange, not so early as this!

Looking about frantically, she leapt from the bed, clutching the coat in trembling hands as she sought a suitable hiding place.

The window. Was there any other way? She could think of none, and surely Solange would appear at the door in seconds. She hurried to the window, threw open the sashes, and tossed the coat as far as she could. How successful she was, she had no idea, for as soon as she closed the sashes, a knock sounded on the door and Solange entered without awaiting her response.

"I heard a noise," Solange said, her brow creased with concern. "Are you up so early, my lady?"

Eleanor nodded. "I could not sleep. And look"—she gestured toward the broken pitcher—"I'm so terribly clumsy."

"Don't fret, mum. It isn't such a fine piece as all that. Look how cleanly it broke." Solange bent and retrieved the two halves from the floor, setting them inside her apron. "Shall I light the fire for you?"

"That would be lovely," Eleanor answered. "Though I thought I might lie back down. Will you wake me in an hour?"

"Of course." Solange folded the corners of her apron around the broken ceramic and placed it on the dresser before seeing to the fire. Once the fire crackled in the hearth, she retrieved the apron and headed toward the door. "Now get some rest, mum. You sorely look as if you need it."

Did she? Eleanor frowned, reminding herself that she must look her best today. As her maid departed, Eleanor hurried to the looking glass and peered at her own reflection, brows drawn with worry. Indeed, she looked wan, her eyes shadowed. However would she manage to capture Mister Whitby's fancy looking like this?

Casting one last guilty glance at the window, she removed her dressing gown and hurried back to the warm, inviting bed. As she slipped back between the linens, she couldn't help but silently curse Frederick Stoneham for creating such havoc in her life.

Eleanor stepped out onto the stone terrace with a smile, feeling refreshed yet famished. The scent of eggs and sausages drifted past her on the breeze, and her stomach grumbled in anticipation.

"There she is, awake at last," Selina called out in greeting, waving to her from a round wrought-iron table laid in crisp white linen. Straw baskets and tiered trays filled with savory treats were spread about the table invitingly, and Eleanor hurried to take a seat beside her friend, directly across from George Whitby.

"Coffee, mum?" a serving maid asked, and Eleanor nodded as she peeled off her gloves and placed them in her lap with her napkin.

"What a lovely morning," she murmured. It was true— the sky was gloriously clear, a brilliant shade of azure without a cloud in sight. Terns circled lazily overhead, and the crashing of the sea could be heard over their calls. How she longed to take a walk to the seashore! Perhaps later, she thought, turning her attention to Mister Whitby.

"I hope you slept well, Lady Eleanor," he said, reaching for a slice of toast.

"Indeed I did, Mister Whitby. The sound of the sea is so very soothing. Your home is wonderfully situated."

"I wholeheartedly agree." He paused to slather his toast with butter. "There's wonderful fishing and hunting in the woods nearby, and the proximity to Plymouth is excellent."

Selina set down her cup and smiled sweetly. "If only you'd accept my offer to help with the décor, George. You cannot deny that your home lacks a woman's touch."

Eleanor's eyes widened. How very bold of Selina. Would Mister Whitby take the bait?

He paused only to chew a bite of toast before replying. "True, true indeed. Without a mistress, my home does lack the polish that a woman's touch would afford. Still, I hope you find it comfortable."

"I do, indeed," Eleanor interjected brightly. "Thank you," she added, as a manservant presented her a plate generously laden with eggs and sausage. "So, Mister Whitby, tell me more about your pursuits here in the country. How is the society in Devonshire?"

"Very amiable indeed, Lady Eleanor. The Duke of

Dandridge has an estate nearby, and the Duchess is a fine hostess, quite charming. I dine with them often."

"How lovely that must be," Eleanor said, spearing a sausage with her fork. "I have not made her acquaintance, but the Duchess of Dandridge is known far and wide as a first-rate hostess, and her invitations are eagerly sought. You must be quite in her favor, then."

"I suppose so, as the duke and I often hunt together. His holdings are vast, the game plentiful and his lakes well-stocked."

Eleanor's attention began to wane as Whitby spoke at length about hunting and fishing on the duke's lands, apparently his two favorite occupations if his enthusiasm was any indication. She allowed her mind to wander as she ate her breakfast in silence, marveling at the beauty of the park beyond the terrace. She really was looking forward to exploring the grounds on foot.

"Lady Eleanor is very fond of the sea," Selina said, laying a hand on her wrist and drawing her attention back to her fellow diners. "Are you not?"

"Very much so," she murmured, marveling at Selina's uncanny ability to read her thoughts.

"You must show her the view from the cliffs, George. I declare, Eleanor, it is positively breathtaking."

"Of course," Whitby agreed with a nod. "Perhaps after breakfast you'd both be inclined to join me on a walk about the grounds?"

"I'm afraid I cannot," Selina demurred, shaking her head. "My neck is still tender from our carriage accident. But Eleanor can accompany you, and I'll use the time to catch up on my correspondence." A ruse, Eleanor realized. Just last night Selina had declared that she felt fully recovered.

"Say you will, Lady Eleanor," Whitby pressed, offering her a wide smile. "It would please me greatly."

"Of course." Eleanor took a sip of coffee, examining the man over the rim of her cup. He really was quite handsome in a simple, robust way. His face was pleasing, with soft, hazel eyes and full lips, and his form bespoke health and vigor. His air was jovial and solicitous, and his behavior entirely gentlemanly. Though he was not titled, his future seemed secure, his home grand though not ostentatious, and his connections spoke well of his character. Being asked to dine frequently with the Duke and Duchess of Dandridge was no small matter, and Eleanor was duly impressed. Yes, Mister George Whitby was everything a gently bred lady could want in a husband, and she'd be a fool to lose the opportunity at hand.

"I say, the strangest thing happened this morning," Mister Whitby said, drawing Eleanor from her ruminations. "An intrigue of sorts. A coat was found in the bushes in front of the house, along the drive. A gentleman's coat."

Eleanor sputtered, nearly choking on her coffee.

He shrugged. "We've no idea where it came from, or how it came to be in the bushes."

"How very odd," Selina said, casting a curious glance in Eleanor's direction. "You don't suppose an interloper was sneaking about outside, do you?"

"I doubt it, or my hounds would have alerted me. They're quite sensitive to intruders." He reached down to pat the head of the hound who rested at his feet.

"Perhaps it belongs to a servant," Eleanor offered, perhaps too brightly. Her heart was pounding furiously in her breast, and it was all she could do to remain in her seat. *Let my secret remain safe,* she silently prayed, twisting the napkin in her lap.

Mister Whitby shook his head, his lips pursed thoughtfully. "No, it could not possibly belong to a servant. It was a gentleman's coat of superfine, and well-cut at that. I'll have to ask Henley and Mister Stoneham about it upon their return. I suppose it could belong to one of them, though I've no idea how it found its way to the bushes."

Eleanor cleared her throat uncomfortably, entirely certain that her guilt was evident in her countenance. "I'm sure there must be a reasonable explanation."

"An explanation, perhaps, but I'm not so sure it will be reasonable. Anyway," he said, pushing away his plate and rising. "If you ladies will excuse me, I have some matters to attend to, and then I shall take Lady Eleanor on that walk I promised. Shall we meet up here in an hour?"

"Indeed, Mister Whitby. That sounds lovely." More than anything, she was relieved that the topic of the coat was abandoned. She only hoped it would be forgotten by the time Henley and Frederick returned, otherwise her guilt would surely betray her.

And if Mister Whitby learned what had transpired in his park between Frederick and her, well . . . She shook her head in despair. She would do everything in her power to make sure he did not find out.

She might be weak where Frederick was concerned, but she was not stupid. It was time to secure her future—her future with George Whitby.

Chapter 9

"Just a few more paces, right up here. At the crest of the bluff. Can you make it, Lady Eleanor?"

"Of course, Mister Whitby." Eleanor smiled, striding confidently toward the crest of the rise. "I'm quite fond of taking exercise on foot, and—" Her breath hitched in her chest as her eyes swept across the vista, drinking in the sight before her. The edge of the cliff disappeared into the blue-green sea, sweeping out as far as the eye could see. Frothy white foam capped the waves, rolling toward the sandy crescent that stretched out to the right of where they stood. "It's stunning," she breathed, turning toward Mister Whitby. "Simply stunning."

"Isn't it? Down below, beyond the orangerie, there's a path that leads straight down to the shore itself. Still, I think the sea best appreciated from this particular vista."

"I've never seen anything lovelier." Eleanor lifted her face to the salty breeze, inhaling deeply. "Tell me, do you ever bathe in the sea?"

"Every morning, when the weather permits. Are you fond of swimming, Lady Eleanor?"

"I've not had much opportunity, I'm afraid, though it

does seem something I would enjoy. If the water were warm enough, that is."

"It was quite refreshing this morning. I find it invigorating. An excellent start to the day. I highly recommend it."

Whitby regarded her for a moment, his fists resting on his hips, his ginger-colored hair blowing in the soft breeze. His mouth curved into a smile. "Do you like to dine *alfresco*?" he asked at last. "I could have the cook pack a hamper with sandwiches and tea cakes, and we could picnic here. Tomorrow, perhaps?"

"What a lovely idea. I greatly enjoy meals *alfresco*, something my brother Henry takes great pleasure in teasing me about."

"I cannot see cause for teasing in that. Though I suppose that is what brothers do—tease."

Eleanor shrugged. "Do you have sisters, Mister Whitby?"

"Indeed, two sisters. Fanny and Julianna. Silly women, both of them. I cannot tell you how vastly relieved I was when they found husbands. I have not seen either in several years now."

Eleanor was bewildered. "Not seen them in years? Your own sisters? Come now, surely you exaggerate."

"No, not at all. We're all far too busy with our own occupations. It's a wonder I see Henley as often as I do, as I rather think he finds the sporting life dull."

"Perhaps." Eleanor shrugged, feeling suddenly uneasy in the company of a man who obviously cared so little for his siblings. "Do you often go to Town?"

He absently smoothed down the cuffs of his charcoal-colored jacket. "Now and again, for business purposes. But I vastly prefer the country."

"I'm fond of the country myself," Eleanor said,

happy for the common ground. Still, she enjoyed Town, too—especially since her come-out.

A gust of wind lifted the hem of Eleanor's pale yellow skirts, sending the fabric flapping against her limbs. She reached up to steady her bonnet, its ribbons dancing in the breeze. "The wind is brisk today, isn't it?"

Mister Whitby smiled. "Perhaps there's a storm headed our way." He shielded his eyes with one hand as he peered up at the clouds. "No, perhaps not. It looks rather clear, does it not? A shame. We've such marvelous storms in this district."

Eleanor couldn't help but grimace. A storm, marvelous? "I must confess, I'm not overly fond of violent weather," she said, unable to curb the shiver that raced down her spine. Nothing terrified her more, if truth be told.

"No? Perhaps you'll change your mind on that count once you experience one here in Devonshire. Our storms are truly magnificent. Anyway, tomorrow we shall have our picnic. But for now, we should make our way back to the house as I fear you've caught a chill." He held out his arm, and Eleanor took it, settling her hand into the crook of his elbow.

If he were so worried about her catching cold, he could have offered her his coat, as Frederick had done, Eleanor thought peevishly. Immediately, she scolded herself for such a thought. Frederick might have insisted she wear his coat, but still, he was no gentleman. She mustn't let herself forget that. Frederick was altogether unsuitable, unlike the man whose arm she now held.

"So, Mister Whitby," Eleanor murmured, smiling sweetly at her escort, "you must tell me more about the Duchess of Dandridge. Is her drawing room really done entirely in gold leaf and marble?"

"Indeed it is, Lady Eleanor. The Duchess's tastes run to the height of opulence, and not just in the drawing room. Did you know the Duke and Duchess have a hunting lodge not five miles from here, and . . ."

He continued rambling on, having somehow managed to turn the conversation back to his favorite topic. With a sigh of resignation, Eleanor tuned out the sound of his voice, reducing it to a steady hum in the background as they made their way back down the steep slope toward the house. *A nap,* Eleanor thought with a yawn. *What I'd really like is a nap.*

"Lemme see that portrait again," the grizzled old barkeep grumbled, casting aside the soiled towel and pushing wire spectacles upon his bulbous nose.

Frederick pushed the miniature that his sister had provided him across the bar with a scowl. Was this man playing games with him?

"Hmmm, I reckon I can't be sure. These 'ere eyes are not quite what they used to be, ye know? My specs is old, and I can't afford me any fancy new ones."

His scowl deepening, Frederick retrieved several heavy coins and placed them on the bar, sliding them across the pocked surface toward the man. "Perhaps this will help your failing memory."

The man palmed the coins with a grin. "Why, I believe I do recognize 'im, now that I'm lookin' more closely. Ain't heard him called Eckford, though. Him's a man of the cloth, he says. New to these here parts, sayin' that he lost his living in a family squabble. The missus travels with him, a peacock of a lady if I ever seen one. Way too bright and fancy for a vicar's wife, my own ladybird says."

"Where might I find him?" Frederick asked, his gaze

meeting Henley's. His gut told him that the man told the truth.

"I don't reckon I know where to find 'em. He's within a day's drive, though, that's fer certain. Once a month he comes here to town, with the lady in tow. Always stops in here for a drink, he does, and takes a room for the night now and again. I remember him special 'cause he's so tight with his coins if you know what I mean. Regular as clockwork, though. Once every moon, and always on a Tuesday."

"And when would you say he was last in town?" Henley asked.

The man scratched his head. "Hmmm, well, 'twas likely a little more'n a fortnight ago, I'd say. Not likely to return for another fortnight yet."

Frederick's heart accelerated. "And you're sure this is our man?"

"I'm not sayin' I'm a hunnerd percent sure." He paused and seemed to consider the question. Finally, he nodded. "But I'm a bettin' man, and I'd put my money on it. The Tuesday after next. Come here and ye'll find yer man."

"Thank you for your time, Mister . . ."

"Crosby. Edwin Crosby at yer service, gents." He held out one beefy hand to Frederick.

Frederick took his hand into his gloved one and shook it firmly. "Thank you, Mister Crosby." He reached for several more coins and pressed them into his hand. "If he is indeed my man, there will be more where this came from. If, for some reason, he returns before expected, you must send word to me at once." Frederick produced one of his calling cards and placed it on the bar. "I'll be in residence at Whitby Hall, a guest of Mister George Whitby. Can I count on you, Mister Crosby?"

The man nodded vigorously, pocketing the coins as he did so. "Ye can count on Edwin Crosby. I'm a man of my word, I am. Jes' ask anyone in these here parts."

"Aye, very good. Good day, Mister Crosby." With a curt bow, Frederick turned, making his way back through the dingy public house to his waiting mount. Henley followed suit, and both men took up their reins from the groom in the drive.

"Well, Stoneham, what do you think?" Henley asked as he swung up into the saddle.

"I think we've found our man," Frederick ground out through gritted teeth. He could barely stomach the thought of waiting a fortnight to get his hands on the bastard. Still, searching him out in the surrounding countryside would be like looking for the proverbial needle in the haystack. Crosby hadn't even provided them with a name. But he'd seen the light of recognition in the man's eyes the moment he'd seen the miniature. They had their man; all they had to do was wait.

Henley's horse began to prance nervously in the road. "I don't know about you, my friend, but I could use a night or two in my warm, comfortable bed back at Whitby Hall."

Frederick glanced up the darkening sky. It did look as if a storm were gathering. "Do you think we can outride it?"

"Oh, I can certainly outride it," Henley answered with a wink, swinging his horse's head toward the south. "The question is, can you?"

Never one to turn down a challenge, Frederick tapped his mount's flank with his crop, sending the beast off in a gallop before Henley had the chance to react.

He would have Eckford in less than a fortnight. He was sure of it. In the meantime, he could spare a few days at Whitby Hall, perhaps even get in some pistol practice, not that he needed it. He'd never lost a duel before; he certainly would not lose this one.

Besides, he had had just about enough of listening to Henley prattle on endlessly about his wife—was she eating well, was Whitby boring her, had she taken a chill, perhaps? If Frederick didn't like Henley so much, he'd have throttled the man by now. What in God's name had happened to him? He'd gone and gotten married— to little Selina Snowden, of all the silly chits—and now it appeared that he'd gone soft in the head.

Frederick shook his head in disgust as he reined in the horse, slowing its pace as Henley pulled abreast of him.

"It'll be interesting to see how Lady Eleanor is getting on with Whitby, won't it?" Henley called out.

Interesting, indeed. Had the fair Eleanor managed to capture the heart of the hapless Whitby? He suddenly couldn't wait to get back to Whitby Hall to find out.

Eleanor shrugged into her dressing gown with a heavy sigh. Oh, how she longed for home, for her beautiful rose-and-cream bedchamber back at Covington Hall. For her familiar things, her familiar life. If only she could turn back time, back to the day her papa had told her about the marriage contract with Frederick Stoneham.

She should have told him then and there—in no uncertain terms—that the match was unacceptable. That she could not possibly marry him. Surely Lord Worthington would have released her father from the agreement— the two men were friends, after all. Then Frederick would have remained mercifully in Town, and she wouldn't be here in Devonshire now, forced to do everything in her power to capture the fancy of a man she did not fancy in return. Expelling her breath in a rush, she sank onto the chintz-patterned tuffet before the dressing table.

The past two days had been tedious at best, though she'd put every effort into enjoying herself. Yesterday they had toured the grounds of Whitby Hall on horseback and, though Eleanor wasn't a particularly accomplished rider, she found it pleasurable nonetheless. Today they had picnicked on the bluff, just as Mister Whitby had promised. Though the view of the sea was incomparable and the food delicious, she could no longer pretend—to herself, at least—that she found Mister Whitby an agreeable conversationalist. He somehow managed to turn every polite exchange into a discussion of hunting—fox hunting, quail hunting, duck hunting. It would seem there was far more English wildlife that could be pursued with a gun than she had thought possible.

She reached for her brush and absently ran it through her unbound hair, scowling at her reflection while she did so. At least Selina had joined them on their picnic, else it would have been near enough unbearable. *What am I doing here?* she mused, irritation rising in her breast. This was madness. She could not marry George Whitby—could she? He bored her near enough to tears, and it seemed they shared no common interests.

Then again, there were far worse flaws a gentleman could possess than simply being boring. She knew it to be true—wasn't Frederick's errant brother-in-law a perfect example? She'd heard many a tale of husbands who drank too much, who gambled away their fortunes, who seduced other women, who ruled their wives with an iron fist.

George Whitby would do none of that. Instead, he'd while away his days in the country, off on his favorite hunter with a rifle flung over one shoulder. She would likely not see him for days on end, whilst he spent his time with like-minded men like the Duke of Dandridge. Would that be so terribly unpleasant? *No,* she told herself firmly. No, her lot in life could be worse, far worse than that.

Her gaze moved past her own reflection in the glass, focusing instead on the bed behind her. Yes, there was *that* to consider. The marriage bed. She knew enough of marital relations to know that she would be required to share a bed with her husband, at least often enough to produce an heir. Would it be all that unpleasant?

Her brow creased with a frown. Mister Whitby was perfectly attractive; there was nothing at all repulsive about his looks. Still, the idea of sharing a bed with the man . . . She let the thought trail off, her stomach pitching uncomfortably. She slammed her brush to the top of the vanity, wincing at the sharp crack of heavy silver against marble. Her gaze was drawn to the dancing light of the candle, reflected in the brush's polished handle, and she simply stared at it until her vision began to blur.

Stop this; stop this now, she silently chastised herself. Marriage was not about physical desire, it was about companionship. About comfort and security. Without a husband, a woman had none of those things. Sharing a husband's bed was considered a wife's duty, and English women far and wide did exactly that—their duty. Why should Eleanor be any different? She had just as much chance at happiness with Mister Whitby as she did with any other gentleman her father might choose.

While Mister Whitby's enthusiasm for the sporting life seemed somewhat irritating at present, it would mean that he would remain occupied with his own interests, leaving her free to do what she pleased. She would likely be able to go to Town or visit Selina or Henry whenever she took a notion to do so. Truly, what more could she ask for? He would not mistreat her, of that she was sure. He was boring, yes, but gentle and kind. Only a selfish woman would wish for more.

Feeling restless, she rose and strode to the window, pulling back the drapes and peering out at the drive below. *How strange.* She had retired early, just after dinner, and yet it was already eerily dark—the inky sky cast an odd shade of green. Squinting against the night, she noticed a line of trees along the drive, their leaves whipping violently in the wind. She blinked rapidly, her pulse accelerating in alarm. Almost at once, the glass began to rattle, the trees beyond bent nearly in half. A shudder snaked up Eleanor's spine, and she took a step back from the glass.

Lud, a storm. A violent one, too, from the look of it. In an instant, her palms dampened, and she wiped them on her dressing gown as she continued her retreat away from the window, toward the bed. When the backs of her shaky legs bumped the mattress, she sat, her gaze never leaving the now-shuddering glass as the wind grew to a howl.

The hair on the nape of her neck lifted just as the room lit with a brilliant burst of light. The crash that followed sent Eleanor back to her feet, scurrying to the door. Her heart beating wildly, she pressed her back against the heavy oak panel, fighting back the hysteria that rose in her breast.

The wind began to lash at the window, the shutters creaking under the onslaught. Another flash of blinding light. The crack of thunder followed only seconds later, and Eleanor squeezed her eyes shut, pressing herself more tightly against the door. The storm was moving closer, near enough on top of them now.

Opening her eyes, she looked to the bed, considering climbing beneath it till the storm subsided. Just then the candle, still sitting in its scrolled iron holder on the dressing table, flickered briefly, then extinguished itself.

Her panic rose a pitch, her breath coming faster. It was dark now, entirely dark until another flash of lightning lit the room, followed not a second later by the accompanying clap of thunder. As a girl, she would have run to Henry's bed in their shared nursery and cowered beneath the covers with him beside her. But she was no longer a girl, and Henry was not there. The sound of blood rushing through her veins roared in her temples, and for a moment Eleanor feared she was going mad.

The next crash of thunder was so terrifying, so horribly ear-splitting, that she reached for the doorknob and began frantically twisting it, her damp palm slipping and sliding against the cut glass. At last it gave and she rammed the door with her shoulder, scurrying into the hall with one hand covering her mouth. With a strangled cry, she pressed herself against the far wall, her eyes squeezed tightly shut as she sought to regulate her breathing.

"Good God, Eleanor," a male voice called out, startling her so badly that her heart skipped a beat. "Whatever is wrong?"

Chapter 10

Frederick stepped back in surprise, the heel of his boot thumping against the molded baseboard. Eleanor stared at him mutely, looking like a frightened child as she pressed herself against the wall. Her dark hair tumbled over her shoulders in glossy waves, spilling across breasts that rose and fell with rapid breaths.

As a flash of lighting briefly illuminated the corridor, Frederick allowed his hungry gaze to travel down her form, to her bare feet and back up again. The scent of her, clean soap and lemon verbena, filled the air, warming Frederick's flesh. What the devil was she doing, standing out in the hall in her nightclothes?

A crash of thunder shook the house, and he heard Eleanor's sharp gasp, watched as she squeezed her eyes shut and bit her lower lip. *The storm.* She was frightened of the storm? A woman like Eleanor Ashton, so terrified that she would venture out into the hall wearing naught but a dressing gown? It seemed unlikely at best, but what other explanation was there?

He took a step toward her, brushing a lock of hair from her shoulder as he reached for her. She was trembling. "Eleanor," he said softly, reaching for her hand, "are you unwell? Shall I send for a physician?"

She opened her eyes and raised her chin, her wild-eyed gaze meeting his, and his pulse leapt in alarm. "Fred . . . Frederick?" she stuttered, as if just realizing his presence there beside her. A faint flash of lightning skittered across the wall, weaker now. The storm was moving away. The thunder that followed was nothing but a low rumble in the distance, barely discernible over the steady staccato of rain against the roof.

Still clasping her hand in his own, he rubbed her palm with his thumb, as if trying to awaken her. "That's it, love. The storm has passed."

Her free hand moved to the neckline of her wrapper, her trembling fingers tracing the lace that trimmed it. "I . . . I don't know what . . ." She cleared her throat. "I did not realize you had returned."

"Aye, Henley and I returned not an hour ago, just before the storm. Are you certain you're well? You're shaking."

She pulled her hand free from his grasp, and he heard her swallow before replying. "Yes, I'm well enough. The lightning . . . it seemed so very close that I grew concerned, and . . . and—"

"Don't worry yourself, Eleanor. Your secret is safe with me."

She shook her head, her unbound hair floating about her shoulders. "Secret? I don't know what you mean. I was just . . . that is . . ." She turned away from him, her hands balled into fists by her sides.

Frederick couldn't help the low chuckle that rumbled up from his chest. It was true, then—the stoic and sensible Eleanor, her composure felled by a storm.

"Please don't laugh at me, Frederick," she said, her voice such a gentle plea that he felt immediately contrite for having done so. "I'm humiliated enough as it is," she added softly.

He reached for her hand, bringing it to his lips. "Please forgive me, Eleanor. I should not have laughed. You've no cause for humiliation."

"Don't I?" she asked, her voice sharp now. "A grown woman, trembling like a child because of a storm."

He grasped her chin and forced her eyes to meet his, her lashes fluttering like butterfly wings. "A violent one, Eleanor. It passed directly over Whitby Hall and moved away as fast as it came. I've no doubt that Whitby's gardeners will be busy tomorrow removing tree limbs and branches that did not hold up under the onslaught."

She nodded, sending a lock of hair across her flushed cheek. He took it between his fingers, surprised at how soft and silky it felt, then tucked it behind her ear.

"But the storm has passed and you, my sweet, are safe," he added, giving her hand a reassuring squeeze.

"Thank you, Frederick," she said, her voice a husky whisper. "I . . . I feel much recovered already."

"You've stopped trembling." He raised her hand, still clasped tightly in his. How often did he get to hold a lady's hand without the barrier of a glove between them? The forbidden nature of the touch, innocent though it was, made it somehow erotic, stirring his desire.

Eleanor must have sensed it, because she began to look about furtively. "What if Selina or Lord Henley were to see us here? This is most improper. I suppose I should ask you to unhand me."

"Have no fear, Eleanor. I can assure you that Henley and his wife are well occupied at the moment. The man was chomping at the bit, desperate to get back to her side. You can rest easy that they will not discover us here."

A faint smile curved Eleanor's mouth, the color in her cheeks deepening. "But what of Mister Whitby?"

"Yes, what of Mister Whitby? What do you suppose he would say were he to find us here like this?"

Eleanor arched a brow in reply. "I'm certain he would somehow liken the situation to a hunt of some sort; a fox hut, perhaps. And then he'd prattle on endlessly about it."

Ah, so she wasn't so smitten with Mister Whitby, after all. How very interesting. Whitby must be a bigger fool than he'd supposed.

Eleanor's brow suddenly creased with a frown. "If you've returned, does that mean you've found Mister Eckford?"

"We found a man who recognized him, a barkeep at an inn just north of Plymouth. He claims that the man he believes to be Eckford patronizes his establishment the fourth Tuesday of every month and isn't due back for a fortnight. Still, Henley and I will return there early next week, to be certain."

"I'm surprised you found such a promising lead so easily."

"As am I. It troubles me that it was perhaps far *too* easy. Which is why I plan to continue my inquiries in the meantime."

"I've . . . I've been so worried these past few days. I only hope you'll be careful."

"I'll do what needs to be done," he answered, far too sharply. Instantly, he regretted it. She had worried— over *him*?

The words barely registered in his mind before Eleanor tugged her hand from his. "I should go."

"I suppose you should, as much as it pains me to say so. Shall I help you to bed? Perhaps I could come tuck you in?" he offered with a grin.

"I believe I can manage, sir." She bit her lip and he imagined her trying to suppress a smile.

"*Sir?* Now you fall back on propriety? After standing about in your dressing gown, conversing with me for nearly a quarter hour?"

Eleanor shrugged, then tightened the belt on her wrapper. "You make me forget myself, that's all."

"I'm glad to hear it," he said, rubbing his stubbly cheek with his palm. "I must live up to my reputation, you know."

He could have sworn he saw Eleanor roll her eyes heavenward before she reached for the doorknob and opened the door to her bedchamber.

"Good night, Mister Stoneham," she said, looking back over her shoulder at him, her dark hair framing her face in tumbling waves.

He wanted to remember that image of her—to burn it into his memory so that he could recall it later while lying alone in bed.

He shook his head in frustration. Damn, but he needed to get back to London, to Molly—and soon. "Good night, Lady Eleanor," he said, sighing in relief as she hurried through the door and closed it softly behind herself. Frederick let out his breath in a rush, reaching up to loosen his cravat. A *click* broke the silence as Eleanor turned the key in the lock.

What the bloody hell does she think, that I'm going to force my way in and have my way with her if she doesn't lock me out? He almost laughed aloud at the thought. Perhaps she knew him better than he thought.

Unbuttoning his coat, he continued on toward his own guest chamber. In minutes he stood in nothing save his breeches and boots, one polished Hessian propped on the low stool before the window as he gazed out on the night. Heavy, gray sheets of rain continued to pelt the window, a steady drum that he found soothing. Unlike Eleanor, he enjoyed a good storm. The power of the winds, the ferocity of lightning—they awed him, impressed him, made him feel powerful yet insignificant, all at once.

He raked one hand through his hair, exhaling slowly as he did so. Devil take it, but he needed to get away from Eleanor Ashton, and fast. He should never have agreed to Henley's help in the first place, and then he would not have found himself in this predicament—and it certainly *was* a predicament.

How had he managed to underestimate Eleanor so entirely? Why had he remembered her as a biddable type of woman? The type that would inspire lust in no one, that he could shuffle off to rusticate whilst he continued to live his life the way he was accustomed to living it—recklessly, dangerously.

He had no use for proper ladies. The innocent misses of the *ton* had never held an appeal for him, with their submissive, compliant natures, their useless talents. Whores and courtesans were far more interesting, unencumbered as they were in their efforts to live their lives in a way which pleased them rather than blindly following the dictates of society, of their families, their husbands.

But Eleanor . . . Eleanor was different. Nothing like the debutantes of his acquaintance who giggled behind fans, pretty smiles painted on their lips as they simpered and flirted in hopes of snaring a man with a title or fortune.

No matter how hard he tried, he could not possibly imagine Eleanor behaving in such a fashion. She was likely too tall, her features too bold to be considered a great beauty amongst the *ton,* and yet she took his breath away. How had he not anticipated that it would be so? After all, he'd kissed her all those years ago. Had he been so full of youthful swagger, so full of himself and his ability to win a wager, that he had failed to notice the diamond in the rough that Eleanor must have been at six and ten?

When he remembered the careless words he'd spoken to Molly not so very long ago, a stab of shame pierced his gut. Clenching his fists by his sides, he turned from the window, his gaze drawn toward the door. No doubt Eleanor was lying in bed right now, thinking him an irredeemable cad, an unforgivable rogue. And how right she was—how goddamned right. His stomach began to churn uncomfortably. He'd told Molly that Eleanor had a huge portion behind her, that he could use his wife's dowry to buy her trinkets. What kind of man was he, to say such things? To speak so dismissively of a woman like Eleanor, a woman who was everything a woman should be and more?

He turned back toward the window where the patter of rain was now more irregular, nothing but the occasional thump against the glass. He'd been a fool to agree to the marriage contract in the first place. As soon as he located Eckford and dealt with the bastard, he'd return to Essex and speak to Lord Mandeville himself, tell him exactly why he could not marry his daughter. And then he would forget her—forget the way she looked at him with no guile in her eyes, the way she spoke her mind, the way she set his blood afire like no one else ever had.

Eleanor deserved better than him, after all. The insipid George Whitby would likely make a good, solid husband.

At the very least, Whitby would not break Eleanor's heart, would not fail to live up to her expectations, as he surely would.

A coldness settled in the pit of his stomach. Yes, he would tell Mandeville exactly what sort of husband he would be—one who kept mistresses, who took his pleasure at every given opportunity, who spent as much time away from his wife's company as possible, propriety be damned. What kind of man would force his daughter to marry a man who confessed to such things?

After all, it wasn't as if he were in line to inherit a dukedom. Nothing but a modest barony, profitable though it might be, lay in Frederick's future. He was no great catch for a marquess's daughter, even had his character been unimpeachable—which it most certainly was not.

Frederick crossed the room in several strides, moving to stand before the crackling fire. Reaching up, he pinched the bridge of his nose, wishing to relieve the dull ache in his head. While they remained there in Devon together, he must resist the temptation to seek Eleanor out. No use torturing himself with more images like the one that now held his fascination—her in her dressing gown, belted tight, the bodice hugging her breasts. Her hair loose and unbound, longer than he'd imagined it, framing her face in ebony waves. And even more fascinating—more attractive than her beauty— was the feeling of camaraderie he felt whenever he was with her. Exactly when it had blossomed, he could not say. But at some point Eleanor had gone from being a woman he simply desired to a woman he truly *liked*. Tonight she had been afraid, and he had comforted her. She had worried about him when no one else had. Was that not a friendship?

The log on the fire snapped and hissed, shooting up a starburst of light. As the ash settled back to the grate, Frederick slumped into the worn leather chair beside the hearth with a groan. This was going to be difficult, far more difficult than he'd imagined.

"You look exhausted, Eleanor." Selina laid down her embroidery, her brows drawn in concern over her pale blue eyes. "Have you not slept well?"

Eleanor set aside her own embroidery hoop with a sigh. She would have to pull out all her clumsy stitches and re-do them, anyway. She simply could not concentrate, try as she might. "I've slept well enough," she answered, knowing it wasn't entirely true. She'd lain abed the past two nights, wishing in vain for sleep to come easily. It hadn't. Instead, she'd tossed and turned, her entire being distracted by the thought that Frederick slept nearby, naught but two doors separating them. She knew she should not care. Truly, she shouldn't think of it at all.

But she did, weak, foolish woman that she was. Her traitorous mind imagined him lying in bed, bare-chested—not that she'd ever before seen a man bare-chested, of course, but it did not stop her from imagining it. Her cheeks warmed at the memory of the conjured image, his skin a warm, honeyed brown, the muscles beneath hard and taut, tapering down to a narrow waist before disappearing beneath the bedclothes . . .

"Shall I speak with Mister Whitby?"

Eleanor realized Selina was speaking to her, and the heat intensified in her cheeks. "You must forgive me, Selina. I'm afraid I was woolgathering."

"Don't apologize, dearest." Selina leaned over and patted Eleanor's hand. "I was only asking if you thought I should send for an apothecary. Perhaps you could use a sleeping tonic." Selina turned toward the door where a low rumble of male voices gained on them, then faded away as footsteps continued down the corridor. Returning her gaze to Eleanor, Selina smiled weakly. "I know this must be a trying time for you. Though I cannot say I'm sorry to have my Henley back with us again, I *am* sorry that Mister Stoneham's presence is forced upon you. At least you can take comfort in the fact that he has left you in peace these past two days."

He's avoiding me, Eleanor thought, *though I cannot say why.* They'd last exchanged words the night of the storm. Friendly words, for the most part. Since then, he had kept a respectable distance from her. He had not dined with them, nor did he join them in the drawing room after dinner. She had no idea how he occupied himself when he was not cloistered away in Mister Whitby's study with Henley.

As if Frederick's dismissal were not enough, Mister Whitby had suddenly begun to act less like an amiable host and more like a suitor. She liked him well enough—truly, she did. It was exactly as she'd wished for, and yet his efforts at courtship brought her no pleasure.

"Indeed," Eleanor lied, retrieving her embroidery. "I am quite relieved that Frederick has been so accommodating." She busied herself with imprecise stitches, unwilling to meet Selina's knowing gaze.

"Frederick's return has not been without its benefits, though. Why, I do believe Mister Whitby has finally found his wits and begun to properly court you."

"Mister Whitby's attentions have become quite enthusiastic, though I cannot credit Frederick's return as the cause. Ow!" Eleanor dropped her hoop and stared at her fingertip where a single drop of ruby-red blood appeared.

Selina handed her a linen handkerchief. "Oh, but of course you can. He only needed some competition, is all. Perhaps you will have his offer before we return to Essex. Exactly as you'd hoped for, Eleanor."

She pressed the ecru handkerchief to her pricked finger, watching as the single drop stained the fabric a bright red. "I'm so clumsy," she said, wishing to divert the conversation.

Selina moved to sit directly beside her. "Tell me, Eleanor, you *do* still hope to gain Mister Whitby's affections, do you not? You have not allowed Frederick's presence to distract you, have you? I know he can be charming, but you must realize—"

"You must excuse me, Selina." Eleanor rose sharply,

her stomach pitching uncomfortably. "I'm suddenly feeling a bit dizzy."

Selina smiled up at her. "You've never been able to endure the sight of blood, have you?"

Eleanor's first instinct was to correct her friend—to tell her that it was not the sight of a mere drop of blood that had her so discomposed. *Let her think it so,* she resolved upon further reflection. Far better than her knowing the truth, that her conflicting emotions about Mister Whitby, about Frederick, were near enough driving her to distraction.

"I only need a bit of air," Eleanor said, forcing a bit of cheer into her voice.

"Are you certain? Perhaps you should lie down instead."

Eleanor reached for her friend's hand and gave it an affectionate squeeze. "I'm certain, dear Selina. A turn about the garden will set me to rights in no time."

"I would join you, but I promised Henley I would take tea with him."

"Do not trouble yourself. Of course you shall stay indoors and take your tea with that charming husband of yours. Besides, you know how briskly I take my exercise. You can never keep up, always begging me to slow down."

Selina laughed, a bright, tinkling sound that made Eleanor smile in appreciation. "It's true. But you must see, I'm forced to take two steps for every one of yours."

"True, indeed. Someday I shall learn to promenade in a more ladylike fashion—"

"—but not today," Selina finished for her.

"Precisely."

"Go, then, Eleanor. Enjoy the outdoors."

In minutes, Eleanor had changed into a sturdy walking dress and boots and set out on an unfamiliar path, one that took her past the stables, along a low fence that bordered a grassy field. On the crook of her arm she carried a small wicker basket containing paper and ink, thinking she'd find a quiet spot to sit and write a long letter to Henry.

Her step was brisk along the path where hardy, late-blooming sweet-pea and hollyhocks grew in profusion. Now and then Eleanor stopped to pick a fragrant bloom, laying them in her basket to bring back to Selina.

Perhaps a quarter mile down the path she paused before a particularly lush clump of hollyhocks, their heart-shaped petals a pleasing purplish-pink. She reached out to snap off a bloom, but leapt back in surprise at the sound of gunfire up ahead, so loud that a flock of birds scattered through the treetops beside the path, squawking loudly as their wings beat the leaves.

Whatever was that? Mister Whitby was back at Whitby Hall, shut inside his study with his steward, not out in his park with a gun, chasing down whatever could be had.

Another shot fired, the smell of gunpowder carried on the breeze. Whomever it was, they were just over the rise ahead of her, and she hurried on, the hollyhocks all but forgotten.

As soon as she crested the rise she saw him— Frederick, in his shirtsleeves and waistcoat. Holding a gun, his arm outstretched, taking aim at what appeared to be a fence in the distance. Another shot fired.

She knew she ought to turn back, but curiosity got the best of her and she approached silently, watching as he reloaded his weapon and took aim once more, firing toward the fence in a puff of smoke.

Eleanor tried to stifle a cough as the gunpowder drifted her way.

Frederick whirled toward her, his eyes narrowing when he spied her there. "Good God, woman!" he barked. "Don't you know better than to sneak up on someone when they're firing a pistol?"

"I did not mean to sneak up on you," she said, approaching him. "I was only out for a walk, and I heard shots being fired."

"And you thought to come investigate?" He tucked the pistol into the waistband of his fawn-colored breeches. "Normally one would go in the opposite direction, you know."

"I *am* sorry for startling you. Whatever are you shooting at?"

He pointed toward the fence. "Do you see the line of crabapples, there on the railing?"

Eleanor squinted, barely able to make out the row of tiny fruit sitting atop the fence's uppermost rail. "You're shooting at such a small target as that?"

"With astonishing accuracy, I might add." He patted the pistol.

"I suppose I should be impressed, then. You've been avoiding me?" she said at last, phrasing it as a question rather than a statement.

"I have been, yes," he answered, entirely unapologetic. "But since you found me here—"

"I did not come looking for you," she interrupted, her cheeks flooding with heat.

"I do not doubt it." He peered over her shoulder. "What do you have in the basket?"

"Pen and ink. Some paper. I planned to write a letter to Henry."

"Henry?"

"My brother. My twin, actually."

"Oh, yes, that's right. Though I did not realize he was your twin."

She nodded. "Eight minutes my junior, if I'm not mistaken."

"And I suppose you think those eight minutes entitle you to boss him around whenever you wish. Am I correct?"

"Of course," she said with a laugh. "I suppose your sisters bossed you around, as well?"

"Indeed they did, all five of them."

"Five? I did not realize you had quite so many."

"Katherine, Emma, Isabella, Anne, and Maria," he ticked off. "All born after Charles but before me. And all as bossy as fishwives, each and every one of them."

"I'm sure Henry would say the same of me." Her gaze trailed back to the fence, to the tiny little crabapples sitting there. "I did not mean to interrupt your practice. I still cannot see how you can possibly hit such a small target as that at such a distance."

"Shall I show you?" He removed the ivory-handled pistol from his waistband and held it out to her. "Or perhaps you'd like to give it a try yourself?"

She shook her head, taking a step backward. "Thank you, but no. I've no interest in firearms."

"No? Have you ever held a pistol?"

"Why ever would I?" she asked.

He shrugged, turning over the pistol in his palm. "I thought perhaps your brother might have taught you to shoot."

"In case you were not made aware of it, Frederick, ladies are not generally taught to shoot."

"A shame, really," he drawled. "Come, I'll show you."

"No, really I—"

"Here, like this." He loaded the pistol, then came to stand behind her, reaching for her hand and placing the cold, hard metal in her grasp. "That's it, finger on the trigger. Take aim. No, it's not really necessary to close one eye."

She barely heard his words, so focused was she on

the fact that his entire body pressed against hers, his masculine scent overpowering her senses and making her pulse leap. Still, she attempted to point the pistol's barrel at the leftmost crabapple.

"That's it, love." He steadied her arm with his own. "Now go on, squeeze the trigger."

She did, the blast causing her to stagger backward against him as the fence rail exploded into splinters with a loud *crack*. She could only stare in astonishment.

"Hmm. Well, that was close. I suppose we'll have to tell Mister Whitby that you shot his fence. Think how excited he'll get, imagining you firing a pistol. Next thing you know, he'll give you a hunting rifle with your name engraved on it."

Eleanor could not help but laugh at the image.

"Come, we should get you back to the house." He bent down and retrieved his coat from the grass, along with her basket. "No doubt that arm's going to hurt. I'm afraid I hadn't considered that."

It already did, she realized with a frown, clutching at her elbow. And her clothes smelled of gunpowder. However would she explain that?

Still, in an odd way she'd enjoyed it, firing the pistol. It had made her feel somehow empowered. Was this why men became so obsessed with shooting, fleeing Town in droves come August, off to hunt grouse?

"Upon further thought, perhaps this should remain our little secret," Frederick said, falling into step beside her as they made their way back toward the house. "You firing the gun, I mean. I wouldn't want to give poor Henley an apoplexy, after all. Propriety and all that"

Eleanor only nodded, glancing back at the shattered fence. After all, what was one more secret, where Frederick was concerned?

Chapter 11

"Are you sure you won't join me, Mister Whitby?" Eleanor asked, reaching for her heavy woolen cloak. The day was mild, but it would be much cooler where she was headed, up on the bluff.

"I wish I could, but I'm expecting my solicitor. But thank you for your company at breakfast, Lady Eleanor. I must confess, I'm glad that Henley and Selina did not join us, as I enjoyed having you all to myself."

"Why, thank you, Mister Whitby," she murmured, tucking a book of poetry beneath her arm.

"Go on, then," he said with a smile, bowing sharply. "Enjoy your exercise."

Eleanor nodded, then hurried out, eager to feel the warm sunshine on her face. Her feet seemed to skim over the lawn as she hurried across the grounds, through the copse of trees, and across a marigold-filled meadow that led toward the sea. As she drew closer to her destination, she hurried her step in anticipation.

Almost there! With a total loss of decorum, she dashed up the bluff, her heavy woolen cloak billowing out behind her. What a breathtaking day! All morning she'd been itching to escape the confines of the house, to breathe in the briny air and watch the waves crash against the shore. She could sit there on the bluff all day, reading poetry or simply staring at the sea. As much as she hated to admit it, she was infinitely glad that Mister Whitby had not joined her.

Indeed, it was a spot best enjoyed alone, she thought, cresting the rise at last. Her gaze swept appreciatively over the vista before her as she inhaled the salty air, a slow smile spreading across her face. She raised one hand to shield her eyes from the near-blinding sun which reflected off the blue-gray water below.

This was, without a doubt, the loveliest place in all of Devonshire. She could not help but laugh aloud in pleasure, the sound carried off on the breeze.

"Lovely, isn't it?"

Eleanor gasped, whirling toward the voice. *Frederick?* She looked about wildly, seeing no one. Had she imagined it? Was the sea playing tricks on her? Her pulse raced, her breath coming far too fast.

"Up here," came the voice again, and Eleanor raised her gaze.

At last she found him, perched in the lowest branches of a tree that was gnarled and bent away from the sea. His boots dangled several feet off the ground, reflecting the sun in their luster.

It took several seconds for her to find her voice. "What in God's name are you doing up there?" she finally managed, near breathlessly.

"What does it look like I'm doing?" he called down as Eleanor took two cautious steps in his direction. "I'm enjoying the view."

"From a tree?" she asked, unable to hide the disbelief in her voice. It was . . . unseemly. A grown man, sitting in a tree? She'd never heard the likes of it.

"The view is incomparable. Would you care to join me?"

"In the tree?"

"Precisely that, yes." His laugh was a low rumble.

She could enjoy the view well enough from where she stood, her feet planted firmly on the ground. "You've lost your wits, Frederick Stoneham."

"I'm not certain I ever had them to begin with. What is that you have there in your hand? A book?"

Eleanor looked at the leather-bound volume she carried. "Yes, just some poetry. I . . . I came up here to read."

"Read aloud, then."

She shook her head. "Perhaps I should go and leave you to your solitude."

"I enjoy your company far more than my own."

For a moment, Eleanor said nothing. Shielding her eyes from the unrelenting sun, she stared at the sea. "I thought you were avoiding me."

"I was," he answered. "For your own good. But just like yesterday you found me, and—"

"Are you really so conceited as that? To think I would search you out, two days in a row? Besides, it would seem you knew I favored this spot."

"Very well, perhaps I did." He shrugged. "So now that we've established that I'm a selfish bastard, why don't you stay and read to me."

Eleanor looked at her book again, Wordsworth's and Coleridge's *Lyrical Ballads*. Dare she? She often read aloud to Selina, to Henry as well. But this was altogether different. The very idea made her feel somehow . . . exposed. "I should warn you that it is nothing so bawdy as what you read to me the day our carriage lost a wheel. I'm afraid you'll find these verses far less titillating than those you favor."

"Or perhaps I'll surprise you with my excellent taste.

Come now, Eleanor. Be a sport. Sit, and pretend I am not here. I'll remain in my perch, a safe distance away."

Eleanor bit her lower lip, considering his request. "Very well," she said at last, unfastening her cloak and spreading it out upon the grass. Suddenly very aware of her ungainly height, she sat on the cloak with as much grace as she could muster, tucking her long legs beneath herself.

Opening the book, she flipped through the gilt-trimmed pages, searching for just the right verse to suit the day. At last she found it, the very last poem in the collection. She took a deep, steadying breath and began to read, raising her voice to be heard over the sound of crashing waves below them.

> *Five years have passed; five summers, with the*
> *   length*
> *Of five long winters! and again I hear*
> *These waters, rolling from their mountain-springs*
> *With a sweet inland murmur. Once again*
> *Do I behold these steep and lofty cliffs,*
> *Which on a wild secluded scene impress*
> *Thoughts of more deep seclusion; and connect*
> *The landscape with the quiet of the sky.*

She continued on, her voice growing increasingly steady and clear as the beautiful words slipped off her tongue. Perhaps ten minutes later she came to the final verses, her voice thick with emotion. With enormous restraint, she held the tears in check as she read the final words.

> *If I should be, where I no more can hear*
> *Thy voice, nor catch from thy wild eyes these*
> *   gleams*

Of past existence, wilt thou then forget
That on the banks of this delightful stream
We stood together; And that I, so long
A worshipper of Nature, hither came,
Unwearied in that service: rather say
With warmer love, oh! with far deeper zeal
Of holier love. Now wilt thou then forget,
That after many wanderings, many years
Of absence, these steep woods and lofty cliffs,
And this green pastoral landscape, were to me
More dear, both for themselves, and for thy sake.

Softly, she closed the book and set it down beside her. Such beautiful, romantic words! Eleanor never tired of them; they never failed to bring a tear to her eye, a longing to her heart.

Summoning the courage to do so, she raised her gaze to the tree where Frederick sat silently. For several minutes, he simply stared out at the sea with his hair blowing behind him in the breeze. In profile, he appeared older than his twenty-three years, his noble blood more obvious. His dark whiskers outlined his strong, angular jaw, his lips full beneath a perfectly-shaped nose, his nostrils slightly flared. She turned away, unable to bear the now-familiar wave of desire that crashed over her.

And then he spoke, breaking the heavy silence. "That was exquisite, Eleanor. Perhaps the loveliest reading I've ever heard. And so very fitting, too. Was that Wordsworth?"

Eleanor cleared her throat. "Indeed it was. Do you enjoy his work?"

"Never before did I find it as enjoyable as that. Your voice is beautiful, and you infused his words with such passion. You'll make a devoted follower out of me yet."

Eleanor felt her heart swell with the compliment. "Then I am glad I chose it. Shall I read another?"

"Indeed you shall, and I shall once more be your captive audience. However, I do believe I will join you there on *terra firma,* if you don't mind."

Eleanor shook her head, watching him as he grinned down at her. "I don't mind. Really, Frederick, have you any idea how silly you look, perched up there like a boy?"

"Look at that ship," he called out, his attention returned to the sea. "It's enormous. Not a packet, I would wager."

Eleanor scrambled to her feet, peering out over the edge of the bluff toward the bluish gray waves. "Where?"

"There," he said, pointing toward the horizon.

Craning her neck, she rose on tiptoe but saw nothing save the open sea. "I don't see anything," she said, shaking her head.

"Likely an American ship." One hand raised to shield his eyes, he squinted against the sun, the corners of his eyes crinkling ever so slightly with the effort. "Look at the sails."

"What of them? I see nothing but water, as far as the eye can see."

"Here," he said, reaching a hand down to her. "Can you climb up here, to the lowest branch? I'll assist you."

"You want me to climb the tree?" Eleanor's voice raised a pitch. "Are you mad?"

"You want to, don't you?" he drawled seductively. "Come, climb up here and take a look. There's some sort of design on the sails, something I've never before seen. I won't tell a soul," he added with a wink.

For the briefest of moments, Eleanor thought to refuse. Then again, it would not be the first tree she had climbed. As children, she and Henry had whiled away many a pleasant summer afternoon perched in the branches of a tree at Covington Hall. Eleanor had never been afraid of scraping a knee or taking a tumble; it had been her frail brother she had worried over, not her own safety. She had been strong, able. And she could most certainly climb a tree.

"Very well," she said, reaching up to take his proffered hand. The gnarled tree offered plenty of footholds and in seconds she reached the low branches where Frederick sat. As if settling herself into a swing, she lowered her bottom to the thick, sturdy branch beside him, one hand still clasped in his.

Immediately she spotted the ship off near the horizon, its brightly patterned sails billowed out on the wind as it sailed for Plymouth.

"There it is. You're right, it *is* enormous."

Frederick regarded her with one raised brow. "You climbed up here remarkably fast."

"I did, didn't I?" Eleanor smiled, pleased with herself. "You must promise that you will not tell Selina. My dear friend would positively die of vexation to learn just how hoydenish I've become."

"I remembered you to be quite the hoyden, dashing through meadows, splashing in the river's shallows. Do you remember the time we raced across a field on horseback, you in the saddle beside me?"

"I'd entirely forgotten about that," she said, the memories flooding back. She'd banished them, once she'd heard him laughing about her with his friends, once she'd realized that their friendship had been nothing but a sham. "Anyway, that was so very long ago. I was only a girl. I'd never dare to behave like that now."

"Are you always the proper lady, then?"

"But of course. It's what's expected of me. I am the daughter of a marquess, in case you have forgotten."

"I have not forgotten. But you didn't used to be so . . ."

He trailed off, shaking his head. She was right; she'd only been a girl then, when he'd first met her. He could not compare it. "Never mind. Tell me about your father," he said instead. "What is Lord Mandeville like?"

Eleanor dropped her gaze to her lap, carefully considering the question. "He is a passionate man," she said at last. "A philosopher at heart. He cares deeply for those he loves, and gives freely of himself. Those who know him well would say he is kind, generous, and magnanimous."

"I've heard it said that he does not often take his seat in Parliament, but when he does his speeches are moving and effective."

Eleanor nodded. "There is no doubt that my father has a way with words. I think perhaps he should have been a poet."

Frederick snapped off a small twig, twirling it in his fingers. "And what of Lady Mandeville?"

Eleanor's stomach lurched. "What do you wish to know?"

"What kind of woman is she really? Rumors and hearsay aside, since those things are often based in half-truths and lies."

If only that were the case in this instance, she thought with annoyance. Gazing out at the sea, she sighed deeply. "Mama is a proud woman," she murmured, feeling disloyal. "Though not always prudent. I fear that much of what you have heard is true, though it pains me to admit it. I do not model my own behavior on hers, of that you can be certain. Still, she is my mother and so I must love her."

"Simply because she is your blood? That fact, and that fact alone, commands your love?"

Eleanor nodded. "Indeed."

"Hmph," Frederick grunted. "I find you are much more charitable than I am."

"Though not so forgiving. There are some injuries that I can neither forgive nor forget, no matter how unchristian that makes me." *The cruel ways Mama had treated Henry.* "There, now you know my greatest flaw."

Frederick threw his head back and laughed. "My dear, if that is your worst flaw then you are a veritable saint."

"A saint, sitting in a tree?" Eleanor could not help the smile that spread across her face as she swung her feet beneath her, the wind whipping at her skirts. "Surely not." Her eyes scanned the sea before her, looking for the enormous ship, but it had disappeared from sight. "You were correct, you know. The view up here is far more spectacular than down below."

Frederick poked at her skirts with the twig he held, a mischievous glint in his eyes. "I'm surprised your Mister Whitby did not suggest it himself."

Eleanor arched a brow. "Do you suppose Mister Whitby climbs trees? I rather find it hard to imagine."

"I do not pretend to understand the sporting type," he answered with a shrug. He turned, looking off beyond Eleanor's left shoulder. "Look," he said, pointing to a line of silver-barked trees. "Just over that rise. Do you see that sandy trail, just beyond those trees?"

Eleanor followed the direction of his arm, narrowing her eyes. "Beside the silver ashes?"

"Indeed. This morning I followed that trail, perhaps two hundred yards on foot. The brush is far too dense for a horse. Anyway, you would not believe what I found, perched there on the side of the cliff."

"A great bird's nest?" she offered.

"No, nothing like that. Something far more intriguing."

"Well then, tell me. What did you find?"

"I found a wonderful little cottage, nearly hidden from view. Well-kept, though it did not appear inhabited. It's within the grounds of Whitby Hall, though I could not discern its purpose. Inside there's naught but an elaborately draped bed and a chaise longue before the hearth. There were fine linens on the bed and ashes in the hearth, but no other signs of habitation save several candles scattered about. No table, no cooking utensils. Odd, don't you think?"

Eleanor's brow creased with a frown. "You went inside?"

Frederick only shrugged. "A key hung behind the shutter. Not very clever."

"I cannot believe you would be so bold as to trespass on Mister Whitby's property."

"Do not be such a prig, Eleanor. It isn't the least bit becoming. Anyway, one can only suppose that it's some sort of love nest, wouldn't you say?"

Heat flooded Eleanor's cheeks. "How dare you attempt to cast aspersion on Mister Whitby's character in such a fashion!"

"Oh, do not get yourself into a pique. I did not say I believed it to be your precious Whitby's love nest now, did I?"

"You insinuated that it was."

"Well, it *is* on the man's property, after all," he muttered. "Who else's love nest do you suppose it could be?"

"I'm sure there is a satisfactory explanation. For you to jump to such a conclusion is . . . is . . ." Eleanor sputtered, entirely flummoxed by the turn the conversation had taken. "It is coarse and crude for you to even suggest it."

"What? That perhaps the man has a lover?"

Was Frederick jealous? Had he noticed how ardently Mister Whitby had begun to court her, and now wished to paint the man in the most unpleasant light possible? "You impugn his honor, sir, and I cannot abide it."

"Impugn his honor? Why, I meant it as a compliment. Perhaps the man isn't quite the eunuch I believed him to be."

"And that is where we differ, Mister Stoneham. To suggest something so impure about a gentleman is not considered a compliment in polite society."

Frederick grasped the branch beneath himself and swung down easily to the ground. His feet planted wide and his arms folded across his chest, he regarded her with a steady gaze. "Need I remind you that the gentleman in question is nearly thirty years of age?" he asked. "Surely you do not believe him to be a virgin?"

Eleanor rolled her eyes heavenward. "I cannot believe you would say such a thing as that. Must you always go and ruin everything? Here, help me down."

"Why, so you can flounce back to the house in a temper?"

"I'll have you know I do not flounce," she shot back. "And I am not in a temper. Will you at least attempt to act like a gentleman and take my hand? It's far easier to jump than to climb back down."

He moved closer, reaching a hand up to her outstretched one. "Here, your other hand. Don't fret, love. I'll catch you."

"Or let me fall on my face for your own amusement," she said with a huff, warily taking his hands in hers.

"I'm far too selfish for that. I'd prefer your pretty face to remain intact. Very well, I've got you. Now jump."

Eleanor did as he requested. Frederick caught her in his arms, her body pressed against his. Slowly, seductively, he lowered her, inch by inch toward the ground. Her body slid against the hard, muscular planes of his, raising gooseflesh on her skin. At last her toes touched the ground; still, he did not release her. Her pulse leapt, her heart accelerating at an alarming rate. She could feel his heart, pounding just as wildly, as erratically, as her own. His warm brown gaze held hers, his eyes near to smoldering.

"Put me down," she said meekly, not really wishing him to.

"The cottage," he said, his voice a growl.

"What of it?"

"Meet me there tonight."

She shook her head wildly. "No, I cannot."

"You can," he shot back. "You want to, don't you?"

"You are mistaken, Frederick. I have no desire to do something so improper, so foolhardy as that."

"Oh, but you *do* desire it. I can feel it, in every fiber of your being. I can see it, there in your eyes. They are the color of indigo ink, you know," he said, tracing her lower lip with his thumb. "So very lovely."

Eleanor lowered her gaze, shielding her eyes from his view. She said nothing in reply, fearing her voice would betray her just as surely as her eyes had done.

He reached for her chin and tipped it up, forcing her gaze back up to his. "Meet me there, at the cottage," he pressed, sounding far more Irish than before. "After Whitby and the Henleys have retired. Say you will."

There was no denying that she wanted to—desperately. It was foolish of her, reckless, irresponsible. And yet she wished to, more than anything.

"You must dine with us tonight, and join us afterward in the drawing room. Only then will I agree."

"Very well, love," he said with a bow. "If that's the price I must pay, then so be it. I will dine with you, and I will make merry in the drawing room. Any other demands?"

Silently, she shook her head. *Why is she making such nonsensical demands?* she wondered. So that he could watch Mister Whitby court her? So that he would know another man found her desirable?

"No? Hmmm, what an intriguing bargain, then. I can hardly wait."

"Just go," she said, cocking her head toward the house.

"Oh, no. I shall escort you back, like a proper gentleman." He hastily retrieved her cloak and book from the grass, handing her the volume of poetry. In several long strides, he crossed the bluff, toward the edge where he shook out the cloak, the heavy folds snapping in the wind.

Eleanor could not help but admire his form as he stood there perched on the edge of cliff, the muscles in his arms rippling with the effort as he sent blades of grass and particles of sand flying out toward the sea. He appeared in harmony with the wild, rugged landscape— not in contrast to it as so many elegant young gentleman would. Closing her eyes, she pictured him galloping across the bluff on an enormous black horse, wielding a sword like the knights of yore, perhaps even rescuing a fair maiden in distress at the risk of his own life. Yes, her fertile imagination could easily conjure images of Frederick Stoneham engaged in such activities. But dancing the quadrille in an assembly room? Driving a jaunty curricle through Mayfair? She opened her eyes again, watching as he gave the cloak one final shake, then laid it across one arm as he gazed out at the frothy waves, a smile tipping the corners of his full lips.

No, she could hardly imagine him engaged in such pedestrian things as that. And this, she realized, was where the danger lay. Since the day he had first kissed her, her childish infatuation had allowed her to cast him as the romantic hero of every poem, every romantic epic she'd read. He was the brave knight in *Le Morte d'Arthur*. The masked man in *Cecilia*. The romantic soldier in *Romance of the Forest*. For all these years,

Frederick had not been a flesh-and-blood man in her mind, but a romantic notion. The dark, dangerous knight who would sweep her off her feet and love her like no mere mortal man would.

She'd known it was nothing more than idle fantasy. She remembered the cruel words she'd overheard that fateful day. She knew full well that his kiss was nothing more than a means to win a wager. Oh, how she knew.

Still, she dreamt of him, allowing herself to fantasize about a romantic love that would never be a part of her life, of her marriage. Just the fanciful longings of a silly girl, barely out of the nursery.

Yet now the romantic notion stood before her—a real man, not a fantasy. He was no longer an enigma; she knew things about him that gave him dimensions she'd never before fathomed. He dearly loved his sisters, particularly the wronged Maria. He spoke Gaelic, enjoyed the Irish poets. He was not afraid to climb a tree if he desired to do so, if it meant a better view of the sea, of the surrounding countryside. She sensed a surprising gentleness, a vulnerability, beneath the rakish veneer he wore so well, the ne'er-do-well façade he presented to the world.

More frightening than anything was the knowledge that, now that she'd gotten to know the real man, he'd only become more intriguing, not less so. Instead of the idol crumbling to clay as they were wont to do on closer inspection, he'd only become more dazzling, far more appealing than before.

Oh, if only Henry were here. She did not dare talk to Selina about Frederick, for she could bare her soul to no one save her brother. She silently cursed Oxford for taking her brother away just when she needed him most. She would write to him, as she meant to do yesterday. Perhaps the act of putting her words to paper would better help her understand her conflicted emotions. With a nod to herself, she resolved to do so at once, immediately upon her return to the house.

"Here, love." Frederick draped her cloak across her shoulders, startling her with his closeness. He moved closer still, reaching around to fasten it at her throat, his silky hair brushing her cheek as he did so.

A shiver worked its way up her spine. Clutching her book tightly to her breasts, she inhaled his powerfully masculine scent. Soap, grass, sunshine. He smelled of the outdoors, clean and woodsy. Unpretentious. Manly.

She would meet him at the cottage tonight, of that she was certain. For how could she resist a fantasy that had become such a tempting reality?

Chapter 12

"So, Mister Stoneham," Mister Whitby said, laying down his fork. "Henley tells me you've made great progress toward locating your brother-in-law."

Frederick leaned back in his seat, surveying his fellow diners as they all watched him expectantly. Whitby sat at the head of the table, his posture almost unnaturally erect and formal. To his right sat Eleanor in a pale blue silk gown, simply cut yet fetching, the color making her eyes appear a darker, deeper shade of blue.

Though she was smiling, he detected a hint of unease in her demeanor, a tightly wound tension that seemed ever-present in her countenance. His gaze flitted briefly over the fair Lady Henley, seated to his left, before continuing on to Henley himself who hovered protectively near his wife's elbow. A hush descended upon the assembled party, as if they waited for Frederick to do or say something outrageous.

"Aye," he answered at last, sure he was disappointing them. "I'm confident we'll have Eckford in no time." He picked up his wine glass and swirled the scarlet-colored liquid in slow circles, his gaze trained on the drink. He would say no more. Just thinking of Eckford made the blood pound in his temples, but he would not give in to his rage simply to amuse them. Not tonight.

"Good, very good." Whitby nodded enthusiastically. "I only hope the matter can be resolved without too much bloodshed."

The man was certainly trying his best to get a rise from him. No matter. Frederick had other things on his mind. Eleanor, and the cottage. Would she come? Only time would tell. In the meantime, it was all he could do to keep himself from mentally undressing her every time he chanced a glance in her direction. Which he did now, eliciting a stirring in his trousers as their eyes met briefly before she looked away, her cheeks pinkening deliciously. Blast it if his cock didn't harden in hopeful anticipation.

Apparently done baiting him, Whitby turned his attention to Eleanor, smiling broadly as he reached for his glass of wine. "I must say, despite the unfortunate circumstances that have brought you all here to Whitby Hall, I'm finding myself enjoying the company more every day. Perhaps I *do* allow myself to rusticate a bit too much. Henley, I thank you for bringing your lovely wife here, along with the equally lovely Lady Eleanor."

"My pleasure, Georgie old boy," Henley said with a wink. "You simply must get out more, you know."

"True, true indeed," Whitby answered.

"Mister Whitby," Eleanor said, turning toward her host with a smile, "just today at breakfast you were telling me a bit about your recent trip to the Lake District with the Duke and Duchess of Dandridge. You must tell me more."

"It was a lovely trip, a lovely trip indeed. With the Duke and Duchess' connections, we were able to visit several . . ."

Whitby continued on enthusiastically, but Frederick

was no longer listening. Instead, he watched Eleanor as she nodded her head and murmured niceties in reply. She *was* incredibly beautiful, more vixen than virgin in appearance. She appeared far more sophisticated than most well-bred ladies her age—more worldly, though he knew such was not the case. She *was* a virgin, the sheltered daughter of a nobleman. He must remember that.

That he was attracted to her physically was no surprise—he was a man used to enjoying beautiful women, and Eleanor was indeed beautiful. But, he realized with a start, he wanted more than Eleanor's favors in bed. He wanted her to find him worthy, when no one else had. He wanted her to look at him the way she was now looking at Whitby, her face full of admiration and respect. For when she looked at him, her gaze was more often that not filled with scorn, skepticism, even annoyance. Deservedly so, he realized, despising himself and the reckless life he'd led.

Even so, she desired him. He was certain of it. Hadn't her reaction to him this afternoon provided evidence enough? Hadn't she agreed to meet him at the cottage if only he would join their company tonight, as he was doing? And what were her reasons for making such a request? To illustrate just how much more suited she was to Whitby than she was to him? To make damn sure he realized that he was not fit to touch her?

Filled with the familiar rancor of self-loathing, he forced his attention back to the conversation at hand. "Lady Eleanor," Whitby was saying. "I hope you won't think me too bold if I ask my guests to join me in a toast to your beauty." Whitby raised his glass in her direction. "You look positively enchanting this evening. Like an angel, if I might say so."

Frederick's gaze flew to Eleanor's. Her cheeks

flushed a deep rose as the Henleys raised their glasses and joined Whitby as he called out, "To Lady Eleanor."

What the hell, Frederick thought, joining in.

"I thank you for the compliment, sir," Eleanor murmured, dropping her gaze to her lap as any proper lady would. The paragon and the perfect gentleman. Truly, they deserved each other.

Bitter jealousy ate away at his insides, making him ill-tempered and irritable. He could not simply sit there and let Whitby fawn all over her, not without putting up a fight. She had bloody insisted that he join them, so he would damn well make his presence felt—in all his roguish glory, and to hell with the rest of them.

"An angel, Whitby?" he said at last, setting his glass back on the blue damask–covered table. "Surely you can do better than that. An angel is so bland, so banal." He waved one hand dismissively. "I'd say Lady Eleanor looks more the temptress, wouldn't you?"

Whitby's smile disappeared at once. "Are you questioning Lady Eleanor's virtue, sir? Do you dare to—"

"Settle down, George," Henley said. "Stoneham meant nothing disrespectful by it, did you, old boy?"

"Quite the contrary," he said, his eyes locking with Eleanor's smoldering ones. Was she angry? Offended? Aroused, perhaps? "I meant it as a compliment, of course. I've never found angels all that appealing."

"No, you wouldn't, would you?" Whitby challenged, his eyes flashing. "I'll ask that you have a care about how you speak of Lady Eleanor. Surely that is not too much to ask of a guest in my home?"

And so it was true; the man was besotted. Eleanor had managed to gain his devotion, and in so short a time. "I suppose it is not, Mister Whitby," he said, drumming his fingers on the table. "You'll pardon my boorish remarks.

I hold Lady Eleanor in the highest esteem, as I'm sure she can attest."

Everyone looked to Eleanor, awaiting her response. Her eyes flitted briefly to his as she fidgeted in her seat, twisting her napkin in her lap. "Indeed, Mister Stoneham. No offense was taken, I assure you."

"I'm glad to hear it. You see, Lady Eleanor and I are very old friends. Our acquaintance goes back many years, does it not?"

"It does," she said, raising her glass to her lips and taking a slow, leisurely sip.

"Though it has been far too long since we last saw one another," he continued. "Do you remember our last meeting, Lady Eleanor? It was perhaps, oh, four years ago. You were wearing a pale pink organdy dress, with ribbons in your hair and—"

"Yes, Mister Stoneham," Eleanor interrupted, her voice sharp. "I remember our last meeting well enough."

"Your mother was hosting a garden party, if my memory serves me." He paused to take a drink of wine, enjoying the pregnant silence far more than he should. Lady Henley was throwing panicky glances Eleanor's way, her pale eyes as round as saucers.

Whitby's eyes narrowed, his knuckles white as he grasped the edge of table. Preparing to attack, if need be?

Evidently not at all discomposed, Eleanor smiled sweetly at Frederick from across the table. "Indeed she was, Mister Stoneham. Mama *so* loves a garden party in June. The maze at Covington Hall is at its finest then, do you not agree? The foliage grows so thick, so lush in June that the hedges are as solid and impenetrable as a stone wall."

Frederick quirked a brow. This was not the response he'd expected. He'd kissed her in the maze, with naught but the moon as their witness. Naturally, he'd expected her to quickly change the subject, to deflect the conversation away from the maze and the events that had transpired there. How interesting that she was doing exactly the opposite. To make Whitby jealous, no doubt.

"Ah, yes," he said, "the maze. A truly masterful one, as I remember it. One could easily get lost in there and not find his way out for days on end."

"I'd very much like to see this maze," Whitby said, relaxing his posture only slightly. "I have a fondness for such a challenge as that. Quite sporting, isn't it?"

"Oh, I highly recommend it." Frederick nodded, then chanced a glance at Eleanor. When she met his gaze, he winked. "Particularly with Lady Eleanor as a guide."

Lady Henley stood abruptly, nearly knocking over her wineglass in the process. A fork rattled to the floor. "Come, Eleanor," she said, her hands visibly shaking. "Let us retire to the drawing room."

Ah, too bad. Things were just beginning to get amusing.

"Very well," Eleanor said, rising and placing her napkin on the slightly worn table linen with obvious reluctance. "Though I hope the gentlemen will join us there directly." She favored Whitby with a dazzling smile.

"You may count on it, Lady Eleanor," Whitby said, hurrying to her side like a lapdog.

Damnation, would the evening's entertainments never end? Frederick drained what was left in his wineglass, the contents of his stomach feeling suddenly sour.

Casting one last glance over her shoulder at the men who gathered in uncomfortable silence near the head of the table, Eleanor followed Selina out, trailing behind her as they made their way to the privacy of the drawing room. Once they had settled themselves onto the gold velvet sofa and rang the bell for tea, Selina turned toward her with a frown pulling at the corners of her mouth.

Eleanor braced herself, feeling like a naughty child about to receive a scolding.

"Eleanor, darling, whatever were you doing in there? Goading Frederick like that?"

Eleanor shrugged. Truly, she hadn't any idea what she had been doing. Testing Mister Whitby's affection, perhaps? He had leapt to her defense rather easily, hadn't he? Would Frederick have done the same, had the situation been reversed? She did not know for certain. Likely not, as defending a lady's reputation was not the way of the rake. Ruining it was.

Regardless, she could not deny the fact that a part of her had enjoyed the way the two men had bristled at one another, like two dogs fighting over a bone. But admit such a thing to Selina? *Never.* So she simply remained silent instead.

Clearly nonplussed, Selina shook her head, her golden curls dancing beneath her lace cap. "I vow, for a moment there I feared it would come to blows."

Eleanor waved away her friend's concerns with the flick of one wrist. "Come now, it was nothing so dramatic as that."

Selina pursed her lips thoughtfully. "Why do you think Mister Stoneham chose to join us for dinner tonight? He's kept his distance well enough up till now. Best that way, don't you agree?"

"Perhaps." Eleanor shrugged. "Really, he's not as bad as that, is he? I thought his behavior rather civilized, considering."

Selina's reply was delayed by the arrival of a maid carrying a tea tray. Eleanor watched her friend carefully, noting the tears that gathered in her bright blue eyes, glistening like crystals on her lashes.

Why ever was Selina so distressed? Nothing so very scandalous had come to pass—just a bit of harmless banter. Frederick never would have been so reckless as to mention the kiss. At least she didn't think he would have.

As soon as the maid departed, Selina laid a gentle hand on Eleanor's wrist. "It's only that I'd begun to truly hope that we would be sisters. George seems so taken by you, after all. But . . . but . . . oh, please don't be angry at me for saying this, Eleanor. You know I love you dearly. But when you look at Frederick, I see . . ." She trailed off, shaking her head. "Something there in your eyes. Something . . . wistful."

Eleanor said nothing, swallowing a painful lump in her throat.

Selina reached for her handkerchief and dabbed at her damp eyes. "I only hope that I am wrong, that you have not fallen prey to Frederick's charm once more. Tell me it is not so, Eleanor."

Eleanor took a deep breath before replying. "I cannot lie to you, Selina. I . . . I wish it were so, that I were immune to Frederick. But, I . . . I cannot say why, but somehow I'm drawn to him, it's true." She shook her head, biting her bottom lip till it stung. "I know I should not be. I know it's imprudent at best. I'm fully aware I should marry someone like George Whitby, and yet I cannot help my feelings. What am I to do, Selina?"

Selina's lips parted with a gasp. "I confess, I'm astonished. I . . . I do not know what counsel to give." She busied herself with pouring tea, clearly unable to look Eleanor in the eye. With trembling hands, she set a steaming cup before Eleanor, then visibly strove to compose her features before continuing. "I cannot deny that it has become my fondest wish for you to marry

George. Selfish of me, perhaps. I would not wish you unhappy. But I did so think you would suit."

"I'm not so certain we would," Eleanor said hesitantly.

"What objection can you possibly have? He's handsome, wealthy—"

"I'm well aware of his qualifications," Eleanor interjected, perhaps a bit too sharply. "I'm sorry, Selina. It's just that I don't quite understand it myself. Indeed, he is everything you said he was. He will no doubt make an excellent, attentive husband. But suddenly I find myself wishing for more."

"More?" Selina shook her head. "I don't understand. What more could you want? I realize he has no title, but—"

"It's not a title I want. It's something else . . . something I cannot explain. An intangible, I suppose. But the more I think of my future . . ." She trailed off, afraid to voice her fears.

As a woman, what had she to look forward to but being a wife and mother? She would run a household, entertain, bear children. If her sole occupation was to be a wife, then shouldn't she at least enjoy the company of her husband? Shouldn't they share common interests? Shouldn't intimacy be pleasurable, not merely a duty? Her stomach pitched uncomfortably.

Was she hoping for too much? Especially given the fact that she had very little time left? She must either honor the marriage contract with Frederick or find a suitable alternative immediately. And as of now, there was no alternative, save George Whitby. Could he possibly satisfy her? *No.* No, he would not. Yet marrying Frederick held the possibility of becoming far *more* disastrous, didn't it?

Selina cleared her throat. "I do hope you know what

you are doing," she said. "You cannot expect marriage to change Frederick's character. Just imagine the humiliation of having a husband who trifles with other men's wives." She looked around furtively, then lowered her voice many decibels. "He could get himself shot, you know. Or worse."

Worse? What could possibly be worse than that? Still, Selina had given voice to Eleanor's greatest fears about Frederick. Even he himself had said that a leopard cannot change its spots. Even now, he was trying to lure her to an isolated cottage, and for what? Certainly not to converse about the weather.

The sound of approaching footsteps distracted her from her thoughts. Eleanor busied herself with her needlework as the men strode in, the scent of tobacco following them.

"There you are, Henley dear," Selina said, moving her skirts aside to make room for her husband beside her on the sofa.

The cushions depressed as Henley took his seat, stretching his legs out before him. "So, my dear, what shall we do for entertainment tonight? Some cards, perhaps?"

Selina shook her head. "Not tonight, as our numbers are not even." She cast an uneasy glance over her shoulder, her pale brows knitted.

"Feel free to play without me," Frederick offered, his deep baritone voice just behind Eleanor, causing her to start in surprise. "I have some correspondence to take care of. Might I trouble you for a pot of ink and a pen, Whitby?"

"Of course, Mister Stoneham. You'll find everything you need here in the escritoire. Shall I have it sent to your room? Perhaps our merriment here will distract you."

"Not in the least," he said, moving from behind the sofa to stand directly in front of her. "I'm feeling inclined to remain in such pleasant company tonight," he added.

Eleanor took a deep breath, forcing her gaze to remain upon the tips of his scuffed boots. Wishing to effect a mask of ennui, she reached for her needle, pricking her finger in the process. Stifling a gasp, she pressed her wounded finger to her handkerchief beneath her hoop, hoping no one had witnessed her careless blunder.

"Unless, of course, my presence here distracts *you*," Frederick added, a hint of amusement in his voice.

Her cheeks flooded with warmth. Still, she did not raise her gaze.

"Don't be a fool, Stoneham," Henley said, clapping Frederick on the back. "Go. Sit, and write your deuced letter whilst we play a hand or two. You shan't distract us in the least, old boy."

"Perhaps it is a love letter you're so keen on writing?" Selina asked. There was a hard edge to her voice, one which Eleanor had rarely heard her friend use.

"Perhaps it is," Frederick drawled in reply, his boots moving yet another step in Eleanor's direction.

"Do tell," Selina pressed.

"A gentleman never tells," he answered. "Or so the story goes. Pray tell, have I the right of it, Lady Eleanor?"

"I'm sure I wouldn't know," she answered, meeting his gaze at last. In the short time since she'd left him there in the dining room, he'd loosened his cravat and mussed his dark hair. Why, oh, why did his slightly disheveled appearance set her pulse leaping? Her heart beating wildly? Whatever was the matter with her?

"I'll leave you to your cards, then," he said, an easy smile parting his lips and setting his eyes aglow with mischief.

He was toying with her, as always. Fully aware that he discomposed her. Maddeningly arrogant and brash, the beast.

Without sparing him another glance, Eleanor took her seat at the card table opposite Mister Whitby. For perhaps a half hour she tried her best to concentrate on the game at hand, though every fiber of her being was painfully aware of Frederick's presence there behind her at the escritoire, his pen scratching against the paper.

Time and again she fought the urge to glance over her shoulder, wondering just what correspondence had so captured his enthusiasm. He had admitted to one kept mistress in Town—perhaps it was to her that he wrote. *Does a man write to his mistress?* Eleanor wasn't certain.

"Come now, Lady Eleanor. The suit is hearts, not diamonds," Mister Whitby scolded, snapping her attention back to the cards in her damp hands.

"Forgive me," Eleanor murmured, retrieving the card she had just laid on the table's baize top.

Selina tossed her cards to the table with a shake of her head. "Don't fret, Eleanor. I fear I am not inclined to play tonight. I simply cannot concentrate."

Henley sighed heavily, tipping back his chair precariously on two legs. "Very well. What shall we do instead?"

"Shall I ring for some port?" Mister Whitby offered, pushing back from the table and rising to his feet.

"That would be lovely." Selina's eyes scanned the room, settling at last on Frederick where he sat slumped in the chair before the writing desk. A lock of hair had fallen across one angular cheek, shielding his eyes from view and mingling with the dark whiskers that shadowed his jaw as he continued to write, his pen moving in graceful arcs across the paper.

Glancing quickly back at Eleanor, Selina cleared her

throat loudly before calling out, "Mister Stoneham, this must be a very important correspondence of yours to gain such attention as this. You must relieve my curiosity at once and tell me to whom you write so earnestly."

"Selina!" Eleanor warned under her breath, casting a scathing glare at her friend for such impertinence. Whatever had come over her?

Frederick laid down his pen and turned to face them, tossing back the errant lock of hair as a hint of a wry smile turned up the corners of his mouth. "If you must know, Lady Henley, I am writing to my grandmother. In Ireland."

"Your grandmother?" Selina delicately arched a brow in disbelief. Clearly this was not the answer she expected. "I confess, sir, I am astonished," she said.

Frederick laughed aloud. "What surprises you, Lady Henley? That I have a grandmother, or that I correspond with her?"

"Why, that you would correspond with her, I suppose."

Frederick waved a hand over the page in front of him, drying the ink. "Do you not correspond with your own grandmother?"

Selina squirmed in her seat. "Well, yes. Of course I do. But . . . but I am . . . and you are . . ." She trailed off uncomfortably.

"Yes?" Frederick prodded. "Go on."

Selina turned toward her husband. "Henley, dear, you do not correspond with your grandmother, do you? Or any relation, for that matter."

Henley shrugged in reply. "The old bird hasn't much to say. Do you write to her, George?"

"Of course not," Whitby answered, reaching for the bellpull beside the fireplace. "Whatever would I have to write to her?"

Selina nodded her agreement. "And yet you've written how many pages there, Mister Stoneham?"

"Three pages," he answered, completely unembarrassed. "And I'm not yet done."

"It just seems . . . odd, is all," Selina said.

Eleanor shook her head in censure. What a silly thing to criticize a man for! Why, Henry had corresponded regularly with Grandmama, right up until the day she had died.

"Is it odd?" Frederick asked, tapping his fingers against the blotter. "Well, then, perhaps you would be better pleased if I did write a love letter, after all? Tell me, to whom shall I address it?"

The uncomfortable silence that followed was broken only by the return of the parlormaid carrying a silver tray laden with a decanter of port and several small cut-glass goblets.

As Mister Whitby began to pour and pass around the glasses, Henley and Selina gathered about him, chattering happily about nonesuch as if naught was amiss.

Fiddling with the fastenings on her spencer, Eleanor turned to look at Frederick, still sitting at the writing desk watching her, looking every bit the dark and dangerous rogue. Their eyes met, the invitation in his gaze so apparent that it momentarily stole away her breath. Would she meet him at the cottage tonight?

With a nod, she turned back toward her host and accepted the glass of port he offered, sipping it with a smile.

"And now perhaps Lady Eleanor will play for us," Mister Whitby said, raising his glass in her direction. "In fact, I insist."

"Very well," she said reluctantly, eyeing the dull rose-wood pianoforte in the room's corner. Somewhat in need of a tuning, the instrument was a fine one nonetheless, and Eleanor enjoyed playing. If only Frederick's presence didn't unnerve her so.

"What shall I play?" she asked, setting down her goblet and striding toward the long wooden bench while the Henleys and Mister Whitby settled themselves back in their seats.

"Something cheerful, perhaps?" Whitby called out.

Yes, he would no doubt prefer something light, a piece without depth. Something old-fashioned. A lively piece of Mozart, perhaps. Running her fingers lightly over the keys, she glanced up at Frederick, his back to her and his attention returned to his letter.

What type of piece would Frederick prefer? Something rich, somber, full of emotion, her mind supplied. Of course. Something beautiful yet turbulent.

Closing her eyes, she inhaled deeply, laying her fingers on the cool keys. As she exhaled, she opened her eyes and began to play. Beethoven's Piano Sonata No. 14 in C-sharp minor, perhaps the loveliest piece of music she'd ever heard. The fingers of her left hand moved continuously while those on her right slowly picked out the dark and whisper-like melody, full of passion. It was a love ballad, dedicated to the Countess Giulietta Guicciardi. *Quasi una fantasia.* Almost a fantasy. How fitting, indeed.

Perhaps a full minute into the first movement, she noticed that Frederick had risen from his seat at the escritoire and moved to stand at the far end of the pianoforte. Without missing a beat, her eyes met his, holding his gaze for several seconds. He watched her intently, a heat emanating from his person, warming her skin as she played on.

No longer aware of the Henleys and Mister Whitby's presence in the room, she played for *him*—only for him, knowing somehow that he appreciated the beloved piece as she did. *Fiercely.* In an instant, she realized that this was a man who would love exactly that way—fiercely, intensely. But steadfastly?

Of that she was not sure, and therein lay the danger. To love Frederick Stoneham would be a risky endeavor indeed. She pushed the thought away, humiliated by the scalding tears that had suddenly and inexplicably filled her eyes, blurring her vision.

Overcome with emotion, Eleanor closed her eyes once more and allowed her fingers to blindly pick out the movement's final haunting notes. When the last note faded into nothingness, she opened her eyes and found Frederick there at her side, a mere foot away.

The room erupted into applause.

"Brava," Mister Whitby called out, rising from his seat.

"Lovely, wasn't it?" Selina asked.

"Beautifully played," Henley answered with a nod.

"Even if a bit morose," Mister Whitby added thoughtlessly.

Eleanor bit her lip, stifling a reply as Mister Whitby returned his attention to refilling the Henleys' goblets. Remembering Frederick's presence there beside her, she turned to him. "And what of you, Mister Stoneham? Did you find Beethoven's sonata to be morose?"

His gaze swept across her face before he replied. "Quite the contrary, madam. That was . . ." He trailed off with a shake of his head, swallowing hard before continuing, ". . . without a doubt, the most enchanting thing I've ever heard."

"Thank you," she said quietly, lowering her gaze to her own hands, clasped in front of her.

"If you will excuse me, I believe I shall now retire," he announced, bowing toward the assembled party. Before she realized what was happening, he reached for her hand and pressed a folded piece of paper into it. "Perhaps it was a love letter all along," he whispered in her ear as he brushed past her toward the door, his breath warm against her neck.

Her legs suddenly weak, she sank back to the pianoforte's bench. She chanced a glance at the folded square of paper in her hand, "My Dearest Eleanor" written in bold, black script. Hastily, she tucked the missive into her spencer's pocket.

"Shall I play the second movement?" she asked, forcing a measure of cheer into her voice. "It's much more bright, I assure you." Without awaiting a reply, she began to play, her fingers visibly trembling.

One more movement, no more. And then she would excuse herself. Her heart began to pound in anticipation, beating furiously in rhythm to the scherzo she played.

Chapter 13

Eleanor wrapped her cloak tightly about herself and set off across the field, her heart thumping so vigorously in her breast that she feared it might burst. Perhaps one hundred yards from the house she paused, leaning against the wide, swirling trunk of a sweet chestnut tree. This was madness, utter and complete madness. She should turn back immediately, before it was too late. Before she did something entirely foolish.

But, blast it, she wanted to go. Doing so was imprudent, terribly so. Selina would be scandalized were she to find out. She could never tell her. *Never.* She glanced up at the moon and sighed, her breath making a puff of steam in the cool night air. For perhaps the sixth time in the past hour, she pulled out the folded square of paper from her cloak pocket and unfolded the page, now slightly worn and ragged along the edges.

The bright light of a full, harvest moon illuminated the words on the page, though she had memorized them by now—each and every word burned into her mind for eternity.

Her first love letter.

My Dearest Eleanor,

If only I were a poet, I would put lovely words to the page, words that would adequately describe your grace, your charm, your flawless beauty. But alas, I am no poet. I am but a man filled with longing, with desire that knows no bounds. I beg of you, meet me at the cottage tonight at midnight—the witching hour. For you must be a witch to have ensnared me as you have, my thoughts filled with naught else but memories of your face, your smile, your voice. Indeed, my lovely Eleanor, you have bewitched me. I must know if I am to suffer alone, or if you are similarly afflicted by feelings which I dare not name. I will wait for you till the first light of dawn.

Until then,
Frederick

Was this some sort of cruel game he played, toying with her in this way? Or did he mean these words that quickened her pulse, that made her knees go weak with anticipation? She would have no peace till she found out. She must go; she hadn't a choice.

Hastily, she refolded the page and slipped it back into her cloak, glancing up at the moon just as a wispy cloud moved across the lower half of the silvery orb, casting shadows upon the lawn. Looking around to make sure no one was about, she pulled the hood of her cloak over her head and hurried on toward the bluff where she would follow the path to the cottage. It should take her a quarter hour to reach her destination, no more. *Midnight*. The witching hour.

For the third time in the past half hour, Frederick strode to the window and pulled back the drapes, peering out at the sandy path that lay before the cottage where tiny grains of mica twinkled under the light of the moon and stars. He had come to the cottage immediately upon excusing himself for the night.

Once there, he had laid a fire in the fireplace, lit the large candelabra by the bed and several other small tapers throughout the cottage's single room, and waited. His coat and waistcoat lay discarded on the chaise, his cravat untied and hanging still about his neck as he gazed out the dusty window, hope beating a relentless rhythm in his breast.

Seeing nothing out of the ordinary, he released the drapes and returned to the chaise, sprawling distractedly as he continued to wait. Sitting up, he reached for the bottle of red wine he'd brought with him and poured a measure into one of the goblets sitting on the small gilded table beside the chaise. Draining the glass in one long draught, he set it back on the table and laid back against the tasseled velvet cushions, his head propped on a plump bolster, his boots crossed at the ankles. Back to waiting. He was not a patient man, not by any measure, but he'd wait all night if he had to.

Would she come? Devil take it, but he hoped she would. He'd sell his soul for one night with her. Closing his eyes, he inhaled deeply, his thoughts returning once more to the haunting sonata she'd played—*for him alone.* He could not say how he knew it to be true, but he was certain nonetheless.

No one had existed in Whitby's drawing room but the two of them as she'd played. He'd been drawn involuntarily to her side, moving toward the pianoforte before he'd even realized what he was doing. Dangerous, perhaps. Whitby had watched him with narrowed eyes, his features taut. Whitby wanted her, too, though Frederick still could not detect any sexual longing in the man's demeanor. No, he wanted Eleanor like a hunter wanted his prey. He wanted to collect her, to own her.

Frederick had no doubt that women like Eleanor—beautiful beyond measure, uncommonly intelligent, a marquess's daughter, for God's sake—did not regularly enter Whitby's social sphere, offering themselves up as potential brides. Indeed, the man must have realized the rare opportunity at hand. Clearly, whomever he shared this love nest with was not considered marriageable, else such a secret affair would not be necessary. A married woman, perhaps? He vowed to find out.

Not that it mattered. Eleanor would not be marrying Whitby, after all. She would marry *him*. By Christmastide, just as their marriage contract stipulated. He'd resolved as much upon his return from Plymouth. He had no choice now; he knew he must bed her, or die trying. Yet she was no Whitechapel trollop, not the skilled courtesan that Molly was. If he bedded her, he must marry her. Eleanor Ashton was not a woman to be trifled with.

Still, she did not deserve him. She deserved far, far better. But like the true roué that he was, he could no longer deny himself, not when he wanted something as badly as he wanted Eleanor.

A log crackled in the hearth, spewing up red ash that settled back to the grate like spent fireworks. Staring unseeing into the flames, Frederick sat, resting his elbows on his knees and cradling his head in his hands. The waiting was near enough killing him, yet he could do naught else. Every nerve, every cell in his body seemed taut, on edge. Never before had a woman affected him this way. *Never.*

As the clock on the mantel ticked off the passing seconds, the candle beside him flickered, uttering a small hiss. Frederick turned toward the door expectantly. She was here—he could sense it. Springing to his feet, he crossed the room in three long strides, reaching for the door just as a faint knock sounded upon it.

His blood racing through his veins like quicksilver, he pulled the door open, bracing himself in eager anticipation.

There she stood—the woman who had begun to haunt his dreams—looking up at him from beneath the heavy folds of a dark, woolen cloak pulled low over her brow. He searched his mind for a clever quip of some sort, but came up annoyingly blank. Instead, all he could do was stare at her face, turned silvery in the moonlight.

"I've come," she said, her voice a mere whisper.

"You've no idea how glad I am. Come inside, love, where it's warm." He moved aside and swept one arm toward the hearth.

He saw her gaze stray beyond his shoulder, toward the fire that cracked and hissed beneath the mantel. Farther still her gaze traveled, to the chaise and table where the open bottle of wine still sat. She did not dare allow herself to look at the bed.

Her troubled gaze flitted back to his, and she shook her head, taking a step backward while she pulled her cloak more tightly about herself. "No, I cannot. That . . . that is why I came here. To tell you that I . . . I cannot."

He quirked a brow, eyeing her curiously. She wanted to come in, he could sense it in her posture. No doubt she was holding herself in check, but he was certain she did so to prevent herself from running to him, not away.

"Liar," he said, daring her to prove him wrong.

"Oh!" Her dark brows drew together. "How dare you?"

"How dare I what? Call you a liar?"

She only sputtered in reply.

"You are a liar, my dear," he continued. "And not a

terribly good one at that. You want to come in. Terribly so. Will you deny it now?"

"It's . . . well, whatever would Selina say? What if one of Mister Whitby's groundskeepers were to see us, and . . . and—"

"And what? That's beside the point. You said you did not want to come in, and I said you were not being truthful. You do, in fact, want to come in. Very much so."

"Your arrogance never fails to astound me, Frederick," she hedged, changing the subject, as always. He would not let her get away with it.

"Forget Selina, forget witless Whitby and his groundskeepers." He reached out and trailed one fingertip along the line of her jaw. Despite the cool night air, her skin was warm, radiating heat. Her breath came in fast puffs of steam, betraying her calm demeanor. "What do *you* want to do, Eleanor?"

She bit her lower lip before responding. "If someone were to see, to find out, I'd be ruined."

"Answer me, Eleanor. What do you want to do? If you truly want to leave, I will retrieve my coat, snuff the fire, and see you safely back. But I do not believe that is what you want. Stop denying yourself, like some sort of martyr. For once in your life, do something simply because you *want* to."

"That's easy for you to say," she snapped, her eyes flashing. "As a man, you naturally have freedoms I do not."

He reached for her hand, encircling her wrist with his fingers. Even through the kidskin of her gloves, he could feel her pulse bounding wildly. "Come inside, love," he said softly, pulling her toward him, across the threshold. "We can discuss the inequalities of the sexes until the sun rises, if you wish to."

For a moment, she hesitated. Her entire body went rigid, her muscles tense yet quivering. He brought her hand to his mouth and pressed his lips against the inside of her wrist where the kidskin ended and the silky flesh began. Her pulse leapt against his lips, and for a split second he entertained the thought that he might very well die if she denied him.

"What do *you* want to do?" he repeated, his voice a hoarse whisper.

"I want to stay," she answered, her voice so full of longing that it nearly took his breath away.

With a nod, he closed the door behind her. "Let me see you," he said, reaching for the hood of her cloak. She said nothing in reply, standing as still as a statue as he pushed back the fabric, drawing her face from the shadows. He nearly gasped aloud when he saw her hair, loose and uncovered, spilling across her shoulders. Involuntarily he reached for it, combing his fingers through the silky tresses.

"I . . . my lady's maid had already taken down my hair. I . . . I didn't take the time to re-dress it."

"And I am so very glad you did not." He twirled one shiny lock about his finger, amazed at its luster as the fire cast its reddish glow upon it. "Have you any idea how very beautiful you are, Eleanor? How utterly enchanting, how incredibly desirable you are?"

Tears filled her eyes at once, and he watched as she blinked them away. Briskly, she untied the ribbon at her throat and shrugged out of the cloak, allowing it to drop to the floor by her feet. "It is not necessary for you to ply me with pretty words, Frederick. Did I not say I would stay?"

Leisurely, he allowed his gaze to travel downward, to her feet and up again, taking in the plain muslin day gown she wore with a lavender silk pelisse. A simple gown. Likely all she could manage without the help of her abigail, and he was glad for it. She looked far more beautiful in this than she did in her elegant silks and lace—less austere, more vulnerable.

Bloody hell, but she was lovely. He damn well did not deserve to lay a finger on her, and yet he had to—he was compelled beyond measure to. "And why should I refrain from speaking pretty words, as you call them, if they are naught but the truth?"

"I am no longer a girl of six and ten, eager to believe such things about myself. You said much the same then, in my presence, but I cannot forget what you said about me when I was not. However can I trust anything you say?"

He drew away. "I've no idea what you mean."

"Of course you would not. It meant nothing to you, and yet I remember that kiss as if it were yesterday. I remember every word you spoke to me—and about me, to your friends."

"I remember it well enough, Eleanor. A man does not easily forget kissing a woman like you, even if you were only six and ten at the time." A white lie, of course, but unavoidable. How could he possibly admit just how little stealing a kiss from an impressionable young woman— one not yet out in society—had meant to him at the time? "You were beautiful then, but even more so now."

"Do you ever speak the truth? Or just what you suppose I wish to hear? I knew I should not have come here," she said, shaking her head. "I heard you, Frederick. I stood outside your father's study door, and I heard you laughing with your friends. Lord Hartsdale and Sir Gregory, all of you laughing as if it were terribly amusing. You spoke such hurtful words, and now you deny them?"

He searched him memory, suddenly desperate to recall the night in question. He remembered kissing her in the maze, then collecting on his wager with Hart and

Gregory—he could remember nothing more specific than that.

"A 'horse of a girl,'" she continued on when he did not answer. "I believe that was the phrase you used to describe me to your friends."

"Let me assure you that your assessment of yourself is so far off the mark as to be laughable. No one in their right mind would consider you such, as I imagine you are well aware."

"Is that so? Why, I clearly remember you speaking those very same words. A horse of a girl, with a figure to match. Likely the only kiss I'd ever get from a willing participant, you mused aloud. I believe you also wished for some tooth powder."

He shook his head. "I said no such thing." Devil take it, why would he?

"I heard you quite plainly. As did Lady Henley, I might add."

"Lady Henley? Selina, you mean? Heard me say such things?" His mind was reeling. "I cannot credit it."

"Perhaps your wild ways have adversely affected your memory, then. Let me assure you that, in describing me to your friends, you spoke those exact words without taking any pains to lower you voice."

Dear God, had he possibly done so? Called her such unflattering, hurtful things? No, he had no memory of it. None whatsoever. And yet he had remembered her as plain, unappealing. Damn it all, perhaps he *had* said it. And not only had she heard him, but she had remembered the words, all these years. A wave of remorse washed over him as he looked up and met her pained eyes.

She bent down to retrieve her cloak. "Ask Selina yourself, if you do not believe me. Whatever was I thinking, coming here?"

"Good God, Eleanor," was all he could say. He

reached up to rub his temples, now pounding painfully. He reached for her hand, but she snatched it away.

Shaking out her cloak, she moved toward the door, preparing to flee. His gut wrenching, he watched as she wrapped the dark folds about her and hastily retied the ribbon at her throat.

"Don't go," he called out, finding his voice at last. "I was a boy then, full of arrogant swagger, and . . ." He trailed off, unsure of what to say to make it right. How could he ever make up for such a thing? For hurting her like he had? "I'm a bloody fool. A bastard, but that's no excuse. My God, no wonder you've thought so little of me, all this time."

"I had other reasons, besides," she said, pausing before the door. "It is entirely your right to find me unappealing, Frederick. I cannot hold that against you. But your reputation?"

"A reputation does not make a man, Eleanor."

"Perhaps." She shrugged, then wrapped her arms around herself, as if she were cold even as the fire burned hotter in the hearth. "But what I cannot abide is that nothing you say can be believed. And yet you've no idea how badly I *want* to believe you, Frederick."

"And is that what you came here tonight to tell me? That, because I spoke carelessly as a boy of nineteen, you cannot believe anything I say now?"

"Just tonight, in Mister Whitby's drawing room, you claimed to write to your grandmother," she accused, her voice low.

"Aye, and write my grandmother I did. Three full pages, after I finished the letter to you."

She planted both fists on her hips, regarding him coolly with her chin tilted defiantly in the air. "And I'm to believe that?"

A surge of indignation shot through his veins. "It's

back in my room, waiting to be posted." He folded his arms across his chest, returning her challenging glare with his own. "You may within your right call me a rogue, a rake, a shameless flatterer, perhaps. But do not call me a liar, at least not where my grandmother is concerned."

Eleanor blinked rapidly, nibbling on her lower lip as she considered his words. At last, she nodded. "I *do* believe you. You care deeply for your grandmother, don't you?"

He shuffled his feet uncomfortably. "Aye," he said at last, a bit gruffly. His grandmother was the one person who saw past his striking resemblance to his mother, who found a measure of comfort in it, perhaps. Unlike his father and grandfather, she did not hold him responsible for his mother's death.

If she blamed anyone for the loss of her child, it was his father—for seducing her only daughter, taking her away from her home, from Connemara's savage beauty. Fiona had not belonged in England, his grandmother believed, and her untimely demise was proof. Still, she had taken comfort in Frederick, as he had in her. His grandfather, however, was a different matter altogether.

"I wanted to write you a poem," he said, quickly and easily changing the subject. "But alas, I found I had not the talent. I hope you'll forgive my cowhanded attempt at a love letter."

Eleanor reached into her cloak and withdrew the missive in question, fingering the edges with trembling fingers. "Did you mean these words, Frederick? Or is this letter full of your usual empty flattery?"

He started to speak but she held up one hand, cutting him off. "No, I must ask this, and you must answer in all honesty. We cannot proceed, otherwise."

"Each and every word is true, though I am perhaps not so skilled at putting my feelings to the page."

Her eyes widened a fraction, her lashes fluttering like butterfly wings. "You asked if you suffer alone from . . . from . . ." She shook her head, unable to say the words.

He took two steps toward her, reaching out to untie her cloak once more. "Desire, Eleanor? Longing? I cannot sleep for thinking of you. I cannot look upon another without seeing your face. When we are apart, all I can do is wonder when we will next be together. Aye, somehow you've taken over my mind, and in so short a time. Never before has a woman made me feel such things, such longings, such desires. Tell me I am not alone in these feelings, before I go mad with them."

For a moment, Eleanor said nothing. She dropped her gaze to her hands, then peeled off her kidskin gloves, one by one, dropping them carelessly to the floor beside her cloak. Nodding almost imperceptibly to herself, she took two steps toward him, closing the distance between them, then looked up to meet his gaze. One delicate hand reached out, slowly, tentatively moving toward his face.

Gently, achingly so, she stroked his rough jaw with her palm, moving closer still, so that her breasts grazed his shirtfront. The sweet, lavender scent of her overwhelmed his senses, his erection straining near-painfully against the flap of his breeches. Though he wanted nothing more than to gather her in his arms, he dared not move a muscle, unwilling to risk her drawing away in fear.

"No, Frederick," she said, her voice a soft, sensual caress. "No, you are not alone in these feelings."

"Thank God," he said on a breath before savagely crushing her to him, taking her hot, sweet mouth with his own with complete and utter abandon.

Chapter 14

Eleanor gasped as Frederick's lips crushed hers with a near-bruising force, his muscled body pressed so tightly against hers that she could feel the pounding of his heart through the layers of fabric that separated them.

Oh, how she'd wanted this! Each and every kiss had made her hunger for more. She'd told herself that her only purpose in going to the cottage was to find out if he'd meant the words he'd written her—nothing more. But this . . . *this* was the true reason, she realized, as she opened her mouth invitingly against his.

His tongue invaded her mouth, gently at first, then more insistently. Eleanor's knees felt suddenly weak and she swayed against him, clutching the back of his head for support. He tasted of wine and a hint of tobacco, an intoxicating mix, she thought, barely cognizant of the fact that his hands were sliding down her back, moving stealthily toward her backside.

She heard a soft moan and was surprised to realize it had been her own, laced with desire, an almost primal sound. Frederick's mouth retreated, then returned to nip softly at her lower lip, his hands cupping her buttocks, kneading them through her thin gown. A molten heat gathered in her belly, radiating downward, and she realized with a start that she had grown strangely damp between her thighs.

His lips trailed lower, down her throat where he pressed hot, moist kisses to her burning flesh, whispering her name over and over as he did so.

Oh, how she wanted him—terribly so. How would she ever stop, now that she'd tasted the forbidden fruit? She'd never have enough of him. *Never.*

His fingers moved around her waist, beneath her breasts, his thumbs brushing tantalizingly across her nipples, drawing gooseflesh across her skin.

"Frederick!" she said on a sharp gasp, unsure whether she meant it in protest or invitation. Her muddled mind could think of nothing save the sensation of his lips against her skin, his hands on her body, setting every inch of her afire with some unknown sensation.

"What is it, love?" he murmured, his lips pressed just above her collarbone.

"I . . . I'm feeling a bit dizzy." It was the truth, as the ground swayed dangerously beneath her feet.

"Are you, now?" he drawled in reply, straightening to meet her gaze. "I'm glad. I meant to kiss you senseless."

Grasping his forearms for support, she took a step away from him, blinking rapidly. "Truly, I'm feeling a bit . . . faint."

His dark brows drew together at once. "Come, sit down." Reaching for her arm, he led her to the chaise. "A drink, perhaps? I've brought some wine. Not the finest vintage, I'm afraid, but it'll do well enough."

Eleanor nodded, settling back on the velvet cushions. "Just a sip, no more."

Hurrying to the ornate table beside the chaise, he poured a splash of deep red wine into a goblet and handed it to her before coming to stand behind her, his warm hands resting upon her shoulders. She took a long draught, shuddering as the liquid burned a path to her stomach. A warmth stole through her veins at once, calming her racing heart.

"Better, love?" Frederick asked, bending down so that his lips brushed her ear.

Eleanor nodded. "A bit. I vow, I don't know what came over me."

"Oh, I think I do," he answered with a chuckle. "But I did not mean to frighten you. Here." He reached for the goblet and returned it to the table, then scooped her up in his arms, as if she weighed no more than a feather. "Just let me hold you for a moment." Straddling the chaise, he lowered himself to the cushions and settled her between his legs, her back pressed against his chest.

Pressing a kiss to the top of her head, he wrapped his arms around her. Eleanor sighed, never before as comfortable as she was at that very moment. Dear Lord, how *right* this felt. How utterly perfect it felt in his arms, the glow of the fire casting a warm orange light about the room, the wine warming her belly, her skin still tingling from his kisses.

"This is lovely," she sighed, dropping her head back against his chest. She would not consider the impropriety; she couldn't. Not now. It was far too late for that, besides.

"Aye, it *is* lovely," he agreed, resting his chin upon the top of her head. "Have you any idea of the monumental restraint I'm exercising in not ravishing you this very minute? You'd better speak of something else, right away, before I change my mind and take you right here and now."

"Very well. What shall we discuss?"

"George Whitby?" he offered, his voice full of mischief.

Eleanor couldn't help but smile. "Most definitely *not* George Whitby."

"You'd deprive me of such pleasure? Ah, very well. The weather, then?"

"Really, Frederick. Surely you can do better than that."

"Music?" he asked, reaching for her hand and lacing his fingers with hers. The contrast was startling—her hand so pale, his bronzed by the sun. And while she'd never been what one would consider delicate, her hand appeared tiny in his. His grip was strong and sure, entirely masculine. Comforting.

"You can start by telling me the name of the piece you played tonight," he prompted, drawing her from her musings.

A smile spread across her face. "It was Beethoven, his Piano Sonata Number 14. He dedicated it to a pupil of his. Many believe he was in love with her."

"And after hearing it, I'd have to agree. I had no idea you were such an accomplished pianist."

"You've much to learn about me, Frederick. Anyway, I don't play as well as all that. But I do so love that particular piece."

"Aye, and now I do, too. Tell me, just what other secrets have I to discover about you? Are you an accomplished artist, as well? A poet?"

Heat flooded her cheeks as she recalled her awkward attempts at writing poetry. "It's you who remain a mystery. You claim that a reputation does not make a man. So tell me, then, who is the real Frederick Stoneham?"

"Well, let me give it some thought. Hmm, I correspond with my grandmother; that you've learned tonight. She's a grand old bird, and I shudder to think how I would have survived my youth without her. What else? You've already learned of my fondness for Irish poets. I don't believe anyone before you, male or female, has ferreted out that bit of information. What more could you possibly wish to know?"

"Tell me about your father. I've always wondered why the Baron Worthington resides at his modest estate in Essex when his baronial seat is in Oxfordshire."

She felt his entire body go rigid behind her. "I do not wish to speak of my father," he said, his voice tight.

"Nor did I wish to speak of my mother earlier today on the bluff. And yet you asked, and I answered with all honesty about matters which only bring me shame. I am not sorry I chose to speak candidly. If we're to be friends, you might consider doing the same. Besides, the more evasive you become, the more wildly I begin to speculate. Your father's sins cannot possibly be worse than my mother's, now can they?"

"Touché. Since you've put forth such an effective argument, I can't very well deny you. Since my mother's death, my father has chosen not to take up residence in Oxfordshire. Too many memories, he claims. Nothing more than that."

"How long ago did your mother pass? I can't recall ever having met her."

"She died the day I was born," he answered, his voice suddenly gruff. "Complications of childbirth."

"I did not know that. I'm so very sorry."

"Don't be. It was a long time ago, though my father has never fully recovered."

"I suppose he loved her very much, then."

"I suppose he did. Anyway, after my brother's death, my father sent me to Ireland to be raised by my mother's parents."

"But why? Hadn't you older sisters to care for you?"

"Five older sisters and a spinster aunt. My father simply wanted me out of his sight. I reminded him too much of my mother and what he'd lost. When Charles was still living, he was able to ignore my presence altogether. But with Charles's death, I became his heir. He could not live with that knowledge on a daily basis."

"And . . . and your grandparents were kind to you?" she asked tentatively.

"Kind enough. My grandfather was the land steward on my father's estate in Ireland, so it seemed a practical enough matter to have me there, learning the basics of estate management. It lent my grandparents a bit of status, actually. The lord of the manor, their grandson. Still, they disliked my father for having taken away their daughter, and they took pleasure in raising me not as an English gentleman, but as one of their own. I did not go to Eton, did you know that?"

"No, I did not."

"Aye, I was schooled by the nuns in Clifton. It's a wonder I ever got to Cambridge. I was not certain my father would shell out the funds on my behalf."

"I must apologize, Frederick. I did not mean to pry so into your personal affairs."

"And now you know the truth. I was not good enough for my father, nor was I good enough for my grandfather, heir to a barony or not. My father was doing yours no great favor when he signed that marriage contract."

"Most would consider you far too young to settle down. It's expected of a woman my age. But not of a man of three and twenty."

"I am my father's only heir. No living male cousins, no uncles to inherit the barony if I do not produce an heir myself. I'm sure he fears that if he does not see me suitably wed in haste, his title will eventually fall into abeyance. No matter his ill feelings toward me, he does not wish that to happen."

"And there you have it."

"And there you have it," he agreed.

"I vow, I cannot understand why novels and poems romanticize love in such a fashion as they do. In truth, love seems to bring nothing but grief to so many. Both our fathers are excellent examples, are they not? My own father grieves daily for a wife who will never return his sworn love and devotion. Everyone in all of Essex knows it to be true."

"Will you not allow yourself to love, then, Eleanor?"

"How can I? How can you?"

He paused a beat before replying. "All I know is, with you in my arms, how can I not?"

As her mind digested those words, her heart began to beat furiously, the sound of her blood rushing through her veins near deafening. She wanted to believe he meant what he implied . . . wanted to believe it desperately. Still, she didn't dare.

He cleared his throat. "And now what shall we do, my sweet? The night is young."

She turned to face him, both her palms pressed flat against the hard planes of his chest, and pressed her lips against his. "This," she said. "And this." Imitating just what he'd done to her before, she trailed her lips down to his throat, inhaling his clean, woodsy scent as she did so. His skin was hot against her lips, slightly salty. Just as she had imagined it would be, all these years.

Frederick groaned against her ear, doing his best to tamp down his lust. Devil take it, but she was going to be the death of him yet. "You're playing a dangerous game, Eleanor Ashton. Don't begin something you do not plan to finish." In one sharp movement he pulled off his untied cravat and tossed it to the floor, then deftly unbuttoned the top few buttons of his linen. Just as he'd hoped, her sweet lips followed suit, trailing kisses in the wake of his fingers, down the hollow at the base of his throat and to his breastbone. "You're an apt pupil," he murmured, brushing her hair back from her flushed cheeks. "Just as I imagined you'd be."

The soft, wet kisses stopped and her gaze flew up to meet his, her blue eyes round with curiosity. "Is that so? And what else did you imagine about me?"

"Oh, you've no idea the extent of it." He reached for the shiny buttons on her overcoat and began unbuttoning them, one by one till the fabric fell away, allowing her to shrug out of the sleeves and drop the garment to the floor. The bared swell of her bosom rose and fell on rapid breaths, her creamy skin flushed a delicate rose. Only her thin muslin gown now concealed her delicious curves, and damn it, but he wanted her out of that gown.

All rational thought seemed to flee him and instinct took over as he scooped her up in his arms and carried her to the bed, laying her down gently on the coverlet. Her rich, ebony hair fanned out behind her, just begging him to tangle his fingers in it as he laid down beside her, capturing her mouth once more with his own.

The fire behind him hissed and spat as he moved his mouth lower, tugging down the sleeves of her gown as he did so, revealing the gentle slope of her shoulders. Lower still his mouth moved, to the swell of her breasts, his fingers continuing to tug down the fabric of her bodice. Eleanor arched her back in reply, mewling softly like a kitten, her fingers clutching the coverlet beneath her.

His cock throbbed impatiently, desperate for release, and all he could think of was plunging himself into her, losing himself in her for all eternity.

With a groan, he gave her bodice one more tug, at last revealing the breasts he'd dreamt of so many nights now. Perfect, just as he'd imagined them. He captured one pale pink nipple in his mouth, suckling gently, making her squirm beneath him.

"Have you any idea how badly I want you, Eleanor?" he murmured against her skin, his hands slipping beneath her, moving toward the fastenings on the back of her gown. *Must get her out of this thing.* Suddenly he could think of nothing else—it became his silent mantra. One fastening gave beneath his fingers, then another. Satiny skin, warm and flushed beneath his hand, sent the blood rushing to his groin. *A marquess's daughter. An innocent. A virgin.* The unwelcome thoughts came crashing through his consciousness, and suddenly he knew he needed her permission—he needed to hear her speak the words.

He dragged his mouth away from her neck. "Tell me what you want, Eleanor," he asked, his voice rough. "Say it."

"I want you to kiss me, Frederick," she answered, her voice a husky whisper.

He wasted no time in complying.

At last he pulled away, breathless, his gaze seeking hers. Their eyes met and held, hers registering fear, confusion.

"What else, love?" he whispered, brushing a soft kiss across her forehead. "I cannot ravish you against your will. You must say the words; tell me what you want from me."

She shook her head, her dark locks falling freely across her shoulders. "I . . . I cannot. I fear we've done far too much as it is, Frederick."

"So much more I'd like to do," he murmured, nuzzling her neck.

She struggled to sit, and Frederick groaned aloud as she tugged her bodice up to its rightful place. "First we must decide what's to be done."

"Must we? Now? Have you any idea how I've longed

to have you in my arms like this? Would you really be so cruel as to deny me now?" He kept his tone light, teasing. *Must not frighten her.* Not now, not when he'd come so very close to securing his prize.

"Come now, am I the first to deny you so?" she returned playfully. "That which does not kill us only makes us stronger, isn't that what they say?"

He fell back to the mattress with a growl of frustration. "Damnation, but my grandfather used to say that."

She moved to lean over him, her breath warm and sweet against his neck. "But you can kiss me again, Frederick. I vow, call me a wanton if you may, but I cannot get enough of your kisses."

Propping himself up on one elbow, he brought his lips within an inch of hers, then stopped. For a moment he regarded her, her eyes closed, her head tipped back expectantly. "Allow me to make certain I'm understanding you correctly. You *are* requesting my kiss, are you not?"

"Yes," she murmured, opening her eyes and meeting his gaze. "Would you really be so cruel as to deny *me* now?"

"Let me consider the situation. Hmmm." He nipped at her ear, then trailed his lips down the side of her neck. "So you are indeed requesting my kiss, but are you begging for it?"

"A lady never begs," she countered near breathlessly.

"Oh, but you will." He teased her lips with his own, brushing them ever so gently and then retreating again. "Not that I've overmuch experience with ladies."

"You're nothing but a scoundrel," she answered with a smile.

"Indeed. And you're desperate for a scoundrel's kiss."

"Oh, very well, if there's no other way. I beg you to kiss me, then, Frederick. Will that do?"

"That'll do nicely," he growled, then captured her eager mouth with his own.

Minutes later, he pulled away, knowing that his tightly held control was surely slipping away. "You do realize I win the wager, don't you?" he teased, tapping her lightly on the nose.

He heard her sharp intake of breath. "Whatever do you mean?" she asked, her eyes narrowed.

"Remember that day in Henley's park? I wagered that you would beg for my kiss before the year was out. You owe me one hundred pounds, if I remember correctly."

The color drained from her face in an instant, and she struggled to stand, her entire body trembling. "Dear lord, that's it, then. You brought me here to win a wager. What a terrible, terrible fool I am!"

"Don't be ridiculous, love." He reached for her hand, but she snatched it away, taking two steps away from the bed.

"However could I fall for it, not once, but twice now?"

"You cannot possibly believe that this," he sputtered, "all this, was simply an act to win a wager?"

"You just said yourself—"

"Good God," he interrupted, his anger mounting. "I said it in jest. Do you really think me capable of such a deception as that?"

"Yes . . . no," she corrected. "Truly, I've no idea what you're capable of." She hurried to retrieve her pelisse, roughly shoving her arms into the sleeves. "I want to believe it is not so, but I cannot be certain. Can't you understand?"

"No, Eleanor, I cannot." He stood and crossed the room, standing before her with his arms folded across his chest. "Two minutes ago you were lying here beside me, trusting me, letting me touch you intimately. Now you doubt my word? I confess, I'm finding your vacillation tiresome."

"Can you blame me? After what happened . . . before?"

"It was four years ago, Eleanor. Four. I've apologized, and . . ." He trailed off, raking a hand through his hair. "Bloody hell, what can I do? Tell me, what can I possibly do to earn your trust again?"

Eleanor shook her head. "You cannot understand; it's useless."

"Rather than running out the door in a pique, why don't you attempt to explain it to me, then. Yes, four years ago I misused your trust. Terribly," he added, seeing the way her eyes began to flash in the candlelight. "But we are adults now, and I believe you know me better than anyone save my sisters. I'd presumed to call you a friend, at a time when I was much in need of one. I've answered each and every charge you've leveled at me about my past with what I thought to be blunt truths. And still you cannot trust me?"

Tears gathered in her eyes, and she turned away from him.

"You've no idea—"

He reached for her arm and turned her back to face him. "Then tell me, damn it."

"Oh, very well," she cried, shrugging out of his grip. "While that kiss fours years ago meant nothing to you, I've not been able to forget it, not in all this time. All these years, as I listened to the gossip surrounding you, even as I asked my father to choose a husband for me— a sensible husband—I dreamt of you. I longed for you."

She began to pace a circuit before the hearth, refusing to meet his gaze as she continued on. "I didn't dare confess my feelings to anyone. Even Selina thought it nothing but a girlish infatuation, ended the day I overheard you laughing about me with your friends. But, damn you, it didn't end that day, nor the next. Four long years of pretending I didn't care a whit that you were rumored to keep several mistresses at once, to seduce other men's wives, to entertain widows in your bed. Have you any idea how I've suffered? How I've hated myself for such weakness? How I've pretended it wasn't so, that I'm not a silly cow, pining after a man who hadn't given me a moment's notice? Who thought me nothing but a horse of a girl?"

Good God. He didn't know what to say. All these years, she'd hated herself—for pining after *him?* All these years she'd suffered, because of him. Damn it to hell, but everything he touched turned to rot, poisoned by his very presence. He had not been worth a second glance from her, a second thought. Still, he'd brought her pain—and she *still* hurt, if the look on her face was any indication. She would never trust him, never believe him to be anything other than what he was, a careless, callous roué. Whatever had he been thinking, that he could allow himself to love Eleanor?

"I . . . I had no idea," he sputtered. "You must forgive me, Eleanor." He swallowed hard, unable to say anything more on the subject. He reached up to rub his aching throat, suddenly feeling as if he were suffocating. Dear God, but he needed to get out of this place, and fast. He couldn't bear it, couldn't bear to remain another moment in her presence, knowing what he'd done. What he'd almost done. Thank the devil she'd preempted his seduction when she had or he'd have no doubt caused her further grief, beyond what he'd already inflicted.

He turned to face her, still standing beside the hearth, her chest rising and falling at a rapid rate, her cheeks stained an angry red. "I'll see you back safely. Just let me extinguish the fire and we'll be on our way."

And tomorrow he'd be on his way, back to Plymouth and his search for Eckford. No more of this madness. *No more.*

Chapter 15

"Will Mister Stoneham be dining with you this morning?" the butler asked, and Eleanor forced her expression to remain blank as she reached for her coffee.

"No, I'm afraid not," Henley answered, rising from his seat and placing his napkin on the table. "He set off at dawn, and I'm to join him in Plymouth. Don't know why he was in such a dashed hurry," he added under his breath.

Oh, but Eleanor knew precisely why. Her cheeks stung with the memory.

"Eleanor, dearest, you look flushed," Selina said, her brow furrowed with concern. "Are you unwell?"

Were her feelings so very transparent? How close she'd come to giving up her most prized asset—her virtue—the night before. How natural it had seemed, even after a lifetime of treasuring it, keeping it safely guarded. Never would she have thought it possible to throw caution to the wind as she had done, so carelessly, so recklessly. Still, she'd overreacted, hadn't she? After stealing back to her bedchamber and slipping between the sheets, she'd lain awake for hours on end, going over and over each tantalizing moment she'd spent in the cottage with Frederick.

He had been truthful, she'd concluded at last. His seduction *had* been more than an attempt to win a wager; she was certain of it now. She had accused him falsely, and she felt badly for it. She would have told him so today had he not left before she'd had the opportunity. For the first time in their renewed acquaintance, she actually entertained the thought that perhaps there *was* more to Frederick Stoneham than his reputation would lead one to believe.

Still, she couldn't help but remember the look of horror etched into his features when she'd confessed that she'd pined for him all these years. He had all but run from the cottage as fast as he could after that, hadn't he? Oh, to be so silly, so weak and foolish, to love a scoundrel like Frederick Stoneham!

Love? She shuddered at the word. No, she did not love him, did she? Could she? Dear God, whatever would she do if she did?

"Eleanor, did you hear me?" Selina tapped her on the wrist, her voice rising in alarm. "Eleanor?"

Eleanor quickly gathered her wits. "Pray, forgive me. I fear I did not sleep well last night."

"You must go lie down at once, then. George has planned some entertainment for us this afternoon, and you must be well rested in time for our guests."

"Guests?" Eleanor had heard nothing of guests.

"Yes," Henley answered. "The Duke and Duchess of Dandridge, and their son Lord Trelawny."

"Lord Trelawny?" Eleanor asked. "I am not acquainted with him."

"Oh, he's a nice enough fellow, and a good friend of George's." Henley waved a hand dismissively. "I believe they went to Eton together or somesuch. Well, I suppose

I should be on my way to Plymouth. I don't know why we couldn't remain here until that blasted man was expected back at the inn, as we'd originally planned. It's a waste of time, it is, combing the countryside, when we could be here enjoying the company of such lovely ladies. Ah, well." He sighed heavily and bent to place a kiss on Selina's cheek. "If you'll both excuse me, I'd best be off."

Selina pouted prettily. "Oh, Henley, must you go so soon? We've only just finished breakfast."

"I'm afraid so, my dear. I gave Stoneham my word I'd bring the carriage by midday. He'll be chomping at the bit now, I'll wager."

"Very well. Go, then." Selina waved toward the door. "We shall enjoy our day with the duke and duchess, will we not, Eleanor?"

"Indeed," Eleanor murmured. "And this Lord Trelawny too, I suppose."

With a wink, Lord Henley favored his beaming wife with one last smile before he strode out of the breakfast room.

Eleanor turned her attention toward Selina, who sat staring dreamily at the empty doorway. "You love him very much, don't you?" she asked softly.

Selina smiled, her cheeks dimpling with the effort. "You've no idea, Eleanor. He is truly a good man, and I am so very lucky to have him."

"You are, indeed. It gives me great pleasure to see you so happily settled."

Selina nodded. "I never dreamed I'd find such happiness. What good fortune that Lady Irvington invited both Henley and I to her house party last year. If she had not, just imagine whom I might have married instead."

"Indeed." Eleanor widened her eyes with mock

horror. "Why, I remember when you fancied Sir William Bowman, and Mister Melton before him."

"Nothing but girlish infatuation, I vow. Neither of them half as good a man as my Henley."

Eleanor nodded her agreement. "But how did you distinguish love from infatuation?" she asked, then instantly wished she could retract the words. Taking a deep, fortifying breath, she boldly continued on. "What I meant to ask was, did you love Henley straightaway, or did something . . ." What was the right word? "Did something alter your feelings in due course?"

Selina tipped her head to the side, her brows drawn in consideration. "There's but a fine line between infatuation and love, is there not?"

Eleanor shrugged. "I cannot say, though I expected there would be significantly more to distinguish them."

"Perhaps my relationship with Henley began as an infatuation. I suppose I began to love him once I realized that he loved *me*. Why are you asking such questions, Eleanor?" Her easy smile gave way to a frown. "Has this anything to do with Frederick?"

Eleanor only bit her lip in reply, unable to meet her friend's questioning gaze.

"You must see that Frederick is not the same sort of man as Henley is. It is one thing to be infatuated with a rakehell; Sir William was one, I suppose, and yet I fancied him. But you cannot allow yourself to think you are in love with one. This is madness, Eleanor. I won't allow it. I won't see you hurt when there are perfectly acceptable alternatives to marrying him."

"You mean Mister Whitby?" Eleanor asked with a wry smile.

"Well, yes. Mister Whitby, for one."

"But I've already said—"

"I know," Selina interjected, allowing no room for

argument. "You claim you will not suit, though I cannot see why you would not. You seem to get on so well, after all. But what of this Lord Trelawny? An heir to a dukedom, no less. Perhaps he will do, instead."

"Are you so eager to divert my attentions from Mister Stoneham that you would instead offer up a man you have neither met nor know overmuch about? Do you really find Mister Stoneham so very offensive as that?"

Selina sighed exasperatedly. "Henley just said that Lord Trelawny is an agreeable sort, did he not? A friend to Mister Whitby. And as to Mister Stoneham, his behavior thus far has been somewhat respectable, I suppose. Still, have you forgotten his reputation? Or that he is here in Devonshire on a mission to find a man and take his life?"

"That man has terribly misused his sister," Eleanor shot back.

"So he has, Eleanor. But murder him?"

"He is only challenging him to a duel," Eleanor said, though her blood ran cold at the thought. Why, he might very well be doing so at this very moment, for all she knew. The thought of Frederick facing a man across a brace of pistols suddenly brought the taste of bile to her throat. Her hand shaking, she reached for her coffee and took a sip, nearly choking on the lukewarm liquid.

"Henley says Mister Stoneham's marksmanship is rumored to be unparalleled. He will no doubt kill him, Eleanor."

"As would my own brother had I been so mistreated by the man."

"Would he? I am not so certain. Nor were you, a sennight ago."

Eleanor shook her head in confusion. "You cannot fault a man for such protective instincts toward a sister. It is"—she swallowed hard—"only natural. Besides, who is to say what will happen? Perhaps they will come to some sort of agreement instead. Didn't Henley suggest such a thing?"

Selina sighed and reached for Eleanor's hand. "One can only hope. Come now, must we quarrel? Perhaps you should have your nap now."

Eleanor squeezed her friend's hand in reply, hoping Selina would not notice the way her own hand trembled. "Very well. I should love a nap, and then a nice, long bath. What hour are our guests expected?"

"By three, I believe. We shall have tea in the garden, and George has set up an archery range. Doesn't that sound charming?"

"It sounds delightful," Eleanor agreed, valiantly attempting to force away all thoughts of Frederick. "I should like to try my hand with a bow."

"Then you shall. And promise me you will be your usual bright, cheerful self. No more maudlin thoughts."

"I promise I will try," Eleanor said with a nod, though she knew it would require a great deal of fortitude. She certainly did not feel bright and cheerful—far from it.

"Perhaps you should wear that lovely yellow lawn gown, the one with the pale blue ribbons woven through the hem. And for dinner, that exquisite peacock-blue gown you wore the night we arrived here at Whitby Hall—the one with the oval cutouts? I vow, in that particular frock you could not help but have the unwavering attention of every male in England, if you so desired. Except for Henley, of course," Selina added with an impish grin, and Eleanor couldn't help but smile back.

"Of course," Eleanor replied, linking her arm through Selina's. "You've besotted Henley so thoroughly that the man could not possibly notice the presence of any other lady, no matter how much flesh her frock exposes."

Selina nodded. "As it should be."

"Indeed," Eleanor murmured in reply, knowing full well she could never command such devotion. At least not from Frederick Stoneham, and truly, wasn't that all that mattered?

Do not cry, she silently commanded herself. Not till she reached the privacy of her room. Only then would she allow herself the luxury of a good, long crying jag— long overdue, if truth be told.

And then, like a cold and calculated opportunist, she would meet this Lord Trelawny and assess his husbandly potential, even while she still considered George Whitby.

Whatever was her world coming to?

Frederick leaned forward in the saddle, squinting against the midday sun. He watched closely as his quarry, dressed in the simple black garb of a man of the cloth, climbed down from a horse-drawn cart and reached up to hand down a gaudily-clad woman in a purple velvet cloak.

At once his blood began to pound at his temples, his pulse accelerating as he gripped the reins in his hands. "That's him, all right," he muttered, watching the man escort the woman—obviously round with child—up the walk and disappear into the modest stone cottage. Indeed, Crosby had done well. Frederick tossed a purse of heavy coins toward the barkeep who stood two yards away, leaning against a tree with a self-satisfied smile.

Mister Crosby caught the purse midair, then reached up to tip his hat. "It warn't so hard to find 'em, once I started askin' around. So, what's yer next move, if you don't mind my inquiring?"

"I await Henley's arrival in Plymouth, and together we will return and make sure Eckford doesn't flee. Then

I call him out, and, if all goes well, put a bullet through the blackguard's heart by tomorrow morn."

Crosby whistled through his teeth, readjusting his spectacles. "You don't mess around none, do you? Well, I s'pose I'd best be on my way, then."

Frederick nodded stiffly. "Thank you, Mister Crosby. It's been a pleasure doing business with you."

"Likewise," Crosby said, holding up the purse with a grin.

Frederick returned his attention to the cottage across the lane as the barkeep mounted his horse and guided it back toward Plymouth. He saw movement in a first floor window, draperies fluttering as the window was thrown open. Loud voices, rising in anger, carried across the lane on the breeze. A feminine shriek followed, and then the sound of breaking glass. Damn it to hell, but it looked as if Eckford's lady friend was throwing pottery at his head. It appeared to be a spat of some sort, with the woman taking the upper hand if the way Eckford was cowering was any indication.

No matter. It was not his concern. Soon, very soon, Eckford would pay for his crimes against Maria. She deserved no less. And he would be doing this unknown woman a favor—she would be lucky to be rid of such rubbish.

By this time tomorrow, Frederick's business there in Devonshire would be done, and he could return to London posthaste. Or would he? There was still Eleanor Ashton to consider, though he refused to allow thoughts of her to distract his attention from Eckford. Only once his brother-in-law was dealt with could he consider what to do about Eleanor and their betrothal contract.

Usually a decisive man, this waffling back and forth on the matter made him irritable, annoyed with himself. Still, something had to be done, one way or the other, and he was in no way fit to decide at present, not with the man who had wronged his sister just across the lane.

With a nod to himself, Frederick prodded his horse forward onto the dusty road, wheeling the beast's head back toward Plymouth. Tomorrow things would sort themselves out, one way or another, devil be damned.

Chapter 16

Eleanor released the bowstring, watching closely as the arrow sailed through the air with a whistle. With a decided *thunk*, it hit its mark, a mere three inches from the center circle.

"Very nithe," Lord Trelawny lisped with a nod of approval. "Are you thertain you've not more ethperience with a bow than you've let on?"

Setting down her bow, she grinned in self-satisfaction, her hands planted firmly on her hips as she regarded the target from across the width of the range. "I vow, it's naught but beginner's luck. Or perhaps it's just that I've such excellent instructors as you and Mister Whitby."

Mister Whitby nodded, then pulled back his own bowstring and set his arrow aloft with a *thwang*.

"Exthellent," Lord Trelawny cried, clapping Mister Whitby on the back as the arrow struck the target dead-center. "I thay, that hit prethithely in the thenter, didn't it?"

"I believe it did." Mister Whitby ambled to the target and removed the arrow with a flick of his wrist. "Precisely," he added, smiling broadly. The sun reflected off his cinnamon-colored hair, and Eleanor couldn't help but admire the fine form he cut in his camel breeches and deep blue coat. Like a true sportsman, he was entirely in his element and his enjoyment was reflected in his eyes.

Eleanor was enjoying herself as well, she realized. For a brief moment she allowed herself to entertain the thought that perhaps she had been too quick to judge Mister Whitby, after all.

"Your turn, Lady Eleanor," he called out, cocking his head toward the targets.

"Perhaps once more, and then I must rest. I'm positively parched." She eyed Selina, sitting a short distance away under a canvas tent, enjoying tea with the duke and duchess. Their laughter floated across the breeze, inviting Eleanor to join in their merriment. Once she proved that her initial success with the bow was not a fluke, that is.

Retrieving the bow from the grass at her feet, she raised it and took aim.

"No, not like that," Mister Whitby called out, striding briskly toward her. Reaching around her, he repositioned her hands on the smooth wooden bow.

Though not unpleasant, his touch did not stir her blood the way Frederick's touch did. Even as Mister Whitby pressed his muscled chest against her back, his arm inadvertently grazing the side of her breast, her heart continued to beat a normal rhythm. When Frederick had done much the same, her pulse had leapt alarmingly, desire thrumming through her veins. Silently, she chastised herself for allowing her thoughts to travel that dangerous route and returned her attention to Mister Whitby's tutelage instead.

"There, that's it," he was saying. "Plant your feet wider, yes, like that. You'll be better balanced. Now, this hand here, not so tight. Loosen your grip a bit."

She did as she was told, and Whitby nodded his approval. "That's it. Good girl. A light touch is all that's necessary. Go on, pull back, slowly. Now release," he ordered, and Eleanor let go of the string.

She held up one hand to shield her eyes from the waning sun, watching as the arrow flew through the air and struck the target just outside the center ring.

Mister Whitby whistled in approval. "Very good, very good indeed!" he said, awkwardly patting her on the shoulder. "Impressive, Lady Eleanor. Perhaps you are more the sportswoman than you know. I say, she's quite the apt pupil, isn't she, Trelawny?"

"Indeed," the man agreed, bobbing his fair head. "It would theem Lady Eleanor is as capable with a bow as thee is beautiful, and that is thaying a great deal in her favor."

Eleanor took a moment to study the duke and duchess's son as he took up his own bow and aimed. He was short and slight, nearly a full head shorter than her. Riotous waves of sandy blond hair brushed the high, ruffled collar of his linen, nearly overpowering his small frame. His eyes were a soft green, and his features were delicate, slightly effeminate. It was an attractive face, she supposed, though lacking in masculine appeal. Still, Eleanor had liked him straightaway—who could not? His seeming enthusiasm for everyone and everything was infectious.

Eleanor swiped at the perspiration that had gathered on her forehead with the back of one hand. "And now you must excuse me, gentlemen. I'm desperate for a spot of tea."

"Oh, go on, then. Abandon uth," Trelawney exclaimed. "But know that you're breaking my heart, dear lady."

Eleanor laughed merrily as she removed her long,

heavy leather gloves. "I'm sure you'll survive my desertion." Taking a deep breath of the cool, sea-scented air, she ambled across the springy lawn, toward the shade beneath the canvas. Her yellow skirts ruffled in the breeze, sending the ribbon trimming dancing about her ankles, tickling her skin through her stockings.

"At last," Selina called out as she approached. "Have you really attained expert status so quickly? From here, it looked as if your shots were as well-placed as the gentlemen's."

Eleanor only shrugged. "It would seem I've a natural inclination toward the bow. Who would have thought?"

"Indeed," the duchess said, raising her quizzing glass to her eyes and studying Eleanor from head to toe. "Though you do look hardy enough, I suppose. You're no shrinking violet, are you, Lady Eleanor?"

Eleanor did not take offense; she knew the woman—a sportswoman herself, according to her son—meant it as a compliment.

"Not in the least, Your Grace. I enjoy a great deal of exercise, and find the outdoors to be most pleasant, especially on a lovely autumn day such as this."

"I wholeheartedly agree. Come, join us." The duchess indicated the scrolled wrought-iron chair to her right. "Have some tea, and allow us to get better acquainted. Your father is Lord Mandeville, you said?"

"Indeed," Eleanor answered, reaching for the cup of tea that Selina handed her—two lumps of sugar and a splash of cream, just as she liked.

"I'm acquainted with Lord Mandeville," the duke interjected with a nod. "Fine man."

"Handsome, too," the duchess added. "Terribly so, isn't he?"

The duke continued on as if he had not heard his wife's comment. "I heard him speak at length on educational reform just last year in Parliament. An inspired speaker to be sure, though I fear that the time is not yet ripe for the changes he proposes."

Eleanor nodded, setting her cup on its saucer. "Educational reform is a topic my father feels quite strongly about, and my brother along with him." She allowed her gaze to stray to the duchess who sat sipping her own tea with a smile.

She was far more youthful than Eleanor had expected, perhaps a full score younger than the balding duke, she would hazard to guess. Petite and lithe, the Duchess of Dandridge was striking, her wheat-colored hair falling in loose tendrils about almond-shaped green eyes that lent an air of exoticism to her countenance. Her face remained remarkably unlined, her lips as full and rosy as if she were still in the first blush of youth. What a contrast she was to her aging, rather portly husband beside her, Eleanor thought.

"Doesn't get to Town much, does he?" the duke was asking, and Eleanor's attention snapped back to the silver-whiskered man at once. "It would seem that he does not often take his seat in Parliament."

"In his youth, my brother's poor health oftentimes required that we remained in the country. My father was loathe to leave him as often as taking his seat would necessitate." It wasn't entirely the truth, of course, but what could she say? That her mother's cuckolding ways compelled her father to remain in Essex as much as possible? That he worried over his wife's treatment of his only son and heir, were he not around to temper it? "But now that Henry is off at Oxford, I expect my father shall take his seat more often."

"Capital." The duke nodded, refilling his glass with port from a decanter by his side. "Then I shall look forward to more of his inspiring speeches."

"Tell me, Lady Eleanor," the duchess said, turning her back to her husband. "How long ago did you take your bow?"

"Two years past, Your Grace. A most embarrassing moment, too. I'm afraid I tripped over my own feet as I made my retreat. I fell to the floor in a rather inelegant heap."

"It wasn't as bad as that," Selina offered. "You only fell partway to the floor before the Queen's page caught you."

"Lady Henley is being kind, Your Grace. I nearly humiliated myself. Knocked several feathers from my headdress in the process, and dropped my bouquet and handkerchief, as well."

"Bah." The duchess waved a hand in dismissal. "You would not be the first. Walking backward like that while wearing a court train . . ." She trailed off, shaking her head. "Happens all the time. I'm told several young ladies have fainted from sheer anxiety alone whilst making their retreat. I would not worry yourself over it."

"Yes, after all, it's barely mentioned any more, is it?" Selina smiled sweetly as reached for a tea biscuit. "Until you bring it up, that is."

The duchess swept her gaze down to Eleanor's delicate pale yellow slippers and back up again to her face, nodding approvingly. "With two Seasons behind you, Lady Eleanor, I must assume that your hand is spoken for?"

"No."

"Yes." Both Eleanor and Selina answered at once. Eleanor scowled, silently chiding herself. Why ever had she admitted such a thing? Hadn't she meant to keep the betrothal a secret?

The duchess regarded them both with pursed lips, glancing from one to the other with a look that bespoke her annoyance.

"Well, which is it?" she snapped. "Please do not tell me that you are one of those silly chits hanging out for a love match?"

"Not at all," Eleanor answered. "My father has entered into an agreement of sorts on my behalf, though I would not say that I am precisely betrothed—not yet, at least."

"A wholly unacceptable arrangement, Your Grace," Selina offered, a bit too cheerily, Eleanor thought.

The duke began to snore softly, his chin resting on his breastbone.

The duchess reached over to *thwap* her husband with her fan, eliciting a snuffle of protest.

"Yes, yes, capital," he muttered before dropping his chin back to his chest.

With a shrug, the duchess returned her attention to Eleanor. "You find the arrangement unacceptable on what grounds, I might ask? After all, marriage is, at its heart, a business arrangement, is it not? One should not allow something as arcane as matters of the heart to get in the way of an advantageous match."

"He's the worst sort of rake, Your Grace," Selina interjected before Eleanor had the opportunity to speak. "A libertine, if you will."

"Your father betrothed you to a libertine?" the duchess asked with the arch of one delicate blond brow. "Is he truly dissolute, or just your typical rakehell youth? There's quite a distinction, you know."

Eleanor's cheeks grew warm, and she dropped her gaze to her lap. Why did Selina feel the need to so thoroughly disparage the man? "Really, Your Grace, he's not as bad as all that," she said, startled by the strength of her desire to stand up for him.

The duchess swung her gaze from Eleanor to Selina, and back again. "Well, is he or isn't he?"

"Yes."

"No." Again, both Eleanor and Selina spoke at once.

"No," Eleanor repeated, more firmly this time. "Lady Henley exaggerates greatly. Mister Stoneham is perhaps many things, but he is decidedly *not* a libertine."

"Stoneham?" the duchess asked, the corners of her mouth drawn into a frown. "Surely you don't mean Mister Frederick Stoneham, the Baron Worthington's son?"

Oh, blast it. Had she actually said his name aloud?

Selina nodded, leaning forward in her seat. "That's precisely the one. Mister Frederick Stoneham of Essex, though his father's baronial seat is in Oxfordshire."

"La! Surely you're not serious? I suppose he *is* quite the wastrel, if the rumors are true. Someone should have a talk with Lord Mandeville, then, before it is too late. Did you say the betrothal contract has already been signed?"

"It has, Your Grace," Eleanor murmured. "Though I've spoken with Mister Stoneham, and we've concluded that perhaps the agreement is not to our tastes." Oh, how it hurt to say those words aloud. A sharp pang of regret shot straight through her heart, stealing away her breath and making her slightly dizzy.

"I should say not," the duchess agreed with a nod.

"Though we have not entirely decided the matter," Eleanor added peevishly. Truly, what did it matter to this woman whom she married?

"Well, whatever are you doing here at Whitby Hall, frittering away your time in Devon rather than seeing to this most unpleasant business straightaway?"

"Why, Mister Stoneham himself is here in Devon at pres-ent," Selina interjected, "also a guest of Mister Whitby's. We traveled here together not a fortnight ago."

"No!" the duchess gasped, one slender hand clutching her throat. "Is he really? Why, I'd dearly like to make his acquaintance and see just what all the fuss is about. Is he really as wickedly handsome as they say?" The tone of her voice changed perceptibly, now nearly a purr, and Eleanor did not like the twinkle in the duchess's eye that accompanied her question.

"He is in Plymouth at present with Henley," Selina offered when Eleanor did not reply. "But, yes, suffice it to say that the gossips have not exaggerated his exceptionally favorable looks."

"Hmm, fascinating, indeed. I must say, his reputation is near legendary, even if he hasn't been in Town but these past six months. Well, if what they say is true, Lady Eleanor, then you'd best extricate yourself from the contract as expeditiously as possible. Those like Frederick Stoneham are best left to women with more . . . er, shall I say, more *experience* with men like him. Besides, isn't he but three and twenty?"

The duchess seemed to know a great deal about Frederick, Eleanor thought, her stomach pitching uncomfortably. All based on rumor and supposition, of course. Though she *did* have his age correct. "He is indeed but three and twenty," she murmured over the rim of her cup, eyeing the woman suspiciously now.

"There you have it. Far too young to marry. Why, I'd send a letter to Lord Mandeville myself, were we better acquainted, advising heartily against the match."

I'm sure you would, Eleanor thought, rather uncharitably. *And then you would seek Frederick out for yourself.* The thought that a beautiful, experienced older woman like the duchess was perhaps the type that Frederick normally consorted with flitted across her mind, making her cheeks warm. Hadn't he once mentioned a widow in Shropshire? Would he succumb to the Duchess of Dandridge's advances, were she to sink her claws into him?

No. No, he would not. She wanted to believe it. Truly, she did. And yet, as always, a niggling doubt destroyed her faith in the man.

"Oh, Mister Whitby!" the duchess called out shrilly, startling Eleanor and causing Selina to nearly spill her tea down the front of her gown. "Put down that blasted bow and join us over here in the shade. You've barely spared a word for me since our arrival," she added petulantly. "Let him be, Trelawny. Must you hog his attention all afternoon? Haven't I taught you to share nicely?"

Masculine laughter drifted on the scented breeze, and soon Mister Whitby was at the duchess's side, reaching for her gloved hand as he bent to kiss her, his lips just barely grazing the corner of her mouth. "My dear duchess," he said. "I'm only surprised that you did not join us on the range. I know you take great pride in your skills as an archer."

"Indeed, but I was far too busy acquainting myself with these two lovely young ladies. Why, I've a mind to organize a house party, and invite both Lady Henley and Lady Eleanor."

"A fine idea," Lord Trelawny said, joining the party beneath the canvas. "I thould like that very muth."

"Oh, Trelawny, dear, can you not dispense with that maddening lisp? He only does it to be fashionable, you know," she added. "Dandridge, wake up." She poked her snoring husband with her fan, and the man sat up and stifled a yawn. "I was just saying we should host a house party," she told him, "and invite these young people here to join us."

"Capital," he said with a snuffle. "A fine idea, fine indeed. Shall we organize a hunt?"

"Yes, whatever." The duchess waved one slender hand

in dismissal. "And I've a mind to become acquainted with Mister Frederick Stoneham, who is currently here in Devonshire. We shall invite him, as well." Nodding to herself, she absently stroked Mister Whitby's arm as he stood close by, a surprisingly intimate gesture and one that made Eleanor more than a bit uncomfortable.

Eleanor could have sworn that a hint of suspicion darkened Selina's features, echoing what she was thinking herself. The image of the cottage on the cliff flashed across her mind, reminding her of Frederick's thinly veiled suggestion that Mister Whitby entertained a lover there. She glanced back at the duchess, watching as she and Mister Whitby conversed quietly, his head bent down toward her fair one.

Was the duchess his secret lover? Silently, she cursed Frederick for planting such a notion in her mind, for now her fertile imagination was taking flight, picturing the two in the throes of passion atop the lavishly draped bed. Dear God, what a thought!

Struggling to banish the unpleasant images from her mind, she looked entreatingly to Selina, who mercifully found her voice at last.

"Your Grace, while the idea of a house party sounds lovely indeed, I am afraid that we shall be returning to Essex, as soon as Mister Stoneham's and Henley's business is concluded here. Within a day or two, I should think."

"Can you not extend your stay a few days more?" the duchess asked, dragging her attention away from Mister Whitby. "It would give me such pleasure. Tell them they must, Whitby."

"Indeed, you must," he agreed, wiping a stray blade of grass from his breeches. "You will not find a more gracious hostess than Her Grace, I vow."

"I'm sure it is so," Eleanor said. "But we really must

get back to Essex posthaste. I'm afraid we cannot tarry a day more than is necessary. Perhaps another time, if you would be so kind as to repeat your invitation at a later date?"

"Oh, very well. It will be up to you and you alone to amuse me then, Whitby." The seductive smile she favored the man with all but confirmed Eleanor's suspicions.

And yet, both her husband and son were looking on, smiling as if it mattered not. *Odd.* Very odd, indeed. At least she was not alone in entertaining such thoughts— she could see Selina's confusion as her friend contemplated the very same thing, no doubt.

"Still, I would very much like to make Mister Stoneham's acquaintance," the duchess added.

Eleanor's enjoyment of the afternoon ebbed away, leaving her feeling weary, cold, burdened with a vague sense of unease. Just what was Frederick doing now, as they all sat around drinking tea and discussing him as if he were naught but an idle curiosity? For all she knew, he had located Mister Eckford by now and the two had battled it out on the field of honor. Who would be left standing at the end of the day?

A silent sob tore at her throat. Never before had she felt so helpless, so utterly and completely at a loss. Her world was topsy-turvy, her future, once so bright, now a muddled blight. She could not trust the man she loved, could not confide in her dearest friend, and the one person who might be able to help her sort things out, the single person whom she trusted implicitly and entirely— her brother Henry—was away at Oxford, enjoying the many freedoms afforded his sex, whilst she remained caught in the noose of the feminine plight, afraid to maneuver this way or that for fear of being strangled.

With a small, choked cry, she rose from her seat. "If you'll excuse me," she said, hurrying away from the assembled party as fast as her feet would carry, nearly twisting her ankle in the process.

She must do *something*. She hadn't a clue what, but she could no longer sit idle, waiting for something to happen, for everything to sort itself out. But what? What could she possibly do to make certain that everything would end satisfactorily, that she would make the right choice regarding Frederick, and that he would agree to whatever choice she made? If he hadn't gone and gotten himself killed already, of course, and that was an all-too-real possibility.

She skimmed the stairs, her breath coming faster as she ran down the corridor, opened the door to her bedchamber, and hastened inside. "I've a terrible headache, Solange," she told her startled maid. "You must tell them that I shan't be down to dinner." Instead, she would think. She would search her soul, if need be, and then, by God, she would do *something* to make her life right again.

If only she knew what.

Chapter 17

Eleanor stood at her bedchamber's window, watching as the duke's carriage clattered down the drive, the moonlight reflecting off its dark exterior.

She had joined them for dinner, after all. Solange had convinced her that hiding away in her bedchamber would have been a terrible affront to Mister Whitby's esteemed guests, putting her host in an awkward position. As loathe as she was admit it, her maid had been correct. So, not a half hour after she'd dashed off so indecorously, she'd come back downstairs, claiming a headache had briefly incapacitated her but that she had quickly recovered.

Dinner had passed in an unmemorable blur. Lord Trelawny had sat beside her and spent the meal doing his best to entertain her. And he had, somewhat. She'd been far too distracted to follow the vein of conversation and had been accused more than once—by the duchess, no less—of woolgathering. She had been lost in her own thoughts, of course. As soon as the meal had ended, Lord Trelawny had declared that Eleanor looked frightfully wan, fawning and fretting over her like a lisping nursemaid. She'd wanted to kiss him in gratitude when he'd suggested that she forego the remainder of the evening's entertainments and retire. And so she had.

She'd spent the past hour standing at the window, doing naught but stare at the night sky as her mind cast about for a suitable plan. She would speak candidly with Selina, she'd resolved. No more pretending that her feelings for Frederick were mere trivialities. She would confess her true feelings, her concerns, convince her friend that Frederick Stoneham was a far better man than Selina believed him to be.

Not that he did not have flaws—serious flaws, perhaps. She would risk her friend's censure and tell her what had transpired in the cottage. And then she could only hope that Selina would advise her well, for where else had she to turn?

Nowhere. Her situation was intolerable, and she could no longer bear to suffer through it alone.

No time like the present, she thought, stepping away from the window and letting the drapes fall back against the glass. Minutes later, she rapped on the door to Selina's bedchamber.

"Selina, dearest," she called out, her voice tremulous. "Might I have a word with you before you retire?"

Eleanor heard the tap-tapping of footsteps, and then the door swung open. "There you are," Selina said, her fair head appearing in the doorway. "Oh, dear. You still look dreadfully pale. Please, come in and tell me what's the matter."

Eleanor silently obeyed, entering the room and shutting the door softly behind herself.

Selina threaded her arm through hers and escorted her to a settee in the room's far corner, her brow knit in obvious concern. "I do not like the look about your eyes, either. Have you not been sleeping well? Did you not nap before the guests arrived?"

"I tried to nap, but sleep would not come," she answered, sinking gratefully onto the soft, worn velvet beside Selina. "I must speak with you, but you must give me your promise of complete and utter confidence first."

"But you've always had my complete confidence, Eleanor." Selina reached for her hand, and Eleanor noticed that her friend was blinking back unshed tears. "You must tell me at once what's troubling you. Please, you're frightening me."

"It's nothing so very dreadful, I vow. Only my own . . . indecision. On delicate matters, I fear."

"Has this to do with George? And the duchess? For I, too, was made uncomfortable by their seeming familiarity. I spoke with George, just now, you see, and he vows that nothing—"

"It's to do with Frederick Stoneham," Eleanor interrupted, giving Selina's hand a reassuring squeeze.

"Oh, dear."

"Indeed. But I vow he is not the vile debaucher you believe him to be, Selina," Eleanor said earnestly. "I think I am in love with him."

"Oh, no. Not again. You believed yourself in love with him once before, did you not?"

Eleanor shook her head. The sound of hooves in the drive briefly drew her gaze to the window, and she heaved a sigh before returning her attention to her friend. "Perhaps I did, but it was nothing more than a girlish fascination. I did not know him then."

Selina appeared unconvinced. "And you do now? You've only spent, what? A day here and there in his presence? However could you allow yourself to fall prey—"

"I haven't fallen prey to anything. You must believe me, Selina. I do not say this lightly, as I still have my reservations, but I believe his reputation has been highly"—she swallowed hard—"exaggerated."

Selina nibbled on her lower lip before replying. "Are you certain? Truly certain, Eleanor?"

"I wish I could say that I am entirely certain of his character. I *want* to be sure—"

"But you're not," Selina cried. "Let that be your answer, then."

If only it were as easy as that. "There *is* more to Frederick than meets the eye. There are things about him to be admired, and I think perhaps I know him better than most, even after so short a time. I know how naïve that sounds, truly I do. But . . . but I believe it to be true."

Selina shrugged. "I suppose it could be," she conceded.

"I realize you want to protect me, that you have my best interest at heart."

"Precisely, Eleanor. I only want to see you happily wed, protected, cherished as Henley cherishes me. Just now George assured me that there is nothing between him and the Duchess of Dandridge; in fact, he laughed at the very suggestion of such a thing. What's more, he told me quite plainly that he believes you to be everything he could want in a wife."

Eleanor shook her head, a bittersweet smile upon her lips. "But you must see that I cannot marry Mister Whitby, not feeling as I do about Frederick. It would not be fair to him."

A single tear escaped Selina's cornflower blue eyes, and she quickly wiped it away. "No, I suppose it would not. Oh, Eleanor, do you truly love him? Frederick, I mean."

Eleanor met Selina's questioning gaze and smiled. "I do. Perhaps I've turned into a bedlamite, but I do."

A harsh knock on the door made both women start in surprise. "Lady Henley?" the housekeeper called out.

"You may enter," Selina answered, rising and moving briskly toward the door which swung open at once.

The gray-headed housekeeper stood on the threshold wringing her hands, her lace cap slightly askew. "Forgive me for disturbing you, my lady, but Mister Stoneham is downstairs, asking—nay, *demanding*—to speak with Lady Eleanor."

"Is Lord Henley with him?" Selina asked, the color draining from her face.

"No, my lady. Mister Stoneham arrived alone, and in a bit of a state, I must say."

Eleanor was on her feet at once, moving to stand beside Selina. "Whatever do you mean, 'a state'?"

"He reeks of liquor, miss," the housekeeper answered coldly.

He was foxed? Eleanor's heart began to race. Frederick downstairs, at this hour, foxed? It didn't signify. "If you'll excuse me," she said, brushing past the housekeeper and into the corridor.

"Shall I accompany you, Eleanor?" Selina called after her.

Eleanor continued on toward the stairs, her palms dampening in fearful anticipation. "No, I shall see to him myself."

Frederick paced back and forth before the fire, his anxiety mounting with each second that passed. Damn it, what was taking so long? Surely he'd been waiting a full quarter hour. He shook his head, still slightly muddled from the fair amount of gin he'd consumed before leaving Henley to watch over Eckford.

He'd jumped on his horse and ridden to Whitby Hall

like a man possessed. And perhaps he was. Reaching into his coat pocket, he fingered the crude pouch that held the ruby ring—the ring he hoped to slip onto Eleanor's finger before the night was out.

He realized, perhaps a bit too late, that he hadn't a choice in the matter. He could no longer play the role of long-suffering hero, keeping the woman he desired above all else at arm's length in order to protect her, to save her from himself. The devil knew what would happen on the morn, and he wanted this settled now.

True, he was an excellent marksman. Hell, he was more than excellent; he was superb. He would not have the slightest trouble disposing of Eckford with a single, expertly placed shot, straight through the blackguard's heart. If Eckford followed the dueling code of honor, that is. But, as his brother-in-law was nothing short of a goddamned coward, there were no guarantees.

If he were to die tomorrow, he would bloody well die knowing that Eleanor knew he meant to honor their betrothal contract. And, damn it, not only would he honor the contract, but he would mean every word of his marriage vows, too, including the one that stipulated he remain faithful to his wife as long as they both should live.

Molly would be sent packing straightaway, and she would be the last of her kind. With Eleanor by his side, he would not want for anything. He was sure of it, more sure than he'd ever been of anything in all his sorry, misbegotten life.

He'd spent the better part of the day attempting to push aside all thoughts of Eleanor, but it was useless. Knowing that nothing was settled between them was distracting him from his task at hand—ridding the world of Eckford. Henley had finally convinced him that he was no good until he set things to rights, and so, by God, he was going to set things to rights. *Tonight.*

He pulled out his watch and checked the time, then shoved the heavy timepiece back into his waistcoat. Where the bloody hell had the housekeeper gone off to? Where was Eleanor? For all he knew, she was off with witless Whitby somewhere, reciting poetry as the man made calf's eyes at her. That thought alone made his blood boil, and he tightened his hands into fists, stopping to stare blindly at the fire in an attempt to rein in his emotions.

"Whatever are you doing here, Frederick?"

Frederick whirled toward the familiar, feminine voice, his greatcoat billowing out behind him. Relief coursed through his veins, a sudden calm washing over him, taking him entirely by surprise.

By God, but she was beautiful. His breath hitched in his chest as his hungry eyes devoured her. His gaze raked over her quickly, from head to toe, before he permitted himself to study her more leisurely, beginning with the mass of dark curls gathered at her crown, to her inky blue eyes, slightly shadowed beneath her lower lashes, down to her full, rosy lips, and lower still to the generous swell of her décolletage. Damnation, but she was wearing that same indecent frock, the exotic blue-green confection that nearly bared her breasts. Had she worn it for Whitby? For she certainly had not expected *him* tonight.

The bitter taste of bile flooded his mouth, and he turned away from her, back toward the fire. He did not want her to see his expression as he struggled to stay the demons of self-doubt.

"Answer me, Frederick," she demanded, her voice as hard as flint. "Why are you here, your hair more disheveled than usual and your person reeking of spirits?"

"Shut the door, Eleanor." He turned back to face her, amazed that his voice sounded so commanding.

"No," she said, shaking her head. "The door remains open."

"Goddamn it, Eleanor," he roared. "Shut the bloody door."

Her eyes widened, perhaps with fear? He hadn't meant to frighten her. Damn it all, but he was losing his mind. He took two steps toward her, bridging the distance that separated them. "Unless you wish that the entire household hear us discuss what transpired last night at the cottage, I would suggest that you shut the door, love," he said softly, gently.

She eyed him sharply for several seconds, then turned and shut the door. "Shall I lock it, too?" she asked, her tone cold, clipped.

"That won't be necessary." He took two more cautious steps toward her.

Looking much like a cornered animal, she fled behind the sofa. "I see no reason to discuss what happened last night, Frederick," she said, leaning against the heavy piece of furniture as if she needed its support. "You certainly did not have to return from Plymouth to do so."

"I've found Eckford, just outside Plymouth. Henley is there now, making sure the coward doesn't flee."

"Then . . . then you have not killed him?"

"I've challenged him to a duel. Tomorrow, at dawn. The gauntlet has been thrown down."

"And you will kill him then?"

"That's my intention."

"And you've come here tonight to tell me this?"

"I've come here to give you this." He produced the pouch from his pocket.

"What is it?" she asked, not moving from behind the sofa.

Releasing the drawstring, he dropped the ring into the palm of his hand. "A betrothal ring."

"Why would you give me this?" she asked, clutching the back of the sofa. She was not wearing gloves, he noticed, and her hands were trembling. "Why now?"

"Because I want to make my intentions clear. Now. I want to marry you, Eleanor."

"You're drunk," she said, shaking her head. "You don't know what you're saying."

He threw back his head and laughed. "I'm not so drunk as that. I found my way here, did I not? Indeed, I know precisely what I'm saying, love. I want to marry you, and I vow to make a good and proper husband. A faithful husband," he added, knowing how important that would be to her.

And he meant it. Devil take it, but he meant it. "Will you come over here? I have no plans to accost you, though if I did, the sofa would not afford you much protection."

"I . . . I do not know what to say," she stuttered.

"Say that you will take the ring. Take it, and think about what I've said tonight. Think about the way it felt last night, your body beneath mine."

He heard her sharp intake of breath, and knew she was indeed remembering. Just as he was. How would he ever forget?

"Think about that," he continued, "and about how it felt to sit perched beside me in the tree, gazing at the sea. Think about that haunting piece of Beethoven you played, for me and me alone." Slowly, cautiously, he moved toward her, around the back of the sofa.

"In the meantime, I will see to Eckford. If all goes well, we will be on our way back to Essex in no time. I will give you three days, no more. You think about what I've said tonight, and decide if you can trust my words, if you can believe that there is more to the man than the reputation, that a leopard can indeed change its spots."

"You're the one who said it could not," Eleanor interjected.

"Indeed I did. I was wrong on that count. I was wrong about many things, it would seem. I had no reason to believe it possible then. But now," he said softly, still moving toward her, "now I have so very many reasons to do exactly that, to change my spots. And if you can believe it possible, too"—he reached her side at last—"only if you truly believe it, then you shall slip this ring on your finger, and we shall marry by Christmastide, just as the contract stipulates."

He reached for her hand, opened it, and laid the ruby ring in her palm. "And if things do not go as planned with Eckford," he said with a shrug, "you can do what you wish with the ring, and no one will be the wiser."

"However can you say that so calmly, so dispassionately?" she asked, her eyes suddenly damp. "Please, Frederick, do not go through with this duel! Take him to London, make him pay restitution, punish him in any way necessary. But do not go through with this madness!"

"I haven't a choice, love," he said quietly, stroking her flushed cheek with the back of his hand. "You must understand that."

"No." She shook her head so wildly that her carefully coiffed hair began to fall from its bindings, several dark tendrils floating about her face. "No, I cannot. I cannot abide it. I cannot marry you if you've just killed a man."

Defeated, he dropped his hands to his sides. "Then I shall be very sorry. Now if you'll excuse me, I must go."

"Go then!" she cried out. "Leave at once. I wish you'd never come." Tears were spilling down her cheeks now, unchecked. He hadn't any idea if they were tears of anger, of sadness, of fear. He hadn't the time to stay and find out. The hour grew late, and dawn would come soon enough.

He turned sharply and strode toward the door, pain tearing at his lungs. Reaching for the doorknob, he paused, steeling himself to walk out the door, knowing the possibility remained, however slight, that he might never see her again. Damn Eckford and his cowardice.

"Please don't do it, Frederick," she called out on a sob. "Please, I beg of you. He might very well kill you instead."

He took a deep, ragged breath before turning to face her once more, his hand still on the door.

"Please," she repeated, weeping openly, and the pain in her countenance near enough killed him.

In mere seconds, he closed the distance between them and gathered her in his arms, kissing her ruthlessly, mindlessly, grasping the back of her head and pressing her to him like he'd never let her go. Deeply, thoroughly, he kissed her, not daring to take his lips from hers until he heard her cry out his name on a whimper, felt her legs go weak. Only then did his mouth retreat.

Dropping his hands to her shoulders, he steadied her, then captured her wavering gaze with his own, forcing her to meet his eyes, to look deeply into them, to see everything he felt for her, there in his gaze. And then he released her.

"Do not fret, love. If by chance I am killed on the morrow, everyone will say how better off you were for it, won't they?" He took two steps back, away from her, his heart pounding so furiously against his ribcage that he feared it might very well burst. "Good-bye, loveliest Eleanor."

With a sharp bow, he turned and left.

Chapter 18

Eleanor stood paralyzed, watching Frederick leave her there in Mister Whitby's salon without a backward glance. He loved her; she'd seen it there in his eyes, just after he'd kissed her. But not enough to call off the duel, to keep himself safe from harm. Oh, dear Lord, whatever was she to do?

"Frederick!" she called out, dashing through the open doorway, lifting her skirts as she ran out into the front hall, the heels of her slippers clattering loudly against the marble. She couldn't let him leave, not like this, not without him knowing how she felt. She would *not* be better off without him, not at all.

Rushing past the startled housekeeper, she hurried to the front door, reaching for the handle with slippery, shaking hands. In seconds, she flung open the door, just in time to see Frederick charging down the drive atop an enormous black horse, his dark overcoat billowing out behind him as his mount kicked up a cloud of dust.

She stood silently, watching until he disappeared entirely from sight, her heart near to bursting. He was gone. *Gone.* For a moment, she considered going to the stables and requesting a mount—following him out into the night. But of course she could not.

A sharp pain in her palm drew her attention away from the road, and she unclenched her fist and stared in surprise at the ring she saw there, the setting biting into her flesh. She'd all but forgotten it, clutched in her hand all this time.

It was exquisite. A generously large but simple, round ruby flanked by two slightly smaller diamonds on either side. Three stones in all, set in filigreed gold. She'd never before owned a piece as lovely as this, stunning in its stark simplicity. Wherever had Frederick purchased this, and when? It seemed far too well-crafted to have come from anywhere but a London shop. Shaking her head in confusion, she closed her fingers back around the gem.

Tears welled once more in her eyes, and she suddenly felt as if she were suffocating. She could not go back inside and face Selina, not yet. Instead, she would take a turn in Mister Whitby's garden, get some exercise, clear her head.

Nodding to herself, she hurriedly made her way back though the front door, across the marbled front hall, and down a long corridor toward the drawing room. Quickly, quietly, she crossed the room and let herself back out into the night through a pair of French doors. Her slippers skimmed down the wide, stone stairs, and moments later she found herself shivering in the neatly manicured garden where large, fragrant chrysanthemums and marigolds bloomed in profusion, the yellows, reds, and golds brilliant even in the moonlight.

Her breath produced puffs of vapor as she walked briskly in silence, her mind far too numb, her thoughts too jumbled to make sense of anything. But bit by bit, her racing heart began to slow, to beat a steady rhythm, her breath coming slower now. The scent of the garden was calming, as it always was, whether here on the Devon coast or at home in Essex.

Spying a lone bench beneath a crabapple tree, she hastened to it, sinking to the cold, stone seat with a heavy sigh. If only she'd put on her overcoat before she'd run out of the front hall.

With an almost fearful reluctance, she opened her fingers and stared at the ring in her hand once more, willing herself to think through the muddle. She recalled Frederick's words as he had placed the ring in her hand, his insistence that she remember things she'd considered best forgotten. But how *could* she forget the way she felt in his arms, warm and comfortable in his embrace? How could she forget the way her skin tingled beneath his touch, beneath his mouth? However would she survive, if she could never again experience such things?

She needed his touch, his kiss, just as she needed air to breathe and water to drink, she realized. And where would that leave her if Eckford killed him, instead of the other way around? A sharp pain tore through her chest, momentarily stealing away her breath.

She looked up at the moon, bright in the sky, and said a silent prayer. *No matter what happens, please let Frederick remain unharmed.* She couldn't bear it otherwise, regardless of whether she chose to wear his ring or not. She could barely imagine a world without Frederick in it—a world devoid of his wicked laugh, missing the mischievous twinkle in his warm, chocolate eyes, the wry curve of his lips. For four long years she'd dreamt of nothing but him—however would she fill her dreams if he were suddenly gone?

"May I join you, Lady Eleanor?"

Eleanor looked up in surprise at Mister Whitby, standing not three feet away and smiling down at her warmly. For the briefest of moments, she'd thought perhaps it had been Frederick, back again. Valiantly she sought to school her features, to hide her disappointment.

"I thought you might be cold, so I brought you your cloak," he said, holding out the garment. "I'm sorry to intrude."

She *was* cold, the chill of the stones beneath her penetrating the fabric of her gown, making her limbs feel numb. Eleanor gratefully took the cloak and wrapped it about her shoulders, stiffly tying the ribbons at her throat and then tucking the folds beneath herself. "Thank you, Mister Whitby. Please feel free to join me, though I fear I'm not good company at present."

"Yes, I assumed as much. I saw Mister Stoneham leaving just now," he said as he took a seat beside her on the bench, so close that his shoulder brushed hers. His presence was surprisingly welcome, comforting. Whatever his faults, George Whitby was a good and kind man, a generous man. Selina had not exaggerated on that count.

"And I thought perhaps we could talk candidly," he said, then cleared his throat. "I spoke with Selina after our guests departed, you see. She told me of your betrothal contract with Mister Stoneham, and of your desire to extricate yourself from it. I wonder, though, if Selina overestimates your desire to do so?"

Eleanor swallowed hard before replying. "I confess, at first I did hope to extricate myself from the agreement. I thought it wholly and entirely unacceptable. But now I . . . I'm not so certain."

"Please do not be uneasy, Lady Eleanor, but I must also confess that Selina expressed her hope that perhaps you and I would suit, instead."

"I did not want you to think this visit a calculated attempt to ensnare you," she answered, dropping her gaze to her lap, her cheeks growing suddenly warm. "Or we would have told you straightaway about my betrothal. I only hoped to make your acquaintance, and see if perhaps we *would* suit, as Selina felt so certain that we would."

"I'm only flattered that Selina should think so highly of me. Why, to think that I might suit a woman as lovely, as warm and intelligent as you are is indeed a compliment. Truly, I could do no better."

A wave of indecision washed over her. What should she say to that? She did not want to lead him on, to make him think that she still hoped to gain his affection. Nor did she wish to hurt his feelings. Remembering her mother's careful instructions, she dutifully murmured, "I thank you for the compliment, sir."

"But you are in love with Frederick Stoneham, are you not?" he added, taking her entirely by surprise.

Eleanor's stomach fluttered uncomfortably. "I . . . I suppose I am," she confessed, entirely mortified. What a strange discussion to be having with a gentleman!

"And do you think him worthy of your love? For I confess, at first glance I did not believe it to be so."

"I'm not . . . not entirely certain. I believe that he is. Still, he has challenged a man to a duel at dawn, and no matter the outcome, I . . . I fear I shall lose him. I cannot condone his taking a man's life, no matter how well deserved. Yet the alternative . . ." She trailed off, unable to voice her worst fear.

"I will offer you another alternative, Lady Eleanor. An escape plan, if you will." He reached for her hand, and Eleanor allowed him to take it, glad for the comfort his touch offered. "I offer you my hand in marriage, if you decide you cannot marry Mister Stoneham."

Eleanor drew back in surprise, a small gasp parting her lips.

Mister Whitby continued on. "You are everything I could desire in a wife, and I vow I would make you a good husband, a gentle companion. A constant and true friend. I find myself in an awkward predicament, you see. I will not attempt to hide the fact that my heart lies elsewhere, as it has for years, and likely always will. So, you see, we will be equals on that count, and I will not hold it against you if you will not hold it against me. I'm certain we can still enjoy a happy marriage, despite the circumstances.

"I've the unfortunate luck to have given my heart to someone I can never marry, you see. If you find yourself similarly afflicted, if you decide that you cannot marry him, then perhaps we can bring comfort to one another."

"I . . . I don't know what to say," she stuttered, entirely flummoxed by his speech.

"I have no doubt I would grow to love you, Eleanor," he continued on. "A companionable love, if you will. This is what I offer, if you decide you cannot marry Mister Stoneham."

Good Lord, she had never in a million years expected such a proposal as this. He loved another, he'd confessed. But to whom had he given his heart?

"The Duchess of Dandridge?" she wondered, barely realizing she'd spoken the thought aloud.

Mister Whitby laughed, a deep, booming laugh that temporarily muffled the sound of the sea in the distance. "So you came to the same conclusion as Selina, then. No, let me assure you it is not the duchess I love." He glanced heavenward, drawing a deep breath. "How close you are to the truth, and yet so very far," he said quietly, his gaze meeting hers.

"But are you certain that . . . that you and she—"

"Oh, entirely so. There is no hope for us, none whatsoever. The situation is far more impossible than if it were the duchess herself that I loved and not her—" He cut himself off abruptly.

Eleanor's brow furrowed in bewilderment. Whatever had he meant to say? Not the duchess's . . . what? Friend? Had the duchess a daughter? She'd only heard of a son, Lord Trelawny, and surely . . . she allowed the thoughts to trail off. *Impossible.*

"No matter," he continued with a sigh, shaking his head. "I've always hoped to marry, and soon after making your acquaintance I realized how enjoyable it was having you here at Whitby Hall. Indeed, my home seemed to come alive with you in it."

"So . . . so you are suggesting a marriage in name only, then?" she asked.

He shook his head. "Not at all. I hope to have children someday, and I have no doubt I could perform my . . . er . . . marital duties when called upon."

Heat flooded Eleanor's cheeks and she nodded, unsure of what to say to that.

"Anyway, before you entirely dismiss Mister Stoneham's suit, let me give you one small piece of advice. It is a sad and sorry thing to know you cannot marry your one true love. Leaves one feeling interminably lonely and bereft, I vow. Under the circumstances, I have no choice. But you, my dear, you *have* a choice." He gave her hand a friendly squeeze. "If Frederick Stoneham is indeed your one true love, then do not allow yourself to suffer my fate. Unless you think he would mistreat you or humiliate you, that is."

"No, I do not believe he would do either," she said, surprised by the degree of certainty she felt. Hadn't Frederick said he would be a good and faithful husband? What's more, she believed him. With all her heart, she believed he meant it.

"Nor do I believe he would. From what Henley tells me about Mister Stoneham, he is man who has enjoyed very little love or acceptance in his life. Perhaps your feelings for him have changed him, for the better. Henley seems to think it so, and Henley knows Mister Stoneham far better than I do."

Henley? Henley knew how she felt about Frederick? How utterly humiliating. Things were going from bad to worse, if that was at all possible. And tomorrow at dawn things would get decidedly worse still.

"Might I ask a favor of you, Mister Whitby? I realize it's a terrible imposition, but still, I must ask."

"Of course," he said, releasing her hand and rising to stand beside her. "Your wish is my command, my lady."

She rose on unsteady legs, looking off toward the stables. "I need to get to Plymouth, and long before dawn. I must find out where the duel is taking place, and I must get there in time to stop it."

He shook his head. "Do you really think that wise? Truly, I do not think the field of honor is any place for a lady. In fact, I'm sure that bringing you there would be breaking some gentleman's code or other. That wouldn't be very prudent of me now, would it?"

"Field of honor, you call it? *Honor?* Hah. It's stupidity, is what it is. A barbaric, outdated practice."

"Perhaps," Mister Whitby said with a shrug. "But didn't the man desert Mister Stoneham's sister, leaving her in dire straits? At the mercy of creditors? Bruised, perhaps by his own hand?"

"Apparently so, but is that reason enough to kill a man? Not to mention taking the risk of getting yourself killed the process?" As the words left her lips, she realized that this was her true fear—that Frederick did not care enough for her to keep himself out of harm's way, that he would risk leaving her to mourn him. Did that make her selfish?

"Most men would say it is indeed reason enough," he answered with a nod.

"And what is your own opinion on the matter, Mister Whitby?"

He stroked his whiskers, appearing to consider the question for nearly a full minute. "That I'd likely do the same, were it either of my own sisters," he said at last. "And I don't even particularly *like* my sisters, silly chits."

Eleanor shook her head. "I simply cannot comprehend the workings of the gentleman's mind."

"Well, take heart. The lady's mind is equally confounding to us gentlemen, for the most part."

Eleanor glanced down at the ruby ring she still clutched in one hand. Whatever outcome tomorrow might bring, she would be there to witness it herself—with this ring on her finger. "So, Mister Whitby, are you going to take me to Plymouth?"

"I suppose I am. I'll have the carriage ready by four; that should give us plenty of time. I expect this means you will not be accepting my offer of marriage?"

"I'm afraid not, thanks to your own excellent advice to the contrary. You are a kind and generous man, Mister Whitby."

"I've been called worse," he quipped. "Try to get some sleep, then. No doubt you'll need it."

Frederick shrugged out of his greatcoat, carelessly tossing it to the grass beside the mahogany pistol case as the first rays of light pierced the murky dawn. As if he were simply preparing for bed, he unbuttoned his coat, his fingers remarkably steady considering the lack of sleep he'd suffered.

After slipping off the coat, he reached up to readjust his collar as Eckford's second, a weasely looking man called Blackburn, examined the pistols. Frederick's own second—Henley, of course—had already examined them and given his approval. Across the dewy meadow stood a handful of spectators, along with a surgeon, all chattering away in eager anticipation. Next to Blackburn stood Eckford himself, glaring openly at him.

Interesting that so many had gathered there in the field, considering Frederick was not known in these parts, and considering he and Henley had told no one of the duel save the surgeon. Given the illegal nature of the morning's activities, they had not wanted to stir attention, of course. Regardless, it would be done, on *this* day, at *this* appointed hour. No matter the witnesses.

Watching Blackburn nod his approval and hand a pistol to Henley, Frederick yawned, straightening the ruffled cuffs of his linen shirt. He was ready to get this business over and done with. Henley ambled back across the meadow and handed him the weapon, one of a silver-mounted pair Frederick had bought from the Manton brothers in Berkeley Square. They'd cost a near fortune—worth every pence, in Frederick's opinion.

"How much do you reason Eckford paid this Blackburn chap to act as second?" Henley asked, nodding his head in the pair's direction.

"Not enough, I'd wager," Frederick answered, turning the pistol over in his palm, admiring it. Indeed, it would do its job, and do it well.

Henley looked over his shoulder at the sullen Mister Eckford, now doffing his own coat. "Do you really mean to kill him?" he asked, his brow furrowed. "If he shoots first and misses his mark, choosing to delope would be insult enough, would it not?"

"I'm not here to insult him," Frederick bit out. "Go tell Blackburn that they have procrastinated long enough."

With a nod, Henley hurried over and relayed the message to his counterpart, who then, in turn, relayed it to Eckford himself. Moments later, Henley arrived back at his side, mopping his brow with a handkerchief despite the chill in the air.

At last, Eckford took his place. Frederick followed suit, moving to the center of the field with his back to Eckford, ready to begin counting off the paces. The rising sun warmed his skin; a bird chirruped in the distance. Frederick felt remarkably calm, relaxed.

And then, without warning, Eleanor's face swam into focus in his mind's eye. Her taste, her scent, the feel of her body pressed against his—all flooded his consciousness at once. The memory of her kiss had haunted him, tortured him the long, seemingly endless night. Would that kiss be their last? Would that last glimpse of her—standing there on the front steps of Whitby Hall, tears streaming down her lovely face as he rode away into the night—be the last ever he saw of the woman who had captured his soul?

With a silent oath of frustration, he forced away the images, banishing them from his mind. Damn it to hell, but this was not the time to be thinking of her. Not now. He could not afford the distraction, not at a time like this.

At last, the call was given. A hush descended upon the assembled crowd as Frederick and Eckford began to count off their paces, slowly, leisurely. Once he'd reached the required distance, Frederick turned, his body sideways, his feet planted wide, and took aim.

His blood thrummed through his veins, his pulse a

near-deafening roar as he focused on nothing save his opponent and waited for Blackburn to drop the hand-kerchief.

Instead, a shot fired. Frederick felt a glancing blow to his shoulder as outraged cries of "badly done" and "for shame" rang out.

What the hell? The smell of gunpowder filled the air and Frederick looked down sharply, surprised to see a spot of bright red staining his linen, the circumference increasing slowly but steadily.

"You cowardly bastard," he roared, charging toward his opponent with his pistol still drawn.

Confusion reigned, the crowd abuzz as Frederick knocked Eckford's now-spent weapon from his hand and grabbed him by the throat. "You worthless, filthy piece of horseshit. What have you to say for yourself before I blow your brains out?"

Eckford's eyes were as cold and flinty as steel. "You'd kill me just because I tired of fucking your sister?"

Rage nearly blinding him, Frederick tightened his grip on his throat, pressing the pistol's barrel against the side of Eckford's head. "I'll see you in hell for that," he ground out through clenched teeth.

Eckford's bravado disappeared in an instant. He began to tremble, his gaze darting about wildly like a trapped hare as he realized at last that Frederick meant to follow through on his threat. "Don't kill me," he choked out, his eyes beginning to bulge. "I'll do any-thing you ask. Please, I beg of you."

Frederick watched in disgust as the man pissed him-self. And damn it, but thoughts of Eleanor pushed their way right back into his consciousness. As if she were there in his head, he could hear her pleading with him to spare Eckford's life. His determination wavered, and he slackened his hold on Eckford's throat.

"We're alike, you and I," Eckford rasped as he attempted to back away from him, his boots kicking up bits of earth and grass as he scrabbled backward. "Cut from the same cloth. You like your women as much as I—"

Frederick had him by the throat again, pulling him up so that the tips of his scabbed boots barely touched the ground. "By God, you'd best shut your mouth, man. I'm nothing like you, you hear me? *Nothing.*" The blood roared so loudly in his ears that Frederick could barely hear, the burning sensation in his shoulder now an excruciating distraction. Bloody hell, but he needed to end this. He raised the pistol and took aim, only to hesitate once more as the man whimpered pitifully, now reduced to a blubbering, sniveling coward.

A wave of nausea washed over him, and he stumbled back, releasing his hold on Eckford who slid limply back to the grass, gasping for air. The scent of burnt flesh, of damp earth, of urine reached his nose, making Frederick gag.

Good God, he couldn't do it. Couldn't bring himself to kill the man who had misused Maria and cast her aside like rubbish. What the hell was wrong with him? He'd gone soft, weak. With an oath, he tossed the pistol to the wet grass beside him.

"I speak the truth and you know it, brother-in-law," Eckford said, eyeing him coldly now that Henley had retrieved the pistol from the grass and tucked it safely into the band of his breeches. "We are one and the same—weak, a slave to our vices. Did you hear what became of your recent conquest, Missus Cornelia Darby of Shropshire? Miscarried a babe and bled to death, not long after you left her bed, I'm told. Who are you to judge me?" he spat, his face a mottled red and his eyes full of hatred.

"No." His voice a strangled cry, the air left Frederick's lungs in a *whoosh*. Cornelia Darby, miscarried? Dead? It could not be so. She'd sworn she could not conceive, said he needn't worry. He stumbled backward, his lungs burning. His arm felt weak, his sleeve now stained red from shoulder to elbow. By God, if it were true, then he *was* no better than Eckford. He fell to his knees with a groan.

Chaos. The surgeon hastened to Frederick's side as the swelling crowd of onlookers circled about like a humming swarm of locusts.

"It's naught but a flesh wound," the surgeon pronounced, and Frederick realized he'd been divested of his linen. "You've only been grazed by the bullet, though you're losing a fair amount of blood . . ."

Frederick stopped listening to the surgeon's words, focusing instead on Henley who looked surprisingly comfortable standing over Eckford, pointing the pistol at the cowering man with a sure and steady grip. "You'll go to London at once at make full restitution, return any of her jewels you might still have," Henley was saying. "I don't give a bloody damn if you're forced to work the docks, but you will repay Missus Eckford what is owed her. You'll satisfy your creditors and pay a living to your wife and children. Do you hear me, man? And if you don't, by God, I will blow your brains out myself. Let this be a warning." Henley fired a shot into the grass not three inches from Eckford's right kneecap, causing the crowd to leap back with a collective gasp of surprise.

Frederick's attention snapped back to his wound as the surgeon poured some foul-smelling liquid over his shoulder that burned like hell. "Good God, man," he roared. "Are you trying to kill me?" It suddenly felt as if someone had prodded his torn flesh with a hot poker, and a wave of dizziness washed over him.

"Lie back," the surgeon ordered. "I need to apply pressure, and I cannot have you thrashing about. Drink this," he ordered, pouring a generous draught of some unidentifiable spirit down this throat.

Without argument, Frederick did as he was told, now mercifully rendered incapable of thinking of anything save the searing pain as the surgeon pressed forcefully on the gaping wound with fabric torn from someone's coat. Likely his own, he realized. The situation was so absurd that he almost laughed.

Instead, he remembered Eckford's words, words the pain had mercifully erased, if only temporarily. Cornelia Darby, dead. Entirely his fault.

"Here, have some more of this," Henley said, pressing the liquor bottle to his lips. He drank thirstily, hoping the numbing effects would leave him senseless.

And then, just as he was thinking that the situation could not possibly get any worse than it was, he could have sworn that he heard Eleanor's voice rise above the din of the crowd, calling out his name.

Bloody hell, what next?

Chapter 19

While Mister Whitby secured the carriage, Eleanor
dashed across the road toward the meadow, her skirts
raised high above her ankles most indecorously. Her
pounding heart kept rhythm with her half boots as she
ran, the din near deafening. She had to hurry. *Hurry.*

They'd heard a shot as they'd approached, then another. *We've come too late*, her mind cried, over and
over again as she reached the meadow at last, her fear
mounting with each passing second.

"Frederick!" she called out, her voice unnaturally
shrill. She paused, her eyes scanning the chaotic scene
before her. Where was he? Where was Henley? Whatever had happened?

One hand flew up to cover her mouth, to stifle a cry
as her searching gaze spied a dark-haired man lying
prone in the grass, not twenty feet away. Several men
knelt over him, others were standing about, nearly
blocking her view. It simply *had* to be Mister Eckford.
Her stunned mind could accept no other alternative.

She almost breathed a sigh of relief, until a memory
of Mister Eckford at the house party in Kent swam into
focus in her mind's eye, a man of medium height and

decidedly *fair* hair. Her heart nearly stilled, her blood turning to ice in her veins.

Dear God, no. *No.* It was Frederick, lying there in the grass. Felled by a bullet.

"Frederick?" she whispered, unable to take a single step closer, terrified of what she might find, what she might see. *Frederick, dead.* No, it could not be so. She couldn't bear it, she thought, feeling suddenly ill, as if she might vomit.

She clamped a hand over her mouth, the ground tilting dangerously beneath her feet as she took several deep, gulping breaths of air. Blurred images of him rushed through her mind, Frederick standing in Mister Whitby's parlor in his long, dark greatcoat, not so many hours before. Telling her good-bye, a sardonic smile on his lips. Strong and well. Alive.

Just then, someone turned toward her. *Henley.* It was Henley, in his shirtsleeves, a pistol tucked into his breeches, the bright sunlight glinting off its handle and hurting her already stinging eyes. "Lady Eleanor?" he called out, his voice laced with incredulity.

As Henley strode toward her, the crowd cleared and afforded her an unobstructed view of the lone figure on the ground—now propped up on one elbow, she realized, her heart skipping a beat in elation and causing her breath to hitch in her chest. He was alive! She nearly wept with relief and mumbled a prayer of thanks, not caring who might hear her.

"What in God's name are you doing here, Lady Eleanor? Where's Selina?" Henley looked past Eleanor's shoulder with a scowl. "George? What's going on?"

Ignoring his barrage of questions, Eleanor brushed past him, continuing on toward Frederick's side in hopeful anticipation. He was clearly injured; how badly, she could not tell. But he was alive! A gray-haired man—

a surgeon, perhaps—knelt over him, pressing something to his shoulder.

And, dear Lord, but there was blood everywhere. The sight made her stop dead in her tracks, her stomach pitching uncomfortably. She could smell it—the blood. Frederick's blood. For a terrifying second, she swayed on her feet once more. *Do not let me faint. Not now.*

"It's just a flesh wound," Henley said, coming up behind her and placing a firm hand on her shoulder, steadying her. "Let the surgeon do his work."

She shrugged off his hand, shaking her head. For all she knew, his life's blood was ebbing away at that very moment. "I must go to him."

"Eleanor?" she heard Frederick call out. "What the devil are you doing here?" His words were thick, slurred.

In seconds she was by his side, kneeling in the wet, blood-soaked grass, not caring if her dress was ruined. "I had to come," she said, reaching for his hand. "Whatever happened?" she asked, her voice a hoarse whisper as she fought to steady her nerves. *Blood everywhere.*

"The bastard fired before the signal was thrown, that's what," he snapped, his eyes looking unfocused, slightly wild. A lock of unruly hair fell across one darkly shadowed cheek, and Eleanor gently pushed it away, his skin stubbly beneath her shaking fingers. Suddenly aware that he was entirely bare to the waist, a shiver worked its way down her spine.

She swallowed the lump in her throat and took a deep breath before speaking. "And where . . . where is Mister Eckford now?" Had Frederick killed him? A part of her almost wished he had, and that thought brought with it a pang of guilt. She shook it away, reminding herself that he'd almost killed Frederick, and dishonorably, too.

Frederick tipped his head to the right. "He's over there, the sniveling coward."

Eleanor followed the direction he'd indicated and saw a man in his shirtsleeves, with close-cropped blond hair—looking much as she'd remembered him—struggling against two men who restrained him.

Returning her attention to Frederick, she saw him wince as the surgeon began to wrap the wound with lint that smelled faintly of camphor.

"You should not be here, Eleanor," he said through gritted teeth. "Go back to Whitby Hall. Henley will take you home to Essex."

"And where will you go?"

"To London, with Eckford. Dammit, man, that hurts," he groaned, coldly eyeing the surgeon as he finished wrapping the bandage and securing the ends.

"So long as it does not get putrid, you should heal well enough. You must change the dressing daily, madam," the surgeon said, turning to address Eleanor. "Clean it each night with warm, soapy water, and then re-dress it, but not too tightly."

She shook her head, confused. "No . . . I . . . I'm afraid you're mistaken." A blush warmed her cheeks and she dropped her gaze. The sight of the hard, muscled planes of Frederick's bare chest, his skin surprisingly bronzed, made her cheeks grow hotter still. Involuntarily, her gaze traveled lower, to the fine line of dark hair that ran from his navel downward, disappearing into the band of his breeches.

She quickly averted her gaze, silently scolding her boldness. "I am not his wife, you see," she said at last. "I . . . I am . . . we are betrothed." Her heart soared as the halting words left her lips. How good it felt to say them aloud!

"Are we?" Frederick slurred, a wry smile upon his lips as he pushed himself to a seated position.

"I believe we are," Eleanor murmured, holding up

one bare hand—her gloves forgotten in her haste to depart Whitby Hall. The ruby and diamond ring caught the rays of the early morning sun, reflecting them in colorful prisms onto the grass.

"Good day, Mister Stoneham," Mister Whitby drawled, strolling up with Henley beside him. "How good to see you've all your limbs intact."

"I should throttle you for bringing her here," Frederick growled, his face paling as Henley helped him to his feet.

"Ah, but you've far better things to do. You've a fine woman here, Stoneham. I hope you realize just how lucky you are."

His face alarmingly drawn and pale, Frederick looked from Eleanor to Mister Whitby, and back to Eleanor again. "I've the idea of it," he said softly, understanding shining in the depths of his dark eyes. Bracing his injured arm, he tipped his head toward the road and the waiting carriage beyond. "Will you see her back, Whitby? I'll need Henley's assistance here for several more hours, at least."

"With pleasure," Whitby answered jovially, reaching for Eleanor's arm.

"Go, then, love," Frederick said, then turned and walked stiffly away without so much as a glance back in her direction.

Eleanor hastened up the bluff, her breath coming fast as her frustration mounted. The sight of the sea would calm her, and she hurried her step toward her destination. How she wished to entirely forget the events of the day, to lose herself in the exquisite view, instead. For what else could she do?

Frederick was gone, off to London with Mister Eckford in tow. They had quarreled before he left. Terribly so, for more than an hour. Frederick had insisted that she remain there at Whitby Hall with the Henleys until the morrow, then travel back to Essex and await his return there. Eleanor wanted to go to London. With him. He was injured; who would change his dressings?

It was not her place, he'd argued, nor did he need the distraction as he sought to deal with Eckford, to force him to settle his debts and make restitution to Maria. He'd all but ordered her to obey him.

Harsh words, indeed. Worse still was the look in his eyes when he'd spoken them—distracted, defeated. He had barely been able to meet her gaze, and that troubled her more than the words themselves. Even more alarming, he'd kept a careful distance from her, as if he were suddenly a paragon of propriety. Not a single embrace, no kiss good-bye. Not even a touch.

She could only wonder what had changed him so, there on that grassy meadow near Plymouth. Whatever it was, he was not the same man who had left her there at Whitby Hall the night before, who had kissed her so passionately, so boldly.

At last, she crested the bluff, the stiff breeze blowing her cape out behind her. The sun had begun its slow descent, coloring the sky with wide swaths of orange and pink. As she gazed out to the deep blue sea, a feeling of helplessness washed over her. How lonely the seemingly endless water made her feel, how tiny and insignificant. How much less she enjoyed the view, without Frederick there to enjoy it with her.

Glancing up at the gnarled tree beside her, she had the sudden urge to climb up to the same low branch she'd sat on before, to experience once more that wondrously liberating feeling. Yet, deep in her heart, she knew it would not be the same. Nothing in her life would ever be the same, without Frederick by her side.

She dropped her head to her hands, sighing in despair as a lone gull called out, circling above, its wings flapping on the wind. Something was not right; Frederick was not himself. And, oh, how she wanted to follow him to London, to find out why. How would she bear it, the long, lonely trip to Essex, the wait for him there, with this odd, uncomfortable feeling, niggling at her mind, making her doubt his affections for her?

"I thought perhaps I'd find you here," a voice called out, startling her so badly that she bumped against the tree.

She turned and saw Selina there on the bluff, stray blond locks whipping about her flushed face.

"It's beautiful, isn't it?" Selina asked, wrapping her scarlet cloak more tightly about herself. "If only a bit chilly. I'm sorry I startled you. I hope I'm not intruding on your solitude."

Though she'd come to the bluff wishing to be alone, she was suddenly glad for the company. "Not in the least. I'm happy you've found me," Eleanor said, smiling weakly. "I was thinking perhaps I'd climb this tree. You should join me; the view is extraordinary."

Selina laughed, a bright, cheery laugh. "Climb a tree?" she asked. "Eleanor, are you mad? Why on earth would you wish to do that?"

"Because I want to," Eleanor answered. It was the truth, after all.

Selina chewed her lower lip, then shrugged. "Well, I suppose. If you must. But what shall I do if you fall?" She glanced back over her shoulder, back to the house in the distance, as if measuring the time it might take her to go for help if necessary.

"Don't fret. I shan't fall, I promise. I'm good at this, actually."

Selina ran one hand along the twisted trunk in question, her blond brows drawn into a frown. "I cannot for the life of me fathom why you should wish to climb a tree."

Eleanor tried her best to explain. "Because the view is better. Because it feels lovely to have your feet swinging beneath you, and . . . and . . . well, just because I want to, that's all." She shook her head. "Haven't you ever done something, for no other reason than simply because you *wanted* to?" she asked, realizing the question had been Frederick's.

"I'm not entirely sure," Selina answered, then shook her head. "Very well. Go on, then. Climb your tree. Shall I give you a leg up? Is that the correct phrase, 'a leg up'?"

"I haven't any idea. But look at you, you're shivering. We should go back to the house."

"But what of your tree?" Selina asked, giving its trunk a pat. "We're leaving on the morn, after all. You'll miss your opportunity, if you do not do it now."

"Truly, it does not matter. Besides, it would not be the same," Eleanor said, staring off at the sea, remembering the ship with brightly patterned sails.

"Has this something to do with Frederick? I confess, I heard you quarrelling before he left. Is . . . is everything settled between you?"

"Yes . . . no. Perhaps," she amended, entirely uncertain. "I'm wearing his betrothal ring, so I suppose it is."

"And that is what you truly desire? To marry him?"

"It is, Selina. I love him. I know it is hard for you to understand, after so many years of hearing me say I had no wish to marry for love. But now it is my greatest desire. I could not be satisfied, otherwise. I know you have your doubts, but I can assure you that Frederick is a *good* man. He could have killed Mister Eckford yesterday, but he spared him instead. That speaks highly of his character, doesn't it?"

Selina nodded her agreement. "Indeed, it does. Henley said most men would not have shown such restraint. If you love him, I am happy for you. Truly I am, if you are certain he loves you equally so in return."

A shadow of doubt flickered across her consciousness. He had not said the words, had not declared his love, not in so many words. But he *did* love her. She was certain of it, truly certain. And that was precisely why she needed to go to London rather than rattle about Covington Hall, allowing the chasm of doubt to reopen and grow by the day.

Why had he left her there, worrying over him, ordering her to go to Essex and wait? She could not wait, not when they'd parted under such difficult circumstances, him unable to meet her gaze, to touch her, to declare his love.

"Eleanor?" Selina was saying, and she snapped her attention back to her friend. "He does love you in return, does he not?"

Eleanor swallowed hard before replying. "Indeed he does," she said, her heart swelling with the certainty of it. "Oh, Selina, dearest, you must do something for me. You must ask Henley to take us to London rather than home to Essex. Tomorrow. I cannot explain why, but you must believe me that it's entirely necessary that we go."

"But Henley said—"

"That Frederick wanted me to wait for him at Covington Hall, yes, I know. But I must see him at once; it cannot wait. London is on the way, besides, and I shan't tarry there but a day or two."

"Is it really so important to you?" Selina asked, reaching for her hand. "Whatever it is you feel that you must do?"

However could she explain it to her? That she simply needed to *see* Frederick, to make certain things were indeed settled between them? To make sure that the look of defeat—of guilt, she realized—meant nothing? That his manner upon his departure had only to do with the fact that a bullet had recently grazed his flesh, and nothing to do with her?

How silly that sounded, to her own mind. How selfish. He'd been shot; his sister's welfare was in question. Had she truly expected flowery declarations of love, his fawning attentions while such heavy matters weighed on his mind? Of course he was distracted. How could she have expected otherwise? He'd come to Devonshire for one purpose, and one purpose alone, and it had nothing to do with her.

Still, she wanted to go to Town. And according to Frederick himself, that should be reason enough. She nodded, her mind made up. "It is truly that important that I go. I would not ask this of you, otherwise."

"Then you shall go, Eleanor," Selina said, squeezing her hand with a determined smile. "I will not allow Henley to say no. Oh, I have my ways," she added, smiling wickedly.

"Do you, now?" Eleanor teased, her mood at once lightened.

"Indeed. I'll tell you all about it, once you and Frederick have wed."

Eleanor's smile was a guilty one as she realized that perhaps she already knew a bit more about such matters than any unmarried lady should rightfully know.

Chapter 20

Frederick ducked as a brightly patterned piece of china sailed through the air like a missile, missing his head by a mere fraction of an inch.

Molly was not taking the news well. Not that he'd thought she would, of course, but he had not expected such histrionics at this. This was far beyond the pale, even for the temperamental Molly.

A king's ransom worth of porcelain and crystal lay at his feet, shattered into a million tiny bits. Plates, vases, pitchers—nothing had been spared her wrath. All of it, paid for with his coin.

The last few days had been unpleasant enough, what with dealing with Eckford. He'd quickly and efficiently seen to that business before moving on to his next problem—Molly. He'd thought he would send her packing with a pout, some practiced, deliberate tears, perhaps. He'd expected a whore's trick or two, an attempt to use her physical charms to change his mind. Indeed, he'd been fully prepared for such a thing as that, ready to deflect any advances, to decisively thwart any attempts at seduction.

But this? Shouting, screeching, throwing dishes at his head? Damnation. All he could think of was returning to Essex, to Eleanor as quickly as possible. He wanted this over, done with. *Now.*

"How dare you?" Molly shrieked, her tirade apparently not yet spent. She sent another piece of china sailing in his direction. "How dare you turn me out like this?"

"Come now, Molly," he reasoned. "I'm not turning you out. You might have noticed that I'm the one leaving the premises." He indicated his packed bags, lying in the front hall.

"Bastard!" A flying teacup followed the epithet.

"Bloody hell, will you stop this madness? Calm down, and listen to me. I'm giving you ample time to find other accommodations. I will not simply turn you out on the streets."

"You're casting me aside like yesterday's rubbish, you arrogant . . . arrogant—"

"Arrogant what? I think you've run through all the choices already, have you not?" Devil take it, but he was tired. Weary. Entirely drained. This had to stop, and now.

Glaring at him, she reached for a saucer. He was across the room in an instant, grasping her wrists together, manacling them before she did any more damage.

"Stop this," he said, endeavoring to make his voice gentle, placating. "I've given you my word that I will pay the rents for a full month more, but no longer. Do you understand? Our association ends now."

"You're hurting me, you bastard. Get your hands off me at once," she cried, wrenching her hands free from his grasp.

Bloody hell, but he didn't mean to hurt her. He'd been the cause of enough pain, enough hurt as it was. He raked a hand through his hair, doing his best to ignore the dull ache in his shoulder.

Just that morning he'd received confirmation of Cornelia Darby's death, not three months past in Shropshire.

Lost a babe, likely his own, and hemorrhaged to death. He would make sure that Molly did not suffer the same fate, but that did not mean he would betray Eleanor's trust in the process.

"Our association ends now," he repeated. "Though I will not put you out on the streets."

"You said that your betrothed held no appeal at all, that you would have plenty of time to spend with me, that you would use her money to buy me—"

"Damn it, I know what I said." He did not need any reminders of his cruel and careless words. "But the situation has changed."

"How so? Have you suddenly developed scruples? A conscience? Do not be a prude, Frederick. You would not be the first married man to keep a mistress."

"As I said, the situation has changed." He eyed her coldly, hating the man he'd been not a month before.

"Has this something to do with that tart in Shropshire?" Molly asked meanly, her eyes narrowed to slits. "Are you casting me aside for some shriveled up old prune?"

A vein throbbed in his temple as rage surged through him, nearly choking him. He clenched his hands into fists by his sides, willing his temper to abate before he did something rash. "You'd best shut your mouth right now, by God, or I'll—"

"Don't you dare threaten me, Frederick Stoneham. Is it your betrothed, then? Is she a cruel, heartless woman, one who will keep you on a short leash? Prevent you from seeking your pleasures? No?" she asked when he said nothing in reply.

All he could think of was that he must have been a fool to have ever found her the slightest bit appealing.

"Or is it that you fancy yourself in love with her? Is that what this is about? You've not been away more than a month, Frederick. You barely know the woman. No, I cannot accept it."

"You haven't a choice. You will accept it, and you will begin to look for other accommodations at once."

"That's it, then, isn't it? You think yourself in love with your well-bred lady. I never would have believed it of you. Tell me, how long did it take for her to spread her legs for you? Surely she could not resist a man as practiced in seduction as yourself," she purred, trailing one manicured nail down the front of his coat.

In a flash, he captured her wrist tightly in his grasp. "So help me God, you will not speak one more word about her, do you understand me?" he growled. "I have tried to be fair and accommodating, but you are sorely testing my patience. All association between you and I will cease at once. The rents will be paid for one month, and one month only. If you encounter any difficulties, you may contact my solicitor." He produced a crisp white card from his waistcoat pocket and laid it on the table beside him. "I suggest you do your best to secure another benefactor as soon as possible. Have I made myself clear?"

"You're a fool, Frederick Stoneham," she spat, nothing but hatred in her eyes. "You care for nothing save yourself and your own pleasure. I hope you rot in hell."

With a curt nod, he released her wrist and headed to the front hall to retrieve his bags.

"You're in luck, then," he said, reaching for his hat and tipping it onto his head. "As I'm very likely to do just that. Good day."

"Jermyn Street?" Eleanor asked, unable to hide her astonishment. Releasing the heavy draperies, she turned from the window where she'd stood for the past hour, staring out at the street. "Are you certain? That's not quite . . . well, respectable, is it?"

Selina only shrugged, stabbing at the fabric in her hoop with an embroidery needle. "Henley specifically said 'Number Twelve, Jermyn Street, but you cannot possibly go there.' I suppose it is a bit unsavory, or else he would not have said that."

It wasn't an area that Eleanor was at all familiar with. Still, it was not so far off the beaten path that it should be dangerous. "Why did you not tell me this before now?" she asked. "I've near enough wasted the entire afternoon, sitting here with naught to do but wear the carpet thin waiting."

"Because Henley said we cannot go there, that's why," Selina huffed. "Did I not just say that? He was quite adamant about it. He didn't mean to tell me at all; it just slipped out," she mumbled, dropping her gaze to her lap. "And he made me promise that I would not tell you. I've no idea why, as he would not say."

Why would he exact such a promise from his wife? Whatever were the two of them playing at, Henley and Frederick? It was as if . . . as if Frederick had something to hide. From *her*.

"I can go, and I will. Oh, do not worry. I'll tell Henley that I found the direction elsewhere; I will not implicate you. You will accompany me, though, won't you?" Eleanor hurried across the room, peering down at her friend imploringly. "I cannot possibly go there alone, not without a proper chaperone." Engaged or not, it still was not proper for an unmarried lady to call upon a gentleman alone. She might be eager to see him, but not so desperate as to permanently ruin her reputation.

Selina looked up from her needlepoint, her eyes filled with doubt. "I think perhaps we should wait for Henley to return. Did he not say he would find Frederick and bring him here today?"

"Why ever should we wait? It's a perfectly acceptable hour to pay a call. Besides, who knows when Henley might return. Didn't he say he planned to stop by his solicitor's office?" Indeed, Henley might be gone for several hours more, and she'd waited long enough.

The trip from Devonshire had been tortuously slow, the conversation all but nonexistent as Eleanor had retreated into her own turbulent thoughts, staring out the coach's window without seeing anything except a muted blur. Fitful sleep in shabby coaching inns had left her near enough exhausted, her nerves on edge.

They'd now passed two full days in London, there at the Henleys' small but fashionable townhouse on Hanover Square, with naught a word from Frederick. He didn't know they were there, of course.

Had she any idea where he lodged in Town she would have sent him a missive immediately upon their arrival. But she'd never thought to ask him, and she'd assumed that Henley would know. And apparently he did—Number Twelve, Jermyn Street. She could not imagine why he had kept that bit of information to himself.

"Please, Selina," Eleanor begged. "I cannot simply sit here and wait. Not another hour. Surely you understand?"

Selina rose from the settee, smoothing down her skirts as she sighed resignedly. "I suppose I do. I'll send around for the carriage, then."

A half-hour later, Eleanor sat beside Selina on the worn leather bench, wringing her hands in nervous anticipation as the conveyance clattered down Bond Street toward Piccadilly.

Would he be glad to see her? If he was at home, that is, and she had no assurances that he would be. *Perhaps I should have stayed and waited for Henley, after all,* she thought, an uncomfortable knot forming in the pit of her stomach.

"Are you sure you want to do this?" Selina asked, as if she'd read her mind. "It's not too late to turn back."

"No, I . . . I must go." She tugged her gloves from her hands and stared down at the ring on her finger. Being able to admit her feelings for him—it was all too new, too fresh. She needed to see him, to touch him, to really believe it true. She could not have waited another hour—no, not another minute. Was that so very wrong?

They rode the rest of the way in silence. Eventually the carriage slowed and came to a stop before a narrow gray townhouse that looked remarkably like the ones on either side of it, save the number twelve in brass beside the front door.

The carriage door opened, startling her as she sat gazing out the window, wondering why an heir to a peer of the realm would choose to live *here,* in this nondescript house in an unfashionable part of Town.

Forcing a smile upon her lips, she took the footman's proffered hand and stepped down onto the walk.

"Odd, isn't it, that he would live here," Selina said, echoing her thoughts once more. "I hope Henley had the right of it. I cannot say I know a single soul who resides in this area."

"Nor I." Eleanor reached up to straighten her bonnet, wishing suddenly that she'd taken the time to smarten herself up a bit. "But I'd best get used to the fact that Frederick often does the unexpected. It's part of his charm, really." The forced cheerfulness in her voice sounded false, even to her own ears. "You knock," she said to Selina as they climbed the front stairs. "I'm far too nervous."

"I do not see why you should be. You are engaged to him, after all. We're only here to pay a proper call, nothing at all out of the ordinary. Go on," she said, tipping her head toward the door. "You're the one who insisted this could not wait."

"Oh, fustian!" Eleanor cried, gathering her courage to rap on the door. "I've left my gloves in the carriage." *Coward.*

Just then the door swung open, and both women stepped back in surprise. An elderly woman in a gray dress and white apron stood there in the doorway, examining them sharply from head to toe. The housekeeper, no doubt.

"Did you plan to stand there all afternoon?" she asked impertinently. "Or might I be of some assistance?"

"Indeed you might," Selina answered, bustling into the front hall. Eleanor followed suit, grateful for her friend's presence of mind.

Selina pulled a crisp, white calling card from her reticule and handed it to the housekeeper. "I am Lady Henley, and this is Lady Eleanor Ashton. May we inquire if Mister Stoneham is home at present?"

"Hah, Mister Stoneham!" the woman barked, her cheeks growing red. "I've no idea where he's gone off to, leaving the mistress in such a state."

"The . . . the mistress?" Eleanor stuttered in confusion. "I'm afraid you must be mistaken."

"Thank you, Mrs. Wardley," a feminine voice called out, and Eleanor's gaze flew to the stairs. A petite woman stood there in a red silk kimono dressing gown, long, blond hair falling across her shoulders. "I will see to Frederick's guests," she said.

The housekeeper bobbed a curtsey and disappeared down the corridor.

Eleanor could only stare up at the woman, entirely unable to breathe. Indeed, it felt as if all the air had left her lungs. *Do not jump to conclusions*, she warned herself.

This could all be a terrible mistake. A . . . a misunderstanding. Yes, that was it. It had to be.

"You must pardon our astonishment," Selina said. "We hadn't any idea that a lady—a woman," she corrected, "resided here."

"I suppose not," the woman said, gliding down the stairs at a leisurely pace, her gaze sweeping over them. "Or else you would not have come, would you?"

"Perhaps we should take our leave, Miss . . ." Selina's voice trailed off. "I'm sorry, but I do not believe we are acquainted."

"Delacorte," the woman supplied. "Miss Molly Delacorte. Frederick and I are . . . well, we are dear friends, you might say. Very dear."

She was beautiful, of course. Tiny and delicate, almost doll-like, with round, china-blue eyes and a perfect bow of a mouth. She spoke like a lady though she was clearly anything but. No well-bred lady would greet guests wearing nothing but a dressing gown.

Frederick's mistress, no doubt. There was no other explanation. Eleanor feared she might begin to retch; instead, she cleared her throat loudly, hoping the wave of nausea would pass before she further humiliated herself. And wasn't this humiliation enough, barging into his mistress's house like this? No wonder Henley did not want her to come here. *He knew.*

"We must go," she said, her voice a hoarse whisper. Her eyes stung with the threat of tears, but she would not let them fall. She would not give Miss Delacorte the satisfaction.

"So soon?" the dreadful woman asked with a pout. "You're perfectly welcome to sit and have a cup of tea. Frederick should return directly from wherever he's gone off to. His club, perhaps. You know how men are about their clubs," she added with a smile.

A viper's smile.

Eleanor took two steps back, colliding with a hat stand which threatened to topple over. Quickly, she reached out to steady it, cursing her own clumsiness.

"I'm afraid we cannot wait," Selina said. "We'd best be on our way."

"Very well, then, if you must. I'll be sure to give him your card. Oh, what a lovely ring," she said, reaching for Eleanor's hand. "And such a distinctive setting. Why, I could swear it's exactly like my bracelet." She pushed up one sleeve of her dressing gown, revealing the ruby and diamond bracelet that encircled one slender wrist. "What an odd coincidence, don't you think? Why, Frederick gave me this just this morning, in bed, for no particular reason at all. Isn't it lovely?"

Eleanor blinked repeatedly, but the sight before her eyes remained the same. Miss Delacorte's bracelet was a perfect match to her betrothal ring, a series of rubies flanked by diamonds, the same filigree setting separating each set of sparkling gems.

There was no mistaking the similarity—the two pieces were a matched set, likely purchased together. Frederick had given her the ring, and Miss Delacorte the bracelet. How very cozy, indeed.

A wave of nausea washed over her, making her weak-kneed and queasy. She grasped the edge of a marble-topped hall stand for support.

Could the situation possibly get any worse than this? She'd been wrong, so very wrong. Frederick did not love her. The proof stood before her, admiring the bracelet on her own wrist with a triumphant smile.

"Come, Eleanor," Selina murmured, reaching for her elbow and steering her toward the door. "We must go."

"What a shame you missed Frederick," Miss Delacorte murmured. "I know he'll be terribly disappointed."

Unable to speak a single syllable, Eleanor looked up and met Miss Delacorte's gaze, if only for the briefest moment. The sudden urge to strike the woman, to wipe the coy smile from her painted lips overwhelmed her, forcing her to clench her hands into angry fists by her sides.

She wouldn't touch her, of course. But, oh, how she wanted to! Instead, she straightened her spine, standing tall with her shoulders thrown back and her chin tilted proudly in the air. Offering Miss Delacorte her most regal, haughty smile, she nodded sharply, then followed Selina out and into the waiting carriage.

Thank God she'd learned the truth before it was too late, before she'd married him. She'd come so close— so very close—to losing her heart, losing *everything* that mattered.

Inhaling sharply, she closed her eyes as the carriage lurched forward, the pain in her heart an unbearable ache.

Never again. Never again would she be so foolish, so vulnerable, so terribly naïve as she had been these past few weeks. She was done with Frederick Stoneham, entirely through with love. From this day forward, a wall would go up around her heart, impenetrable as stone, and there it would remain until her dying day—this she promised herself.

And perhaps she would take Mister Whitby up on his offer, after all.

Chapter 21

"I've no idea what's going on, old chap," Henley said with a grimace, raising his gaze to the ceiling where the loud, thumping noises seemed to originate. "All I know is Lady Eleanor is upstairs banging things around, Selina is bawling into her handkerchief, and no one will tell me a bloody thing except that we must leave for Essex immediately on the morn."

Frederick massaged his temples, his head feeling as if it might explode at any given moment. Devil take it, how much more could he endure in one day? It had been surprise enough to learn that Eleanor and the Henleys were in Town, but now she refused to see him and he hadn't the slightest notion why.

If anyone had reason to be angry, it was him, he reasoned. He had told her in no uncertain terms that she was to travel straight through to Essex after leaving Whitby Hall. Just the knowledge that Eleanor was there, close by, would have been far too distracting as he forced Eckford to satisfy creditors and set up financial accounts to see to Maria's living expenses. It was unpleasant business, that, and he wanted Eleanor as far away from such sordid things as possible.

There had been Molly to deal with as well, and new accommodations to secure. The house in Grosvenor Square would become his when he became the Baron Worthington, but until then he and his bride would need a residence in London. He'd found one that would do nicely, a small but elegant townhouse just off Upper Brook Street. An agreement had been struck, but he had not yet had time to have the papers drawn up. Indeed, he still had several days' worth of business left in Town before he could travel on to Essex.

And now this. "Enough nonsense," he barked to Henley, his patience worn thin. "Go up there and demand that she come down at once."

"I'm not entirely sure that's the best course of action, Stoneham. It's quite"—he paused as something banged loudly on the ceiling up above—"a scene up there."

"I don't give a damn if . . ." Frederick trailed off as Lady Henley appeared in the doorway, her eyes red-rimmed and swollen, a handkerchief clutched to her mouth. "Good evening, Lady Henley," he said with a bow. "If you would be so kind as to convince my betrothed to come down here and receive me, I would be most grateful."

"How dare you?" she cried out, her features an angry mask. "How dare you come here? Have you any idea what sort of a state poor Eleanor is in right now? I told her you were nothing but a rogue, but she would not listen to reason, would not believe such things about—"

"If you'll pardon me, madam, but I haven't the slightest idea what I've done—"

"What you've done? No, I don't suppose you would think you've done anything wrong, would you? I suppose you thought your wife would never know about your activities in Jermyn Street, that you could continue on with—"

"Jermyn Street?" He felt the blood drain from his face. "What the hell—pardon me, but what do you know of Jermyn Street?"

"We were there, today, Eleanor and I. We met your Miss Delacorte."

"Didn't I tell you that you could not go there?" Henley blustered, an angry flush climbing his neck. "I specifically said—"

"I know you did, Henley, and I am so terribly sorry for having disobeyed you. If only you'd told me *why* we could not go there . . ." Selina broke into sobs, muffling them with her handkerchief.

Frederick cleared his throat loudly. "And just what did Miss Delacorte tell you?" he snapped, a terrifying fear clutching his heart.

"Just that . . . that you were not at home at present. And she showed us the bracelet. It was dreadful—you should have seen Eleanor's face when she saw it. Her heart is near enough broken, thanks to you."

The bracelet? What in God's name was she talking about?

"I thought you were dealing with that . . . ahem . . . situation?" Henley shuffled his feet, looking uncomfortable as he patted his wife on the shoulder. "There now, love. Don't cry," he murmured.

"That situation *had* been dealt with. Just this morning. I cannot believe Molly would lead Eleanor to believe otherwise." But even as he said the words he realized their absurdity. Of course she would, out of desperation, perhaps, or simply mean-spiritedness. Given the opportunity, Molly would have done her damnedest to ruin his life, for retribution's sake. Bloody hell, it wasn't as if he'd ever expected the two women to meet. And damn Henley for telling his wife the direction. What in God's name had the man been thinking?

"Lady Henley, you must believe that any association between myself and Mol—Miss Delacorte—was ended by me just this morning. It was the first and only contact I've had with the woman since I came to Town, and I made it perfectly clear where I stood on the matter."

Lady Henley glared at him across the distance that separated them. "If you ended your association, why would you give her the bracelet, just this morning, she claims? A perfect match to Eleanor's ring."

The bracelet? *No.* Damn it all to hell, no. His stomach pitched as he remembered the ruby and diamond bracelet he'd bought along with the matching betrothal ring. He'd given Molly the bracelet before he'd left Town, to placate her. A meaningless gift, which was why he had entirely forgotten it.

"I gave it to her long ago, before I traveled to Essex. Before I'd even become reacquainted with Eleanor. It meant nothing—"

"Why should I believe you?" She shook her head, her lace cap fluttering wildly about her ears. "And why ever should Eleanor?"

"You would believe the words of a whore over mine?" Frederick roared, furious at himself, at Henley. At everyone, damn it.

"Oh!" Lady Henley gasped, her face turning white. "You must go, sir. At once. Henley, please," she begged, looking entreatingly to her husband.

"Go upstairs, Selina, dearest," Henley said, nodding toward the stairs. "Allow me to see Mister Stoneham out."

Without another word, Lady Henley dashed out, sobbing as she went.

Frederick turned on Henley, his entire body shaking with rage. "Why the bloody hell would you tell her about Jermyn Street? I told you I would see to that as soon as possible."

"I say, old man, I thought you were. I hold Lady Eleanor in the highest regard, and I will not stand for you trifling with her. If there is a word of truth to—"

"You believe her, then? You honestly think I gave Molly an expensive gift—a piece of jewelry—just this morning? That I planned to keep Molly around a bit longer, to enjoy both a kept mistress and a wife? You believe I would do that to Eleanor?"

"You would not be the first man to do so," Henley said with a shrug. "But Lady Eleanor is Selina's dearest friend, and I cannot allow—"

"Damn you, man!" Frederick advanced on him, one finger thrust accusingly toward his chest. "I though you of all people knew—that you understood just what I felt for Eleanor. You think I would risk something that precious on someone like Molly? On anyone?"

"Look, old boy," Henley said, his tone placating. "I do believe you. Nonetheless, I think you should go. Now. Tomorrow I will take Selina and Lady Eleanor home, and you can finish your business here in Town. We can sort it all out when you get to Essex. In the meantime, I'll try to smooth things over on your behalf."

Frederick only shook his head, attempting to staunch the rage that threatened to overcome him. "Damn it, I'm through with all of you. How many times must I prove myself, to her, to you?" he bellowed, his mind a clouded mess. Again and again, Eleanor doubted him, as did everyone else. Well, damn her to hell. Damn them all to hell.

He stormed out of the drawing room, pausing at the bottom of the stairs. "Enough, Eleanor Ashton. Do you hear me?" He pounded a fist on the wall, so hard that a mirror rattled off the moldings and smashed to bits on the marble by his feet. "I'm through proving myself worthy. Run back to Essex, but do not expect me to come chasing after you. I'm finished with this. With you."

With that, he grabbed his hat from the hall stand and shoved it onto his head before flinging open the front door. It banged against the wall, splintering loudly as he stormed down the stairs and onto the walk. He needed to find a public house, and quickly. All he could think of was getting himself thoroughly and mind-numbingly foxed, as soon as possible.

If everyone was going to think him a debauched, immoral wastrel no matter what he did to prove otherwise, then, by God, he might as well enjoy it. And to hell with the rest.

Eleanor glanced out the church's window at the sky—a heavy, dull gray, just like her heart. Pulling her wrap about her shoulders, she leaned back against the hard wooden pew, doing her best to concentrate on the vicar's sermon. Something about resisting vice? *How very fitting,* she thought, endeavoring once more to concentrate on the man's impassioned speech.

It was no use. Her mind was elsewhere, as it had been these many weeks since she'd returned home to Covington Hall. How many had it been? She'd lost count. More than a moon, she realized, her gaze straying back to the window. She shivered as a chill worked its way down her spine, drawing gooseflesh on her skin.

Just as Frederick had threatened, he had not come chasing after her. True to his word, he remained in London. Apparently he'd sent a message to his father, indicating that he would not honor the betrothal contract, that he wished the agreement annulled. Eleanor had finally worked up the courage to tell her papa the same, that she would not marry Frederick Stoneham if he were the last eligible man in all of England.

Lord Worthington had been furious. Papa had assured the man that he did not wish the match if both parties were no longer in full agreement. There would be no breach of promise suit, no resentment, no recriminations.

She'd wanted to kiss her father, for proving to her that her own welfare—her happiness—was more important to him than the bargain he'd struck with the baron. Still, Papa had seemed saddened, as if he'd somehow failed her. He retreated to his study now more than ever, his nose more often than not in a book. Greek philosophy, most likely. His favorite. Whatever the case, no more had been said about marriage. Not to Frederick, nor to anyone else.

She glanced over at her mama, sitting beside her now in her elegant Sunday silks, her mouth pressed into a tight line. Though her own father had been a vicar, Mama did not enjoy religious services. Still, her position in society often compelled her to attend, and Mama was not one to jeopardize her position. She had insisted that Eleanor accompany her that morning, and she'd readily agreed, thinking it might serve as a much-needed distraction.

Apparently she'd been wrong on that count. Indeed, all she'd done since taking her seat there on the pew was worry over her future—a dangerous occupation, in her current state. She hadn't any idea how much her parents knew of the events that had transpired in Devon, and then in London. She had categorically refused to speak of them to anyone, even Selina. To do so would force her to revisit a series of emotions she hoped to never again suffer through.

Instead she'd pushed it all as far from her mind as possible, remaining numb, detached from her true self. It was all she could do, really—an act of self-preservation. For if she allowed herself to think of him, to think of his betrayal, she'd go mad. The pain was still too fresh, too raw.

Fingering her reticule, her thoughts shifted to the letter her mama had handed her just before they'd left for services that same morning. From Mister Whitby, whom she had been corresponding with these past few weeks. She'd not yet had a chance to read it, but his letters always brought her a measure of comfort. They served as a reminder that something good had come from her trip to Whitby Hall—a friendship of sorts, even if an odd one.

These past few weeks she'd considered how she would respond if Mister Whitby renewed his offer of marriage. He'd alluded to it briefly in his last correspondence, and she'd indicated in return that she might be receptive to such an offer. She was eager to read his reply, yet anxious all at once. Would her future be settled, at last?

And even if it were, would she be content with it, a marriage of convenience, of mutual commiseration? Could she forget Frederick, without having ever allowed him to explain? Selina had relayed to her in detail exactly what he'd said that last night in London, that Miss Delacorte had lied, that he'd never betrayed her. Still, to have come face to face with the woman whose bed he had shared, whose very livelihood he had funded in return for her sexual favors . . . No, she could not bear to think of it.

Still, she could not help but wonder if he *had* been telling the truth. She supposed she would never know, as Frederick remained in Town, and she in Essex. Besides, if he had been innocent, if Miss Delacorte had indeed egregiously misrepresented the situation, he would have come for her by now, wouldn't he? A man in love would have done so, she reasoned, nodding to herself. The fact that he hadn't was proof he did not. Proof that he had gone on with his life. As she should be doing with hers, she told herself, glancing down at the outline of Mister Whitby's letter against the silk of her reticule, her vision suddenly blurred.

Oh, blast it! She had not cried, not once in all these weeks, and now her eyes dampened dangerously, right there in the church for everyone to see. The sudden need to get out, to breathe the fresh autumn air overwhelmed her.

When the congregation rose to recite a prayer not five minutes later, she was afforded the perfect opportunity to escape.

"Mama," she whispered, leaning close to her mother's ear. "I'm feeling suddenly ill. I must go."

"I'm to have tea with the vicar's wife after services. Your father insisted. I cannot leave now," she whispered back harshly.

"I can go alone, Mama, on foot. A brisk walk in the cool air will no doubt revive me."

"Go on, then," she murmured with a scowl. "But be quick, as it looks like rain."

Eleanor nodded, then quickly made her exit, ignoring the curious glances the villagers cast her way as she scurried down the aisle and into the vestibule. In seconds she was hurrying down the lane, glancing up worriedly at the threatening sky.

It did look as if it were going to rain, and she had nothing for protection save her heavy woolen cloak. She quickened her pace, thinking that perhaps this had not been such a good idea, after all. In fine weather, Covington Hall was a good half-hour's walk from the old stone church. Were it to rain, she would be soaked to the bone long before she reached home.

Not a quarter hour later, it began to drizzle. *Fustian.* She paused to pull her hood up over her bonnet, shivering as the icy rain pricked her face. As she trudged onward, the drizzle became a downpour, the lane turning to mud beneath her half boots.

Up ahead, across the wooden bridge that spanned the river, she spied a copse of willows by the side of the road. That would have to do.

Taking a deep breath, she dashed the entire length of the bridge and ducked beneath the bare, drooping branches just as the sound of thundering hooves appeared from nowhere.

Please, let it be someone I know. Someone who would take pity on her and offer her a ride home. She stepped out from under the trees' protection, just as the horse and rider appeared over the crest. In seconds, they were upon her, the horse's hooves clattering across the bridge's wooden planks.

Reaching up on her tiptoes, she waved wildly, hoping to be seen despite the heavy, cloaking mist. The rider raced past in a blur of billowing camel greatcoat, then wheeled the enormous beast around, back toward her.

"What the devil?" the man called out, tugging his tall beaver hat lower on his brow before swinging down to the ground and tossing the horse's reins across its back.

Frederick? Dear lord, no. She took a step back in astonishment. No, her senses must be playing tricks on her—cruel tricks.

"Are you trying to get yourself killed, stepping out into the road like that?" he bellowed, moving closer. "The visibility is next to nothing."

The rain poured off the brim of his hat, partially obscuring his face as he moved closer still. Her hungry gaze traveled over his familiar features—thick brows knitted over dark, penetrating eyes; an angular jaw; full, sensual lips. His wild, dark hair—now fully soaked—brushed his broad shoulders.

It *was* him. Not merely a figment of her imagination, but flesh and blood, there in the road, dripping wet. Looking menacingly large and powerful, devastatingly handsome. As always.

Recognition at last lit his eyes, narrowing them perceptibly. "Eleanor?" he asked, his voice breaking on the last syllable.

Just a single word, spoken with such emotion that her breath caught in her chest. She had not expected that, had not expected the look of pain that darkened his features, if only for a moment.

"What the devil are you doing out here?" he asked.

"I . . . I got caught in the rain," she stammered. "Whatever are you doing here?"

For a full minute he said nothing. Eleanor did not move—waiting, watching, her breath coming dangerously fast. The rain continued to bear down, sluicing off them as they stood there on the edge of the road facing one another silently for what seemed an eternity.

"How is your shoulder?" she asked at last, unable to bear the silence a moment longer.

"Nearly healed, thank you."

"And . . . and how is your sister Maria?"

"She is well," he answered. "My eldest sister and her husband have come to take her home."

Eleanor nodded. "I'm glad to hear it." She looked away, toward the top of the road, wishing he would say something—anything—to make this less awkward. Rain dripped from her nose, and she wiped it away with her sleeve, knowing she must look a terrible fright. "I . . . I must know why you are here, Frederick."

"The truth? Because I could no longer bear to stay

away, try as I might. You did not give me a chance to explain, to have my say."

She shook her head, sending a spray of rain into her eyes, stinging them. "There was nothing you *could* say, Frederick."

"You're mistaken. I had much to say, if only you would have listened. I would have told you that Molly is a damnable liar, that nothing she said to you that day in Jermyn Street was true. Aye, and that you were a fool to believe her."

Eleanor inhaled sharply, indignation surging through her. "How dare you call me—"

"I've never before lied to you, Eleanor. Not once," he snapped, closing the distance between them with long, angry strides. "There's more, and this time you *will* listen. I could have said that you've taken over my heart, my soul, my every waking thought. That each morning you are the first thing I think of, and each night the last."

"Please don't," she cried, not wishing to hear the words. It was too late, far too late. "Don't do this, not now." Not when she'd finally found a measure of peace, a numbness of mind and soul that had served her well.

"You *will* hear me out," he said, raising his voice above the din of the rain. "I've stayed away as long as possible, but it's no use. I'm ruined." He spread his arms wide, then dropped them to his sides. "You've stripped me of my defenses, left me bare, and despite my best intentions . . ." His voice trailed off as he shook his head, looking utterly defeated. "I love you, Eleanor Ashton."

The very words she'd so desperately wished to hear, come too late. She struggled to catch her breath as a flood of emotions engulfed her, catching her in their turbulent tide.

"And even as I say those words, I can see the doubt, there in your eyes." He moved forward, his lips only inches from hers, his gaze scouring her face, lingering on her mouth.

Despite everything, she realized she wanted him to kiss her, so thoroughly and senselessly that she no longer knew up from down, left from right. Right from wrong.

Instead, he staggered back, flexing his hands as if he'd suffered a physical blow.

Eleanor blinked in confusion. This was not the Frederick Stoneham she knew, the arrogant roué with a quip at the ready, who did exactly what he pleased, no matter the consequence.

No, this man was vulnerable, instead. Hurt. Restrained and self-doubting. Was *this* the real Frederick, kept hidden behind the devil-may-care façade, beneath the rakehell veneer? *For protection*, she realized with a startling clarity.

And he loved her. He loved her!

"We must talk," she said quickly, her voice infused with hope.

"Indeed we must." He reached out, as if he were going to take her hand. Instead, he let his arm fall back to his side. "But not here," he added, "not like this, standing out in the road soaking wet."

Eleanor nodded, vaguely aware that the rain had tapered off to a fine mist. Her clothing and undergarments clung wetly to her skin, and her teeth began to chatter.

"Come," he said, gesturing toward his horse. "I'll take you home."

Shivering now, she followed him to his mount and allowed him to hoist her up into the saddle. As she tucked her cloak about herself, he stood below in the road, holding the reins as he gazed up at her, his eyes suddenly as hard as flint.

"We must speak—alone," he said, his voice clipped. "Tomorrow. There's an old artisan's cottage on my father's property; I often stay there when in residence. Henley can tell you its exact location. Tell your parents you are going to pay a call on Lady Henley; tell them whatever you wish. Henley will give you a horse; it's an easy ride from his stables. If you have not come by sunset I will return to London, and that will be the end of this."

Eleanor only nodded, swallowing the lump in her throat.

"But listen to me, and listen well," he continued, a muscle in his jaw flexing perceptibly. "Do not come unless you are entirely prepared to put your fate in my hands, to trust me with all your heart, with every inch of your being. To accept my word as the truth. I do not want you, otherwise."

With that, he swung up onto the saddle behind her, one arm wrapped protectively about her. Kicking his heels into the horse's sides, he spurred the beast into a gallop, off toward Covington Hall.

Chapter 22

Water dripping off her, Eleanor trudged past the twin fountains on either side of the tree-lined drive where Frederick had deposited her just moments before. Her skirts dragged in the mud as she made her way across the flagstones and up the wide stairs toward the familiar, aged yellow stones of Covington Hall. Her mind was still reeling, her heart racing despite her sluggish pace. Her garments were shockingly heavy when wet, and all she could think of was getting out of them and into a hot, steaming bath.

Wondering where the butler had gone off to, she let herself into the front hall and stopped short, gaping in surprise at the sight before her, at the singularly handsome man who stood leaning lazily against the wall, his arms folded across his broad chest as he regarded her with barely concealed amusement in his deep blue eyes, eyes the exact same shade as her own.

"What the devil has happened to you?" he drawled, his mouth curving into a grin.

"Henry!" she squealed, launching herself across the hall and into his arms. "Whatever are you doing here? Oh, don't tell me. I'm just so very happy that you are."

She pressed her face against his coat, smiling giddily as he embraced her. It had been too long—far too long— she realized, stepping away from him at last.

"Perhaps you should go change," he said, brushing off his lapels. "What did you do, fall in the river?"

"I got caught in the rain, you fool. You *did* notice it rained, did you not? Quite heavily, too."

"At least there was no thunder," he teased. "Or you might have perished there in fright, coward that you are. Good God, but you're soaked. Here, let's get you upstairs." He reached for her elbow, guiding her up the wide, sweeping stairs.

"How long can you stay?" she asked, still barely able to believe he was there.

"I'm afraid I must return in the morn, as I'm only here for the night."

"All this way, just for the night? Surely not, Henry. Blast it, but I've missed you. You've no idea."

"I had to come, El. Something about your last letter alarmed me. I wrote to Father—"

"And I suppose he told you everything?" she snapped.

"To the contrary, dear sister. He told me nothing. Go, have a bath. And then you can tell me everything yourself."

Eleanor looked up at Henry and nodded, amazed as always that he had grown so tall since he'd gone off to university. He'd been such a scrawny, sickly boy, always a head shorter than her and trailing a step behind. To look at him now, well over six feet and heavily muscled . . . it made her heart sing with joy. He looked healthy and fit, and she could not have been happier for it.

"I shan't be long," she said, then slipped inside her bedchamber, calling out impatiently for Solange.

An hour later, she joined Henry in his sitting room across the hall, warm and dry, her hair twisted into a single plait that fell across one shoulder. She took a seat on the gold velvet bench beside his dressing table while he sprawled in a worn leather chair, his coat tossed carelessly across the back. His long limbs were stretched out toward the hearth where a fire crackled pleasingly. So many times they'd sat just like this, discussing their hopes and dreams. Henry had talked about his passion for painting; she, of her love for poetry. Life had been so much simpler then. If only she'd realized those years would pass so quickly, she would have savored them more, for now they were lost forever.

Henry cleared his throat, pulling her from her thoughts. "Now, then," he prompted. "Tell me what's troubling you. And please"—he held up one hand—"no tears. You know I cannot understand you when you get all blubbery."

She glared at him across the room. "I do not get all blubbery."

"Yes, whatever," he said, examining his fingernails. "Go on, from the beginning."

She took a deep, fortifying breath. "That would be the betrothal agreement. Papa arranged a match for me, you see. With Frederick Stoneham, of all people."

"Stoneham? The Baron Worthington's son? He can't be more than three and twenty."

Eleanor nodded. "He's precisely that."

Henry shrugged, reaching up to untie his starched white cravat. "Well, I suppose you could do worse than a baron's only son. Worthington is well connected, and rich, too. Successful estates in Oxfordshire, Essex, Ireland." He ticked them off with his fingers. "Whatever is the problem, then? Had you higher hopes than that?"

"It's nothing to do with my hopes, Henry. Oh, you'll never understand." She folded her arms across her breasts and turned toward the fire, staring blindly into the flames. "Never mind, I cannot tell you."

"Of course you can. You better, as I came all the way from Oxford to hear it."

Her gaze snapped back to his. "You'll laugh; you'll think me silly. It's all far too embarrassing."

"I solemnly swear I will not laugh," he said, placing one hand across his heart. "There, will that satisfy you?"

"Have you been painting?" she hedged, noticing a trace of pigment beneath his neatly trimmed nails. "I hope you will not give it up in favor of—"

"Indeed, I have been painting, but pray, do not change the subject. Come now, out with it."

"I . . . I kissed Frederick Stoneham," she blurted, "when I was but ten and six. In the maze. And . . . and I've fancied myself in love with him ever since."

"You what?" he barked, sitting erect at once, his hands gripping the chair's arms so tightly that his knuckles turned white. "You cannot be serious. You, in love? Impossible."

"I told you it was humiliating," she said, her cheeks suddenly hot. "But true, nonetheless."

"Love? Haven't you seen what it's done to our father? Can you honestly wish that for yourself?"

"No, of course not. And I didn't wish for it, not at all. It came . . . unbidden." Yes, that was the word. She'd wanted nothing to do with love, and yet it had found her anyway.

"And did he . . . does he love you in return?"

"He didn't, not then. He kissed me to win a . . . a wager. Do not get angry, Henry," she said, seeing a vein throb in his temple. "Else I will not tell you the rest."

"There's more?" he groaned.

Eleanor nodded, gathering her courage, forcing back the tears that had gathered in her eyes.

"Devil take it, Eleanor, don't tell me he's trifled with

you, that you're in some sort of trouble. Why, I'll kill the bastard—"

"Goodness, Henry," she interrupted with a scowl. "Take a damper. It's nothing so bad as that."

It took nearly an hour for her to recount the past two months' events—liberally edited, of course, as she did not dare tell him of their far-too-intimate encounter at the cottage on the cliff. Heavens, no; her brother would likely have suffered an apoplexy had she done so. Clearly she'd underestimated his protective instincts where her virtue was concerned.

When she finished her tale, ending with their most recent exchange in the rain, Henry merely shook his head.

"Well, go on. Say something," she prompted, his silence making her squirm.

"I . . . I don't know what to say. I'm stunned, to say the least. I thought you far more sensible than this."

"Don't you dare criticize me, Henry Ashton."

"You must admit it sounds insensible," he muttered, raking a hand through his dark hair.

"Oh, very well. I suppose it does." Eleanor dropped her head into her hands, sighing deeply. "My mind tells me that marriage is about security, companionship, about advancing one's position. But my heart tells me otherwise."

"So what will you do?"

"I hoped you'd have an answer, Henry. I . . . I'm to decide by tomorrow."

"Then you've a long night ahead of you, haven't you? I'm afraid I cannot help you with this. I do not even believe such a thing as romantic love exists."

"Nor did I, till now. But now I'm entirely certain that it does. It does," she repeated, "and it is wondrous and frightening, all at once. I fear cannot turn my back on it, now that I've discovered it."

"I suppose Father thought the same thing, so many years ago. Which reminds me, whose bed do you suppose Mother is frequenting at present?"

"Don't be vulgar, Henry," she snapped. "You know I don't wish to hear these things."

"Perhaps you should hear them. I've seen it with my own eyes, Eleanor. For all we know, Father has, too. You've seen how he's suffered, how she's humiliated him, time and again. Can you risk finding yourself in that same position?"

"This is different," she said, pounding one fist on the bench in frustration. "Frederick is not Mama. He loves me, Henry."

"And you're certain of that? Certain it will endure once the novelty wears off?"

She nodded. "Entirely so."

"Well, then, Eleanor, there's nothing left for me to say. It seems that you will get your arranged marriage, after all. Just not quite the one you'd expected." He rose and came to stand beside her, one hand resting on her shoulder, patting it affectionately. "All I can do is wish you luck."

Frederick smiled as Maria wrapped her arms about his waist, embracing him tightly. He bent and kissed the top of her head, relieved to see her so well recovered. He only hoped that, when Eckford came crawling back to her—as he no doubt would, the bastard—that she would have the fortitude to resist him, to send him packing.

"Thank you, Freddie," she said, drawing away from him at last. A lone tear traced a path down her cheek. "Thank you ever so much, for finding him, for making him do right by me and the girls. For sparing him, worthless lout that he is," she added, a bittersweet smile upon her lips. "Truly, I don't know how I'd have managed without you."

"Just promise me that you'll take good care of yourself."

"Only if you'll promise the same of yourself." She reached for her bonnet. "I worry about you, you know. Will you return to Town? Back to your wicked ways?"

He shrugged. "I might go to Ireland instead." In truth, he'd already bought passage to Dublin, just in case. If things did not go well with Eleanor—and he could not allow himself to hope that they would—he would take some time to collect himself at the Abbey, there between the lake and mountains, the most peaceful place on earth.

"You'll write to me, won't you?" she asked, tying her bonnet's ribbons beneath her chin.

"Every week, as always." He watched as his two small nieces skipped down the walk toward the carriage, their ribbons fanning out behind them as they turned and waved.

"Goodbye, Uncle Frederick," they lisped in unison.

"Goodbye, poppets," he called back, leaning against the doorway with a smile. "Safe travels."

Katherine bustled out, tugging on her gloves, her husband trailing behind her. "Marcus, dear, the carriage is waiting," she called out over one shoulder. "Oh, Freddie, darling." She hurried back to embrace him. Standing on tiptoe, she kissed his cheek, her scent—rosewater and soap—so comfortingly familiar.

"You are a good man, Freddie," she whispered in his ear, tears dampening her light brown eyes. "A fine man. I knew it all along."

Damn, but he loved her, the closest thing he'd had to a mother. Thank God he'd returned to Essex in time to see them off.

"You'll write?" she asked.

"Of course," he answered with a mock bow. "Now go, off with you. See that Maria is settled. If you need me, just send word."

"I will. Very well, then, I suppose I'm off." She blew him one last kiss, then bustled down the stairs and into the waiting carriage.

"Drive on," his brother-in-law called out, and the carriage sprang forward, jostling down the drive. He watched until the clip-clop of hooves faded, until the carriage was naught but a speck in the distance, and then he headed back inside.

Just as he feared, his father was there in the front hall, waiting. "They've gone?"

"Indeed. If you'll excuse me." Bowing sharply, Frederick made for the stairs.

"Frederick, I . . . if you don't mind, I'd like a word with you," his father called out after him, his voice sounding strangely tight.

Frederick paused, one hand on the carved newel post. Dropping his chin to his chest, he sighed, not wanting a scene with the man, not now. All he wanted was to go in peace, off to his cottage to enjoy a bit of solitude.

"Please, son," his father added.

"I'd planned to go to the cottage for the night."

"Your mother loved that little artisan's cottage, did you know that? It's no wonder you've always been drawn there."

Frederick stepped back in surprise, one boot on the stair, thinking that hell must have frozen over. The Baron Worthington did not speak of his late wife to Frederick—*ever*. Too stunned to speak, he simply shook his head.

"Indeed," his father continued. "This was our primary residence when we first married, until my father passed and we took up the estate in Oxfordshire. 'Twas

Fiona who had the pianoforte moved out to the cottage."
His eyes took on a misty, faraway look, a faint smile
upon his lips. "Aye, she loved to play, and to paint. The
cottage was her private retreat. One of her landscapes
still hangs there, if I'm not mistaken."

Of course—above the mantel. A bold piece that
always put him in mind of the walled flower garden at
the Abbey. As was likely intended, he realized, given the
artist's identity. He'd passed many an hour staring up at
that painting, wishing it were a portal that could trans-
port him across the Irish Sea, to the place that felt more
like home than any of his father's English estates ever
would.

"Anyway," his father said gruffly, "I realize that I
have not always been the best of fathers, not to you, at
least."

Frederick only shrugged, wishing to put an end to the
uncomfortable discourse at once.

"I tried my best, but you cannot possibly know what
it's like to lose a wife you love so dearly, and then a son."

"You've no need to tell me this," Frederick said
through clenched teeth. He had no wish to hear it.

"Indeed, I must. You're so much like her, you see."
His gaze strayed to the portrait of his long-dead wife,
there in the front hall, and Frederick's followed suit.

For a full minute, both men simply stood there in silence, admiring the portrait of the lovely dark-haired
woman with mischievous brown eyes. Captured for
eternity standing beside a red velvet chaise, a playful
smile tipping the corners of her mouth.

At last his father cleared his throat, turning his attention back to his son. "What I'm trying to say, however
awkwardly, is thank you. Thank you," he repeated, "for
doing for Maria what I have should done myself. There's

no telling what the situation would be now, had you not stepped in."

"I have always held my sisters in the highest regard," Frederick replied softly. "Each and every one of them. Though you might not have noticed."

"Touché." He stroked his long, drooping whiskers thoughtfully.

They were entirely gray now, as was the hair on his head, what was left of it. With a start, Frederick realized his father had grown old.

"I underestimated you, Frederick," the baron said. "And I am sorry for it. I hope you will reconsider marrying Lady Eleanor."

At the mention of Eleanor, Frederick's attention snapped back into focus.

"I do not know under what circumstances the agreement fell asunder, but my greatest hope is that it can be set to rights. I know you think me a cruel, hard man, but, I vow, I entered into that agreement with Lord Mandeville with only the best of intentions."

Frederick could only stare at the man in disbelief.

"Aye," his father continued, shoving his hands into his pockets. "She's an exceptional young lady, a diamond of the first water."

"She is, indeed," Frederick said. At least they could agree on *something*.

"I only hoped that, with some interference on my part, the pair of you might find a measure of happiness together. As I found with your mother, God rest her soul. Anyway, I hope you will reconsider."

"Of course I've reconsidered; I'm not such a fool as that. If you must know, the only obstacle hindering our happy union at present is that the lady in question is disinclined to marry me."

"Hmm, an obstacle, indeed. However, I'm certain

you've the persuasive powers to rectify the situation. Aren't such things rumored to be among your talents?"

"Are they?" Frederick asked with a shrug. "I confess, I'm not precisely up to the rigs on the rumors concerning me."

"Well . . . ahem. I suppose you can go off to your cottage now, though I'm glad we had this talk. I hope that perhaps someday . . . well, never mind. Go on, then, and best of luck winning the hand of your fair maiden."

Luck—that was just what he needed right now. That, and a small miracle.

"I'm so sorry, dear, but I simply cannot allow you to take the carriage, not today." Eleanor's mother generously slathered her toast with butter. "I'm to call on the Duchess of Warburton this afternoon, and I hoped you'd accompany me."

"I'm afraid I cannot, Mama. You see, I promised Selina—"

"Nonsense. You spend far too much time at Marbleton as it is. Besides, you know how Her Grace enjoys listening to you play."

"It's just that . . . that . . ." *Oh, bother.* She hated to lie to her mother, but what else could she do? "Selina is feeling unwell and I promised to keep her company, to read to her today."

"She is so unwell that she cannot read to herself?" Mama asked with raised brows. "If that is so, then you should not be exposed. I do not want you taking ill."

"No, it's nothing like that." Eleanor's hand shook as she reached for her coffee. "She's just feeling a bit . . . poorly . . . is all."

Her mother's eyes narrowed with suspicion. "Does this have something to do with Frederick Stoneham?"

Good heavens, was she really as transparent as that? Blast it, but now what was she to say?

"Oh, don't be such a ninny, Eleanor. Out with it; I can see the truth all over your face. You're a terrible liar, you know."

Eleanor let out her breath in a rush, her cheeks flooding with heat. "Very well, Mama. I had hoped to see Fred—Mister Stoneham," she corrected, "at Marbleton today." *Dear Lord, another lie.* "We have some matters of importance to discuss. Quite urgently," she added lamely.

"I should say so. I suppose this explains your brother's sudden appearance yesterday, and equally abrupt departure at dawn? Asking his counsel, were you?"

Eleanor only shrugged, entirely unsure how to respond. Speaking of Henry always made Mama irritable, and she did not wish to irritate her—she wanted the carriage.

"Well, perhaps I can offer you some womanly advice instead." Mama nodded, fingering her lace fichu. "But first, I've a confession."

"A confession?"

"Indeed. Beneath your feather mattress is not a terribly clever place to hide your diary, dear."

"What . . . whatever do you mean?" Eleanor stuttered. Her mother only arched one delicate brow in reply.

Eleanor's heart skipped a beat as realization dawned on her. Her diary. Her mother had read her diary, and everything in it about Frederick. Foolish words, written when she'd been but a girl.

"There I was, doing you a favor, as it were. Suggesting to your father that Mister Stoneham was just the man for you to marry, when heaven knows there are surely more suitable gentlemen to be had. And somehow you managed to go and ruin it. You could have had exactly what your heart desired—the man you loved. Not every girl is so lucky."

"I . . . I don't understand," Eleanor murmured, shaking her head in confusion.

"Do not be a dimwit, Eleanor. I read your girlish scribblings, you see. Many months ago. I realized then that your Frederick was the only man who would satisfy you, and so I made certain that you secured him. Luckily your father was easy to convince, as he always is."

Why ever would her mother do such a thing? It was not so hard to believe that Mama would read her private writings. Indeed, that was entirely in character for her. But act to secure Eleanor's happiness?

That she could not credit, especially when the match she'd schemed to secure was not what she would have called advantageous. "But you've always said I should marry well," she insisted, "and Frederick is only a baron's son."

"A baron's *heir*, my dear. I've seen Worthington's seat in Oxfordshire, and I can assure you it is quite grand, far more so than his estate here. And here is where my advice comes in. You've been given the chance to marry the one man whom you desire above all others, the man who sets your blood afire and your pulse to racing, if your diary is to be believed. Such a chance only comes along once in a lifetime, and I suggest you embrace it, no matter the circumstances. Otherwise you will never be satisfied. I can assure you of that."

"But what if Frederick—"

"Does not love you? No matter." She waved one hand in dismissal. "You will *make* him love you, Eleanor."

"That hadn't been my question, Mama. Frederick *does* love me. Of that I am certain."

"Then I am bewildered. If he loves you and you him,

why was the betrothal contract ripped in two and tossed in the fire?"

"It's far too complicated to say, Mama. But that is why I wished to see him today, to try to set it all to rights."

"Then you shall. You might have told me straight-away rather than making up a ridiculous story about Selina being ill." She eyed her coldly, her mouth pursed in displeasure. "I suppose I should be glad you're such a poor liar."

"I *am* sorry for that, Mama." And sorry still for the continued lies, as she would not mention the artisan's cottage. "But I suppose I should thank you," she said, realizing with a start that she meant it. "If not for the be-trothal agreement, I don't imagine my path would have ever crossed Frederick's again."

"Likely not," her mother said softly. "I was in love once, you know. Desperately, passionately in love. He was the son of a solicitor, a beautiful boy. And then I caught your father's eye, and . . . well, he is a marquess, after all, your father. It was entirely insensible that your father would wish to marry me, a vicar's daughter, but indeed he did, and there was no arguing with my par-ents. My lover and I hadn't a chance. Anyway," she said with a sigh, "what's past is past. Still, I could not help but wish that you would have *your* chance."

"Thank you, Mama," Eleanor murmured, reaching for her mother's hand.

"Now look at me, all maudlin." Mama reached up to wipe her eyes, though they did not look at all damp. "Enough of this talk. Go on, put on your most fetching frock, and you shall have the carriage take you to Mar-bleton. I cannot possibly let you go on foot and arrive with reddened cheeks and muddy skirts now, can I?"

Chapter 23

The noon sun was high in the sky as Eleanor set off from Marbleton atop one of Lord Henley's mares. He'd given her explicit directions, and assured her it should not take more than a half hour to reach her destination. Her route would take her across a wide field, along the river, and then down a long, narrow lane that wound through the woods that separated Henley's estate from Lord Worthington's.

It was a beautiful day for a ride—sunny and unseasonably warm, the sky a breathtaking blue with nary a cloud in sight. The autumn colors had begun to fade, heralding the arrival of winter in the coming weeks. Still, the countryside was lovely, soothing to Eleanor's jangled nerves.

Whatever would she find at the cottage? The Frederick of old, laughing and teasing, entirely sure of himself? Or the Frederick she'd only just glimpsed yesterday, somehow sad and angry, all at once? Could she convince him of her love? That she trusted him implicitly? He had said that he did not want her otherwise, and she knew in her heart that he meant it.

Just as he had meant it when he'd said he loved her.

She had lain in bed last night, hearing those words again and again in her mind, till a sense of peace had descended upon her. She'd expected a sleepless night; after all, she'd had so many since becoming reacquainted with Frederick. Instead, she'd fallen into a deep, dreamless slumber, surprised to find herself so well rested at dawn when she'd awakened to bid Henry farewell.

Yes, she was making the right decision in going to the cottage, even if doing so went entirely against propriety. More than anything, she wanted to go. She prodded the gentle mare into a gallop, suddenly wishing to race across the field, toward her fate. Whatever it was, she was more than ready to face it.

Not a half hour later, she found the old stone cottage, just as Henley had promised—nestled in the clearing ahead, smoke rising from its single chimney. Somehow it fit Frederick—isolated, unpretentious, and yet appealing all the same. It was larger than she'd expected, likely encompassing more than one room, nothing like the little cottage on the cliff in Devonshire.

And, curiously, she heard music coming from inside. Dismounting, she led the mare around to the watering trough and hitched her there. There was definitely music coming from inside, a pianoforte, if she was not mistaken. Had there been an error, a misdirection of some sort? Perhaps she'd found the wrong place.

Nonsense, she chastised herself as she rounded back to the structure's front façade. She'd followed the directions precisely, and how many gray stone cottages could there possibly be, here in the woods between the two properties? This had to be it.

Tentatively, she took a step toward the front door, her curiosity piqued. *Was it . . . ?* No, it couldn't be. The slow, melodious tune became louder, clearer as she reached for the latch, causing her breath to hitch in her chest.

She'd been correct; it was Beethoven's piano sonata. Number Fourteen, the one she'd played for Frederick at Whitby Hall. But played now by whom? Puzzled, she pressed the latch and pushed open the door—slowly, quietly.

Once inside she froze, rooted to her spot by the door, one hand reaching up to stifle a gasp. Across the width of the room was Frederick, sitting before a mahogany pianoforte, his dark head bent over the keys.

His hair obscured his face as he played, but she was certain his eyes were closed. His hands—so large, so strong—were gently, expertly picking out the haunting notes as if he'd played the piece every day of his life.

She swallowed hard, her mind barely able to make sense of it all. Not daring to move a muscle, she stood silently, listening raptly till the movement's final notes faded away.

At last, his fingers stilled on the keys, and he raised his gaze to hers. He did not appear the least bit surprised to see her standing there, as if he'd known all along that she was listening, watching. She could feel the heat of his stare, boring through her, making her skin tingle with awareness.

"I did not know you played," she said at last, her voice barely above a whisper.

"Aye, taught by the nuns when I was a boy. I was not often grateful for the instruction, till now. I purchased the music in London."

But there was no music on the stand. "And already you play it by memory?"

Frederick shrugged. "The nuns taught me well."

"It's so very lovely, isn't it?" *Particularly when he played it.*

"Aye, I cannot hear it without thinking of you. It's haunted me, all this time."

"Frederick, I . . ." She shook her head, tears stinging her eyelids, her throat aching terribly. "I'm so very sorry, for not trusting, not believing—"

"Shhh, there's no need for that, love. Come here," he commanded, his voice gruff.

Eleanor untied her cloak, dropping it carelessly to the floor with her reticule, then rushed across the room, her lungs near to bursting.

Without rising from the pianoforte's bench, Frederick wrapped his arms around her, his head pressed to her breast. In unison, their hearts beat a furious rhythm, their breathing rushed and ragged.

"You came," he said, his voice muffled, sounding almost strangled.

She ran her hands through his hair, letting the silky strands slip through her fingers as she pressed him tightly to her, her legs growing dangerously weak. "Of course I came, though I don't know how you'll ever forgive me. I was wrong, so very wrong—"

"Don't," he said, shaking his head.

"I love you so very dearly, Frederick Stoneham. I . . . I could not bear to lose you again."

He said nothing in reply, only holding her more tightly. At once the front of her frock felt strangely hot, damp, as if he were . . .

No. Her mind refused to accept the obvious even as his body began to tremble, his hands clutching at her like a drowning man. And then she heard his choked sobs, muffled in the folds of her skirts.

He was crying. Sobbing against her like a child. Deep, gulping sobs that wracked his entire body.

Her heart near to breaking, Eleanor did the only thing

she could think to do—hold him tightly and stroke his hair, as if he were a boy.

Nearly a quarter hour passed, Eleanor comforting him as she tried to staunch her own tears, to remain strong—for him.

At last Frederick stilled in her arms, spent. "You came," he repeated, his voice naught but a hoarse whisper.

"Of course I came," she said, her own voice hoarse. "Did you truly think I would not?"

He looked up at her then, and the pain in his countenance took her breath away. "Why should you believe in me, when no one else ever has?" he said.

She swallowed the lump in her throat before replying. "But I do believe in you, Frederick."

"Thank you," he said, drawing away, taking her trembling hands in his. "I do not deserve you, but thank you."

"Thank you for giving me another chance. I was wrong—terribly wrong. I should have allowed you to defend yourself, to say your piece. Only a coward would have done otherwise."

Frederick took a deep, steadying breath. Bloody hell, but he'd lost it. He wiped his face with his sleeve, embarrassed by his tears, relieved that she had not fled in horror. He reached up to brush her cheek, as soft as velvet beneath his fingers. "You are no coward, Eleanor," he said softly.

"It's only that . . . that Miss Delacorte seemed so very convincing. The very thought of you and her . . ." She trailed off, shaking her head, suddenly unable to meet his gaze.

"She is a part of my past that I am not proud of. Aye, there's much I'm ashamed of. But I vow to you, I am no longer that man."

God knows, he'd tried to be. After she'd so hastily departed London, he'd spent the first two days in a drunken stupor, feeling sorry for himself, hoping to find comfort in the arms of another.

He'd gone to Covent Garden in search of a warm, willing body and come home alone instead, taking refuge at his father's residence in Grosvenor Square. No longer did any aspect of his previous life—drinking, gambling, whoring—hold any appeal for him, none whatsoever. In the end, he'd sobered up, set his financial affairs in order, and purchased the respectable little townhouse in Mayfair.

Not that he'd expected to win back Eleanor's trust, her heart; indeed, entirely the opposite was true. Still, there was no going back to his old ways. That part of him was forever gone, and good riddance.

At last her gaze found his again. "And I vow to you that I will never again doubt you. Never," she repeated, her eyes shining like a pair of deep, dark sapphires.

Which reminded him . . .

Rising, he hastened to the red velvet settee where he'd tossed his coat. Reaching inside, he withdrew the pouch from his pocket. "I've something for you. Come, let me do this properly."

With a curious smile, Eleanor followed him. The fire sputtered, its red and orange flames reflected in her face as he sank to one knee before her, taking her hand and tenderly kissing it.

And then he held out the ring—an enormous square sapphire flanked by diamonds and set in heavy gold. "I hope you will accept this ring as a token of my eternal devotion, of my pledge to love and honor you till my dying breath."

"But . . . but you've already given me a ring," she stammered. "The ruby one. It's there, in my reticule."

"I do not care what you do with that godforsaken thing—it was purchased before we became reacquainted, before I knew that a sapphire suited you far better. This one was chosen for you and you alone, though I dared not hope you would accept it. Will you take it? Will you marry me, Eleanor Ashton?"

"Yes," she said, her eyes suddenly damp. "Yes, of course I will."

In an instant he was on his feet again. She tugged off her gloves, allowing him to slip the ring on her finger. For a moment, they both admired it—a perfect fit. And then he kissed her, tenderly at first, wanting to savor every moment, every taste, every touch.

Her mouth opened against his, his name upon her lips in invitation. Reaching up to clasp the back of her head, his tongue danced along her lower lip, teasing it, then plunged inside. Damnation, but she stole his breath away, her own tongue meeting his in bold exploration.

Together they stumbled backward, toward the pianoforte, their hands everywhere at once. Her backside collided with the keys, discordant notes breaking the silence as she braced herself against the instrument.

His mouth found hers once more, his lips meeting no resistance. As he kissed her, he allowed his hands to roam her luscious body, taking in every delicious curve. He was going to spend himself, right then and there, if he did not stop.

Summoning every bit of strength he could muster, he dropped his hands to his sides, his lips retreating to her throat where her pulse leapt wildly. "You're going to be the death of me yet, woman," he muttered, nuzzling her warm, fragrant skin.

"Do not stop, not this time," she said, her voice breathless as she lowered herself to the pianoforte's bench. Reaching for his linen, she tugged it from the waistband of his breeches. He shuddered as her bare hands glided up his torso, her nails raking his skin, tempting him beyond reason.

"I must stop," he said through gritted teeth, his control teetering on a dangerous precipice.

"Why must you?" Her voice was husky, laced with need.

"To show you that I can, God help me. I will not compromise you. Not now, no matter how badly I want to." No matter that desire coursed hotly through him, nearly making him mad with lust. For once, he would consider the consequence; he would not take her, simply because he wanted to.

Gaining her feet, Eleanor reached behind her and unfastened her gown, allowing it to drop to her feet with a swish. "Oh, yes, you will."

He could only gape in astonishment as she stood there in nothing save a thin chemise and stays, her breasts pushed high and round, her skin flushed a delicious pink.

"You *can* compromise me," she said, her voice a caress, "and you will. Because I wish it, Frederick, and haven't you always said I should do what I wish?"

He let out his breath in a hiss. He could not deny her, not now, not with such an invitation as that.

Eleanor gasped as Frederick's lips trailed a hot, wet path down her throat, toward her breasts, his hands reaching beneath her chemise. Suddenly too weak to stand, she sank back to the bench, leaning against the cool ivory keys which rang out a disharmonious tune in affront.

While one of his hands traced a path up her thigh, the other tugged at her stays' lacings, his mouth moving lower still, pushing away her chemise's fabric. Her heart racing, she tugged at the lacings herself till the stays fell away, dropping to her feet. Tangling her fingers in his hair, she guided his mouth lower still, gasping when his teeth grazed one sensitive nipple, the skin taut with desire.

She shuddered as an unfamiliar heat coursed through her veins, making her suddenly dizzy, her thighs slightly damp. With a sharp tug on her chemise, he bared both her breasts to his hungry gaze. As his tongue made slow, deliberate circles around one nipple, she became vaguely aware of his fingers, teasing her entrance, rubbing against her most private place. Instinctively, her thighs clamped together, but in seconds he'd coaxed them open once more.

A soft moan escaped her lips as he began to suckle her, gently at first, then more insistently. Her head tipped back, onto the keys. Dear lord, but this was wicked. Wonderful and wicked, all at once. She struggled to sit, to reach for him, to beg for . . . something. Something to ease the exquisite ache that was building inside her, making her breathless with desire.

He only pressed her back again, his mouth leaving one breast and moving to the other. Between her legs, she felt one finger slide inside her, and she cried out as he began to stroke her, making her entire body tremble with need. "Frederick, I . . . what's happening? I . . . oh!"

"Shhh, love," he murmured, drawing away from her breasts. His gaze raked over her, his eyes dark with desire. "Damn, but you're beautiful. You must know that I've never . . . it's never . . ." She saw him swallow hard. "I've never before wanted anyone as I want you now."

"Then take me," she whispered. "Now, before I go mad with it."

He nodded, taking a step back from her. His eyes never once leaving hers, he pulled his linen up and over his head, then reached down to pull off his boots and unfasten his breeches. In seconds, he stepped out of them, standing there proudly bare before her.

Eleanor allowed her curious gaze to trail from the hard, smooth planes of his muscled chest downward, to his abdomen, following the thin line of dark hair lower still till it reached his fully erect manhood—splendid in all its glory.

At once her gaze flew upward, back to his face, where amusement lit his features. She smiled in appreciation, in invitation, wishing desperately to feel his mouth upon her once more, his hard body pressed against hers.

Her legs shaking dangerously, she stood, thinking that perhaps he'd carry her to the settee. Instead, he took two long strides toward her, pressing her back against the pianoforte. In one fluid motion, he pulled her chemise over head, tossing it over the music stand behind her. "I . . . I don't see . . . how," she murmured in confusion, the heels of her hands pressing hard against the keys as he fitted himself between her thighs, his hardness pressing insistently against her opening.

With a groan, his mouth captured hers, his body pressing her back so that she nearly sat upon the keyboard. And then he slid upward against her, entering her. Inhaling sharply, she tensed, her muscles tightening against the tip of his shaft.

He stilled, his mouth nuzzling her neck. "I'll try my best not to hurt you, love. I vow to make it as pleasurable as possible."

She nodded, her breath coming so fast now that she feared she might faint.

And then, with one sharp but sure movement, he sheathed himself entirely within her.

She squeezed her eyes shut as a sharp, burning sensation temporarily stole her breath away. But just as quickly the pain ebbed away and her skin began to tingle, her pulse to accelerate as a delicious sensation overcame her.

Grasping her chin, Frederick tipped her face up, his gaze searching hers. "Are you hurt?" he asked, nothing but concern, but love, there in his eyes.

In reply, she moved against him, tilting her hips, seeking a rhythm. Reaching beneath her, he lifted her off her feet, wrapping her legs about his waist as he answered her call, pumping himself into her again and again, till she began to lose her focus, crying out his name, over and over again.

At once it seemed as if the earth fell away beneath her, wave after wave of pure and potent pleasure gripping her. Her insides pulsed against his shaft—still buried deeply inside her—and then his cries joined hers, his hot seed filling her.

"My God, Eleanor," he gasped, his head thrown back as he lowered her back to the bench.

For a moment, she could not speak. Her breath was ragged, her thoughts entirely muddled. She took several deep breaths, forcing her racing heart to slow. At last she found her voice, however tremulous. "Is it always as lovely as that?"

"Never," he said forcefully, clutching her tightly. "Never before."

"Exactly as it should be," she murmured, smiling now.

"You realize we cannot wait till Christmastide now, don't you?"

Releasing him at last, she plucked her chemise from the music stand behind her. "Whatever do you mean?"

"I mean we must marry right away. Without delay. We might have started a child. Devil take it, I hope we *did* start a child," he added, reaching for his breeches.

"Do you really? So soon? I did not know you were so eager for fatherhood."

"The thought of you, bearing my child . . ." He cleared his throat. "Are you not anxious for motherhood? For there are things that can be done to prevent it, if you are not ready—"

"I'm quite ready, Frederick," Eleanor said with a laugh, pulling the chemise over her head. "But I *had* always hoped for a Christmas wedding."

"Had you?"

Eleanor nodded, retrieving her sprigged muslin gown from the floor and stepping into it. "At the parish church, Selina as my bridesmaid. Holly and ivy for decoration—"

"And your belly round with child?" he asked with a laugh.

"No, you rogue. Here"—she presented him her back—"can you fasten this?"

"Must I? I'm not certain I'm yet through with you today."

"Indeed you are. If you do not want me round with child at our wedding, that is. Our *Christmas* wedding," she added.

"Would you really be as cruel as that? Do you know how many weeks there are between now and Christmas?"

"A good many," she answered with a nod.

"Dear God, you *are* cruel." With quick fingers, he fastened up the back of her gown.

"A shrew, I know." She shrugged. "Perhaps you can make it your mission to wear me down, then. Despite what you claim, I'm certain that a leopard cannot *entirely* change its spots now, can it?"

Chapter 24

Exactly nine months later

"Look at her, Frederick! Is she not the most beautiful thing you've ever seen?"

Frederick lowered himself to the bed beside his wife and bundled daughter, her face a lovely pink as she slept peacefully, fully sated. Hair the color of ebony peeked out from her swaddling, as fine as silk. "She is indeed, love. And born not even eight months after our wedding. Think of the scandal we shall cause."

Eleanor reached across the babe to kiss her husband full on the lips. "It's only to be expected from a scoundrel such as yourself," she said. "No one will be the slightest bit surprised, I'm sure."

"Well, if I'm a scoundrel, just what does that make you?"

She shrugged. "A very happy woman. Did you send word yet to Henry? And to the Henleys at Marbleton?"

"I did, indeed. Though I'm not sure Selina will take kindly to you beating her to motherhood."

"Her babe is due any day now. How long do you

think it will be before we can travel there to Essex? Or she here to Oxfordshire?"

"Not so very long, I'd say." He glanced down at the sleeping babe, a smile spreading across his face as he reached down to touch one tiny hand—five perfect little fingers curling around one of his. "She does look rather portable, does she not? What shall we call her, our scandalously early babe?"

Eleanor glanced down at the babe, a warm, sleepy smile upon her lips. "I like the name Katherine, after your sister," she said. "Katherine Fiona, I think."

He nodded, tears dampening his eyes. How very like Eleanor to suggest two names that meant so much to him—his sister's and mother's names combined. "Katherine Fiona it is, then," he said, his voice thick with emotion. "Little Katie Stoneham. I like it."

Eleanor tilted her head to one side, regarding him. "Come to bed, Frederick. Keep us company, though I don't suppose we'll get much sleep. She'll be hungry again soon enough."

Hell, he'd be happy to lie awake all night, simply staring at his daughter. Yet somehow he doubted it would be considered appropriate, given the circumstances. "Perhaps I should leave you two to your rest. The physician said I should not disturb you—"

"The physician? Really, Frederick, whatever has become of you? What do *you* want to do? Stay in here with us, or go to your lonely bedchamber next door, the one you've not slept in a single night before now? I vow, there's nothing wrong with doing something, simply because you *want* to, now is there?"

Put that way, how could he refuse her?

Epilogue

Oxfordshire, 1817

Frederick stood watching as Eleanor laid a bouquet of wildflowers beside the grave, the one marked *Fiona, Lady Worthington,* then moved on to the neighboring graves, those marking his father and brother.

Beyond the churchyard gates, Katherine and Emily dashed around the meadow picking more flowers, young Freddie trailing behind them. Their childish laughter floated on the warm summer breeze, making him smile despite the somber surroundings.

He'd hated this place for so many years—hated it with a passion. He'd never been able to forget that hideous day they'd laid Charles to rest, and for more than a decade he'd refused to set foot there in the churchyard.

Yet, now he found a surprising peace there, with his family surrounding him. He smiled at his wife, knowing she was the one who had brought peace to his life, happiness to his heart where there had been none. She had made him worthy—made him realize he *was* worthy, he corrected.

Across the graveyard, Eleanor wiped her hands on her skirts, returning his smile. "Are you anxious to be off?" she asked, hurrying to his side. "We've still plenty of time before the first guests arrive."

"No," he said, wrapping one arm about her waist. "I'm happy enough here. The children are still collecting flowers to lay on the graves, and Freddie will no doubt return any moment, asking to be fed. Greedy little devil. Until then, let them have their fun." He kissed the top of her head, inhaling her familiar scent—soap and lemon verbena. "Tell me, why was it so important to leave Town in the middle of the Season? Why a house party now?"

"I told you, it's for Henry's sake. He's in love, Frederick," she said, excitement in her voice.

"Henry, in love? Impossible. I cannot believe it."

"Nor does he, which is why I had to have the house party."

He shook his head. "I can't say I'm following your logic, Eleanor."

"Don't you see? I've invited the woman he loves, though he claims not to, of course. Lucy Abbington, I told you all about her. The Rosemoors are sponsoring her; she's the one with the interest in veterinary arts."

"Ah, yes," he said, now remembering hearing something about the girl in question. "The horsey girl."

"She's not a horsey girl. Nor is she a horse of a girl," she added with a grin. "She's lovely, in fact, a perfect match for Henry though he will not admit it. Her father is only a physician, you see, and you know how Henry insists on marrying well, no matter the consequence. Anyway," she waved one hand in dismissal, "you must not tell Henry I've said anything at all about her. Just make sure it's known that you approve of her entirely. Her family, her interests. Even if you do not."

"Why shouldn't I? She sounds like a right sensible girl. How old is she, anyway?"

"Not quite one and twenty," Eleanor answered.

Frederick whistled through his teeth. "So young as that? You're sure she's appropriate for your brother?"

"Entirely sure. Would I resort to such desperate measures, otherwise? He's avoiding her, and this was the only way I could think to . . . well, push him in the right direction. Trust me, he will thank me for this one day. Anyway, make it known to everyone in attendance that you approve of her. Have I your word?"

He nodded. "Indeed you do."

"I'm afraid that, thanks to my mother, there will be some in attendance who will do their best to disparage her."

"Really? Well, it sounds as if this shall be an interesting house party, after all. Lucy Abbington is her name, you say? The one I'm not to mention?"

"Miss Abbington is to be there?" Katherine called out breathlessly, weaving her way through the graves, Emily and Freddie in tow. "And Uncle Henry, too? Oh, how lovely!"

Frederick scowled at his daughter. "What do you know of the situation?"

"Just that Uncle Henry is in love with Miss Abbington, but he does not yet realize it," Emily added matter-of-factly.

"He sent her flowers," Freddie offered. "Though I bet she would have preferred a pastry."

"Good God, is everyone in on this conspiracy?" he asked, shaking his head in amazement as the children gathered around. "Poor Mandeville hasn't a chance."

Eleanor only shrugged. "Can I help it if I wish for my brother to find love? To be as happy as I am?"

"Yes, and isn't it romantic?" Katherine asked dreamily. "Nothing like the two of you, with an arranged marriage and all."

Frederick began to sputter in indignation. "Why, I'll have you know that—"

"Yes, yes, I know," Katherine said with a sigh of boredom, as if she'd heard it a million times. "You fell in love anyway, despite your best intentions. Still, it *did* start as an arranged match, did it not?"

Frederick looked to Eleanor, who only shrugged helplessly, a mischievous gleam in her indigo eyes.

"It did, indeed," he answered, his gaze not leaving his wife's.

"Not very romantic at all," Emily declared. "I shall marry for love, or not at all."

"I'm hungry," Freddie put in.

One day they'd have quite the story to tell their children, Frederick realized. But not today. For now, let them think their parents entirely unromantic.

He and Eleanor knew the truth. And for now, that was enough—lucky scoundrel that he was.